THE IVY LEAGUE CHRONICLES:
9 SQUARES

by E.K. Prescott, Ph.D.

THE IVY LEAGUE CHRONICLES:
9 SQUARES

by E.K. Prescott, Ph.D.

A Division of Five Star Publications, Inc.
Chandler, Arizona

Linda F. Radke, President
Five Star Publications, Inc.
PO Box 6698
Chandler, AZ 85246-6698
480-940-8182
www.FiveStarPublications.com

www.IvyLeagueChronicles.com

Publisher's Cataloging-In-Publication Data

Prescott, E.K.
   The Ivy League chronicles. 9 squares / by E.K. Prescott.

   p. : ill. ; cm. -- (Ivy League chronicles)

   Includes bibliographical references.
   Issued also as an ebook.
   ISBN: 978-1-58985-254-9; eISBN: 978-1-58985-255-6

   1. College teachers--Connecticut--New Haven--Fiction. 2. College students--Connecticut--New Haven--Fiction. 3. Murder--Investigation--Fiction. 4. Amulets--Fiction. 5. Detective and mystery stories. I. Title. II. Title: 9 Squares III. Title: Nine squares

PS3616.R473 I9 2013
813/.6
2012950782

Electronic edition provided by

the eBook Division of Five Star Publications, Inc.

Printed in the United States of America
10 9 8 7 6 5 4 3 2

Cover & Page Design: Kris Taft Miller
Page Layout: Linda Longmire
Editor: Cristy Bertini
Proofreader: Patricia Kot
Project Managers: Patti Crane and Lisa Baumann

MIX
Paper from responsible sources
FSC
www.fsc.org   FSC® C002589

This is a historical fiction mystery novel. Although portions of this work are derived from actual historical events and persons as history reports, each literary character is a product of the author's imagination and has no reference to any person, living or deceased.

Special thanks to my husband Dennis,
my son Doug, my daughter-in-law Sarah,
and my granddaughter Audrey.
Thank you for your continued support in helping
to make my dream a reality.

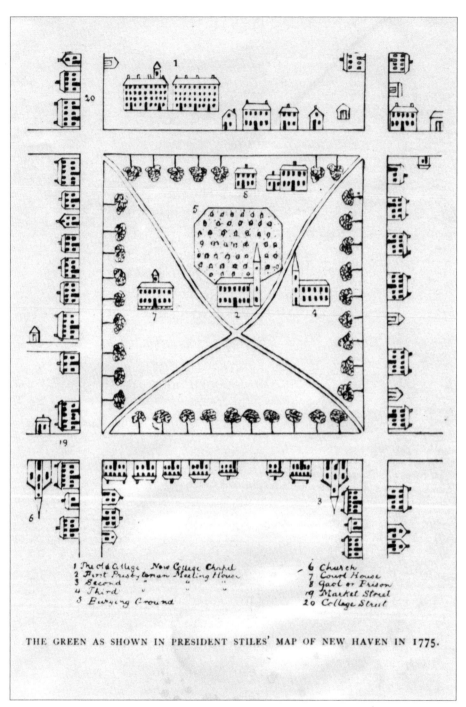

1 The Old College   New College Chapel
2 First Presbyterian Meeting House
3 Second   "   "
4 Third   "   "
5 Burying Ground

6 Church
7 Court House
8 Gaol or Prison
19 Market Street
20 College Street

THE GREEN AS SHOWN IN PRESIDENT STILES' MAP OF NEW HAVEN IN 1775.

From the Archives of the Yale Library

vi

PROLOGUE

No records would be found, and no minutes would be taken of this unofficial meeting called by the Master Prior. Plans must be carried out seamlessly with no stone unturned, no shadows lurking behind closed doors, and no tracks to be uncovered. They must act as one for the good of the country; no sacrifice too great.

The five must unite and act as one; but leave as five individual entities with iron-clad alibis, establishing a safe distance from each other and their patriotic deed. The date and time down to the second must be exact. It must be carried out at the precise point when the electromagnetic field of the earth and the gravitational pull of the moon are at its peak.

"All of us must be in our exact positions in order to unite energies collectively and focus on our united intention," the Master Prior instructed.

Four heads nodded in unison, as the priors realized the scope and depth of their plan. In a few short weeks, the time would come where all of America would benefit from their actions.

George Seymour entered the conference room and sat to the left of the Master Prior. "I have reported our concerns to the Council."

George, a direct descendent of Roger Sherman, the first mayor of New Haven and the only statesman to sign all four documents connected to the Constitution of the United States, is a powerful secret partner of the Priors. George earned a Bachelor of Arts degree from King's College in Cambridge, England in 1904 and earned a second B.A. from Yale in 1908. He went on to earn his Ph.D. from Yale in 1911.

During his junior year at Yale, he was tapped to become an elite member of the Skull and Bones secret society for his senior year,

1907/08. Come Tap Day, if you're a junior and selected by the standing senior members to join their secret society your senior year, a Bonesman (senior) stands by your door, and when the tower clock strikes eight he rushes in and taps your shoulder and shouts, "Skull and Bones! Accept or reject?"

In 1921, George became one of the founding members—among other members of the elite ruling class, which included the Rothschilds of England and the Rockefellers of the United States—of the U.S. Council of Foreign Relations, headquartered in New York City, a few hours drive from New Haven. A subsidiary office was also located in Washington, D.C., which was crucially funded by John D. Rockefeller, Sr., owner and director of Standard Oil, controlling over 80 percent of the world's oil refining.

In the summer of 1921, George traveled to Paris with the newly formed Council members in order to combine their global objectives with England's Royal Institute of International Affairs—previously known as the Round Table Group—which was formed by several elite British dynasties including the Rothschilds, Astors, and Greys.

Presently in 1923, a founding member of The Council of Foreign Relations, George is also a distinguished professor teaching history at Yale University, and an active alumni member of the Skull and Bones secret society.

In 1897, John D. Rockefeller Jr. became the director of Standard Oil in New York City, replacing his father. The senior Rockefeller had situated himself as one of the wealthiest and most powerful men in America by the mid 1800s. Not only did he own a monopoly on oil in America, he also worked closely with America's national banking system and federal political arm.

Being the only son and key heir to the Rockefeller dynasty, John Jr. fell into a powerful mix of money, oil, and politics. In the early 1900s, he was situated to become part of his father-in-law's Congressional

Bill which would elevate the Rockefellers to becoming one of the most powerful families in America. Republican Senator Nelson Aldrich recommended the creation of a central bank—known as the Aldrich bill—the Federal Reserve Act establishing the Federal Reserve System. He rebuilt the American financial system along Progressive lines. Though what many concluded was unconstitutional, as only "The Congress shall have Power To coin Money, regulate the Value thereof ..." according to Article I, Section 8 of the Constitution, the Federal Reserve Act was passed in December 1913; ostensibly to stabilize the economy and prevent further panics, but as Lindberg warned Congress: "This act establishes the most gigantic trust on earth ... the invisible government by the money power, proven to exist by the Money Trust investigation, will be legalized."

John Rockefeller Sr., as one of the main financial backers—J.P. Morgan being another—of The Council of Foreign Relations, and his son John Jr., also son-in-law of the chairman for the Commission of the Federal Reserve Act, became the power behind the Council of Foreign Relations—the promotional arm of the ruling elite in America.

As the last Prior entered, the Master Prior began the spontaneous meeting.

"I'm glad to see all of you could come at the last minute. George has been instrumental in communicating our collective goals and intentions here and across the Atlantic. It seems we are in very good hands. As we requested, George relayed our concerns about President Harding to The Council. He now has a report." Turning his attention to George, Master Prior said, "George ..."

Suddenly, there was an unexpected knock at the door, breaking their focus. A hush came over the room. No one would dare interrupt this meeting but Renold, who was affectionately known as Remy. Renold had been befriended by the Master Prior during the years he spent mingling and hobnobbing with the most powerful political figures in England; not all of whom were necessarily members of the visible ruling class. If truth be known, Remy was the only person in this world Master Prior trusted. Those few years he spent in England were the Prior's breeding ground for his future role as Master Prior in America.

"What is it?" Master Prior sternly asked, obviously irritated with the interruption. As Remy poked his head in the door, everyone relaxed. Master Prior motioned for him to enter and speak. Remy walked confidently towards Master Prior and whispered in his ear. As he delivered the message, Master Prior's face grew from a tight frown to eyebrows raised to mouth open.

"Did they identify the body?"

"No sir, but they have uncovered some kind of green fungus next to the skeleton's head. They think it might provide a clue … probably grasping for straws. It's being analyzed as we speak."

They spoke as if alone in the room. With an extremely intent look on his face, Master Prior commanded with a tone that projected explicit compliance. "Personally relay a message to our source inside, and tell him to meet me at the same time and place later today." He remained seated and continued with eyes of stone, facing the others. "Tell him to keep his eyes and ears open. I do not like surprises."

"It's as good as done, sir." And with that, Remy immediately exited the room.

The four sat quietly, waiting for Master Prior to relay the details surrounding what had just occurred. Upon listening to the details, the four quickly concluded Master Prior had more than one reason to be worried. It was Leslie, his daughter, who discovered the skeleton.

Chapter 1

YES! Yale boys in sleeveless t-shirts on the beach! These were Maize's first thoughts as she awoke in the late morning to a warm spring breeze filtering through the slightly opened window. The smell of summer was in the air. In a few weeks, Yale University would be dismissed for the summer and her favorite pastime would be on hold until the fall semester. But, even more important was the fact that she was going to graduate in a few weeks from the most prestigious secondary girl's preparatory school in the area, The Day School.

She would be a part of one of two remaining classes before the school would be torn down and moved up the hill off The Green. Though The Day School had undergone numerous facelifts over the years, it had proudly stood at the corner of Elm and College Streets behind the United Church on The Green across from Yale University since 1665. It was time for a fresh start. Maize knew each girl in her graduating class extremely well, sometimes too well, being that there were only thirty girls per class who followed each other through the grade levels. Not all of her elementary school classmates, however, continued their education in a private school, but most did, especially in

New Haven, Connecticut. New Haven is an aristocratic town with an up-and-coming middle class, to the chagrin of the elite.

Living in New Haven as the daughter of the owner of the only newspaper in town—*The New Haven Gazette*—was like living in a fish bowl. Maize lived this role since she was five, when her family moved to New Haven from Boston, Massachusetts. Her mother and father wanted to move away from the big city and all its problems to a nice, small, quiet town to raise their three children, Robert, Scott, and their youngest and only daughter, Maize.

New Haven provided a wholesome small town environment which could be interpreted as an elusive façade if one were to look closely. But now in 1923, even small town New Haven was chaotic— embedded around a major Ivy League school and the center of many aristocratic functions from arts to politics, drawing people from New York to Boston. In a few short years, life had changed from the Victorian era with all its rituals and frivolities to a new era—The Roaring Twenties, where life was full of exciting moments and free spirits. Although Maize didn't immerse herself in the hip "flapper" movement, she enjoyed toying with some of its perks, such as wearing makeup, a shorter hair cut, and higher skirt hems. To many, this was scandalous, charlatan behavior. Maize herself had read in the latest *Harper's Bazaar* that some thought "to be a Flapper was to be a whore." Older members of society did not understand the youth of today, particularly the young women and why they wanted the right to vote, to go to college, and to have a career.

As Maize looked out her bedroom window, she smiled to herself. Today there would be no worries of homework, peer problems, or parent issues. She was going to Long Island Sound beach with her best friend, Leslie. Leslie was the only child of the wealthiest man in New Haven, Ron Davenport. His descendants dated back to London, England, when Rev. John Davenport and his partner Theopolis Eaton sailed to the new world to establish a strong Puritan seaport colony in 1638: The New Haven Colony.

Leslie's father is the owner of a prestigious line of hotels, one of which, The Taft Hotel, is located in downtown New Haven across from The Green, or the nine-squares as some call it, on Church Street. Ron Davenport is a member of every political committee, social club, and philanthropic endeavor hosted in New Haven. He knows everybody and everything that is happening. He is highly visible in New Haven, including top billing in Maize's father's newspaper at least twice a week.

Leslie was raised in the highest societal circles of New Haven. Over the years, Maize and Leslie had occasionally crossed paths at social gatherings and became good friends in and out of school.

Maize's father, Jonathan Judson, proprietor of *The New Haven Gazette*, had earned respectability both professionally and politically. He was an accepted member of the high social structure of New Haven; even if it was more from the outside looking in. Although he was invited to most of their functions, who was using whom could be up for grabs any given day.

Maize bathed and dressed before she went downstairs. It was imperative to choose the perfect outfit for her picnic at the beach. Leslie and Maize spent many an afternoon after school poring over *Vogue* or *The Queen* magazines, eyeing the latest fashions. Not concerned about monetary price tags, Leslie always managed to look like she just stepped out of a magazine every time you saw her. Maize, on the other hand, had to be a little more frugal in selecting one or two outfits that best fit her tastes.

As Maize dressed, she was thankful that the corset her grandmother Margaret wore and her mother Virginia still wore on occasion was now replaced by the loose-fitting camisole. She could not imagine being so confined. Maize chose a seaweed-green, lightweight pair of cotton knickers that ended just below her knee, which were set off by a coordinating striped band of material. Her rayon stockings, which had been patted with a powder puff to mask the sheen, were light brown with a hint of seaweed-green horizontal strips. Since it was warm but breezy, she chose a short-sleeved matching shirt with large matching buttons down the front. The short, puffy sleeves gave a sense of femininity to a somewhat masculine look. As Maize topped off her outfit with a matching cloche hat, she took one more look in the mirror. *Humph! Not bad!* Maize had intricately observed how young women dressed at many a social function; they were her teachers.

As she ran down the stairs to fetch the picnic basket their cook Julia had methodically assembled, she heard the phonograph playing "Fluffy Ruffles." Although very trendy, Maize thought it was a highly unusual, lively song for Mother to be playing this early in the day. She peered into the parlor on her left as she walked down the hall towards the kitchen. The sun showed brightly through the window sheers, illuminating Mother's new oval Oriental rug lying in the center of the room covering a small portion of the newly laid hardwood floor. The Judson family had not moved since arriving to New Haven twelve years ago and in the past five years, many new household technologies had been created to make life easier. During the last few years, Virginia had been engrossed with upgrading their home with new technologies, such as replacing the wood burning stove with a gas stove that included a top burner and an interior oven, the ice box with a Frigidaire refrigerator, the addition of a Maytag washing machine, the replacement of carpeting with hardwood floors, and the addition of the latest telephone model, called French, by Bell Telephone. The United States had left WWI behind, and was now prosperously moving into The Progressive Era.

"SCOTT!" Maize yelled as she leaped across the room, giving him a big bear hug. Scott had been living in the dorm his freshman and sophomore years at Yale. As far as Maize was concerned, he might as well have attended college in another country because he hardly came home to visit these past two years. Scott was quite dapper with his blond, slicked-back hair, his collegiate sweater and tan pants, not to mention his two-toned brown and white shoes. Maize shouted with glee, "You're here!" before their mother entered the parlor complaining that the music was too loud and that the neighbors would question the morality of the Judson household. Virginia loved to exaggerate whenever she wanted to make a point with her children. "Need to get their attention," she always said.

As Scott rose to lower the volume on the phonograph, he asked. "Is Father here? I came early, hoping to catch him home on a Saturday morning before he went to the newspaper to finalize the Sunday edition."

"Sorry son," Virginia stated as she left the parlor. "He had an emergency at the newspaper."

Hiding his disappointment, Scott couldn't help but think that there was always an emergency at the paper when he needed his father. But this time it was true. The national news was busting at the seams with Prohibition, Women's Suffrage, the Social Feminist Movement, the Ku Klux Klan, the rise of Al Capone, the entertainment industry, new technologies, President Harding's Teapot Dome scandal, the formation of the newest branch of the Federal Government, The Council of Foreign Relations, and the recent railroad train strike—not to mention reporting the local news.

Scott lamented to himself. Nothing had changed during his absence from home while living in the dorm. Shaking it off, he turned towards Maize and changed the subject, "Well peanut, what's up with you? You look marvelous! Where are you off to?" Maize and Scott were extremely close. Scott was only two years older than her, unlike her brother Robert who was seven years her senior. She barely knew him. Being so close in age, Scott was always there for a laugh or a tear, perpetuating a wonderful brother-sister relationship. But now he was a big shot Ivy League boy, and quite popular with the girls. His suave moves, good looks, and funny jokes captured the young female gender just like it had Maize.

"Leslie and I are going for a picnic near the old lighthouse on the beach. Julia has prepared a wonderful basket, and the weather seems perfect for a day at the beach."

"Sure, sis," he said knowingly, winking at her. "I'm sure the scenery will be marvelous!" Scott was aware that many a fraternity spent Saturdays at the beach playing volleyball and frisbie. His eyes were set upon becoming a member of the ultimate frat his senior year. He spent a significant amount of time during his freshman and sophomore years befriending members and investigating exactly what it took to secure his membership in the most elite brotherhood on the Yale campus, Skull and Bones. He knew where many of the Bonesmen would be today … the beach.

Ignoring his accusation, Maize batted her bright, azure eyes and asked ever so innocently, "Would you be a wonderful brother and bring the car around front?"

Her infectious smile, combined with her gleaming eyes, always made him drop his defenses. He would do as she asked. "Sure Maize, I'm leaving anyway. I'll grab the keys to the Touring from the wall hook by the kitchen door on the way out."

Maize followed Scott to the kitchen where Julia was waiting for her. Virginia was busy planning the weekly meals when she noticed her daughter enter. "Dear, you will need some type of wrap to cover your arms. The sun is deceiving, and there will be a breeze coming off the water."

Maize silently acknowledged her mother. While grabbing her cape hanging on the coat rack near the kitchen door, she smelled an aroma permeating the kitchen. "Julia, something smells really good."

"I thought I would cook you some fried chicken. Fried chicken is always great for picnics on the beach," Julia exclaimed with great satisfaction.

With cape in hand, Maize thanked Julia, grabbed the picnic basket, gave her mom a quick kiss on the cheek, and proceeded down the hallway to the front door. There, she found Scott standing on the curb, leaning against the shiny, candy apple red 1921 Oldsmobile Touring their father purchased for the family the year before. The Judsons lived in a two story eighteenth century Gregorian-gabled home near downtown New Haven on Elm Street. Their small, gated, plush green lawn overlooked one of the three northwest streets that dead-end at The Green.

As Maize closed the front gate and walked across the sidewalk to the automobile glistening in the sun, Scott opened the driver's door. Maize slid into the driver's seat, and Scott proudly declared, "The windows are down, but I left the top up 'cause it's cooler than one would think." He winked teasingly adding with a big smile, "I know you have a father, but it takes a village to raise Maize." Shutting the driver's door before Maize could reply, he smiled and said, "Have fun, sis!" Scott walked toward the massive front porch that surrounded the whole house, making sure he was out of Maize's way. To Scott, his sister was a disaster waiting to happen.

Fun is just what she planned to have. She and Leslie had been planning this outing for two weeks. She knew that Leslie would look like a model. She would not be wearing knickers, but a light, cotton three-quarter length skirt. Even though skirt lengths were moving up and down, as high as above the knee and as low as one's ankles these days, "Three-quarters," as Leslie's mother would say, "is a respectable length for a young socialite."

Leslie had been groomed since birth to prepare for her future role as a proper aristocratic wife. She had been attending numerous finishing school functions since elementary school, preparing for her debutante ball upon graduating from high school. Through the years, she relayed to Maize all of the wonderful ins-and-outs of proper etiquette for almost any social function one could imagine.

Maize was thankful her parents never put her through those boring, torturous lessons. She had no use for them, even though she couldn't bring herself to admit it to Leslie. She was a girl of the twenties. She wanted to go to college—Yale in particular—and have a career and vote. Marriage was not something she wanted in the foreseeable future. Maize believed she had plenty of exposure to the intricacies of New Haven's high society as a part-time assistant society reporter for *The New Haven Gazette*.

During her junior year in high school, Jonathan Judson decided to groom his daughter for the newspaper business as he had with his eldest son Robert upon his return from WWI. Jonathan realized a long time ago that Scott's interests and loyalties lay somewhere else, shying himself away from the family business.

As Maize approached Leslie's house, she recognized the two huge, white pillars that ornamented the front of the house. Leslie also lived on the southwest end of Elm Street in West New Haven. Conveniently, both Elm Streets intersected just before The Green, so it was a straight shot west to her house.

Leslie's house was the largest on the block. It seemed to have been built to be more like a monument to her father's status in the community than a part of the neighborhood. It was amazing to Maize that she and Leslie had been friends for all these years. They had such different lives, but so much in common.

As Maize pulled into the circular drive, she noticed the oversized cement angel waterfall that graced the flower garden. The sun glistened through the trickling water as a slight breeze sprinkled drops like rain over the flowers. Leslie was waving at her from the doorway, motioning that she would be with her in a minute. Soon she appeared, dressed as Maize predicted, which included a full-brimmed, straw hat tied under her chin with a huge, coordinating sash.

"Mother said I should wear a hat since it was breezy today. My hair might not keep its shape," Leslie casually mentioned while gracefully gliding in the passenger's side as Jim, the family's butler, put the picnic blanket in the back seat through the open car window and closed Leslie's door.

"Have a good day girls, and remember Leslie, you must be home in time to dress for your father's dinner party tonight," Jim muttered as he watched them pull away.

The beach near the old lighthouse was at the farthest western tip of East New Haven across the harbor. Maize doubled back, driving around the horseshoe harbor crossing The Green. It was a beautiful day for a drive. Maize had considered taking the ferry across the harbor from West New Haven to East New Haven, but Leslie would not. In any event, driving the family car was a luxury Maize's parents granted only on occasion; she was going to milk this opportunity for all it was worth.

Upon reaching their destination, the girls chose an ideal spot on the beach; close but not too close to the male volleyball game to the east, a somewhat flat spot in the sand with a significant view of the lighthouse, nicknamed The Skeleton. Maize spread the blanket as Leslie took in the scenery.

"Great spot!" Leslie exclaimed. "We have an inconspicuous view of the male gender flexing their muscles."

"Why Leslie, your mother would have a hissy fit if she heard you talk in a manner unbecoming a lady of your stature," Maize chided. Leslie was always complaining about her mother's tirades on proper behavior of a young aristocratic debutante. Leslie found rebellious satisfaction in naming them "hissy fits."

"No mind, let's set up our picnic," Leslie flippantly retorted.

The girls managed to chatter away, discussing Coco Chanel's new Chanel #5 fragrance, Helena Rubinstein's newest Cupid's Bow Sinful Scarlet lipstick, the newest talkie by Valentino, and the true meaning of Fitzgerald's most recent novel, *This Side of Paradise*.

"All this talking has made me famished … let's dig into Julia's masterpiece," exclaimed Maize. As they ate, they continued to keep a close eye on the scenery to the east, both silently wondering when one bold young gent would notice them.

"How is your society reporting doing these days?" Leslie asked, curious for any gossip Maize might have uncovered.

"You know, I actually enjoy it. People are quite interesting to watch. Mrs … oh excuse me … *Lady* Peacock loves to entertain, and her afternoon teas are anything but dull. No one knows why she is called Lady … she's never said … it's quite a mystery. Anyway, she provides me with a continual source of entertainment plus great material, although what I'd like to write and what I do write about are often two different things."

"And?" Leslie asked, coaxing her for any delicious detail.

"Well, although in her sixties, she has moved into the twentieth century unlike my grandmother Margaret."

Margaret moved in with the Judsons two years earlier when her husband died from tuberculosis; a disease that swept the country a few years back. Margaret held firm to her Victorian ideals and the Gibson Girl persona as life around her was changing to a carefree, frivolous lifestyle. Maize loved her dearly and enjoyed her living with the family. As "Grandma's tender flower," she provided a safe haven from many a problem. Maize only avoided her grandmother when she began her tirades about the misguided youth of today.

Continuing, Maize gladly exposed, "Lady Peacock loves to invite psychics and play divinity parlor games to entertain her guests. She is quite the liberal from the point of view of most aristocrats, but too rich and too powerful to refuse, at least in front of her face. She is expecting her nephew from London next—"

Maize caught a glimpse of a volleyball rolling towards them. The ball lost momentum as it approached and stopped at Leslie's feet. Noticing Leslie was uneasily startled, Maize quickly grabbed the ball and tossed it to the tall, sleeveless, and handsome young gent standing before them. Both girls sat silently, staring upward as he courteously asked to be excused for interrupting their picnic.

Before either girl could reply, he realized they were obviously high school girls and nodded cordially before quickly rejoining his senior frat brothers to relay the disappointing scouting report.

Leslie, leaning backwards and placing her hands behind her in the sand to prop herself, laughingly exclaimed, "Well, what do you think—AHHHHH!!!!! ICK!!! What is that?" Leslie quickly moved to her right, shaking her left hand furiously while Maize jumped up to investigate.

The more sand she brushed away from the protruding object that had startled Leslie, the more Maize could hardly believe what she was seeing.

"What do you think it is?" Leslie asked, still shaking her hand. Maize said nothing and continued to cautiously wipe away more sand until she was sure.

"Leslie, why don't you gather what you can carry and return to the car. I will bring the rest."

"Why? What is it?" Leslie's voice was beginning to give way to terror. Maize quickly looked in the direction of the frat boys, and was relieved they didn't notice Leslie's outburst.

"Everything is fine." Maize calmly repeated again that Leslie should return directly to the car. As Leslie did as she was told, Maize refocused her attention to the skeletal hand protruding from underneath the sand. She had brushed away just enough sand to realize it was still connected to the arm. Taking a last glimpse, Maize noticed some type of necklace entwined with its bony fingers. Curious, without thinking, and focused on leaving as soon as possible, Maize put the necklace in her pocket to review later. She knew what she had to do. She had to talk to her father, *now*.

Chapter 2

Professor Detective Richard Wikki swiveled his black, weathered, leather desk chair ninety degrees while gnawing the end of his saxophone-shaped pipe and peering out of his office window that overlooked The Green. The Green—a plush, green, carpet of grass— supported numerous meandering students enjoying the summer air after an extensive, chilly winter. The Green has served as a public park since its conception, dating back to 1641. Placed in the center of New Haven across the street from Yale University, the nine squares—a privately owned park approximately sixteen acres in size—has provided a tranquil respite for many for almost 300 years.

As Richard stared at the summer afternoon rain shower slowly emerging out of the cloudy gray sky, his mind wandered to his first days as a visiting professor at Yale. He had moved across the Atlantic Ocean two years earlier from London, England, accepting a full-time visiting professorship at Yale University Law School. He desperately needed a change in all areas of his life, and his long time confidant and friend, Professor Dunby, now retired Dean of Cambridge Law School in Cambridge, England, provided an avenue to do just that. Dr.

Dunby had been Richard's major professor and mentor while attending Cambridge University, where he worked towards a degree in criminal law. Fatherless, Richard had a constant source of encouragement and support from his mentor while he pursued his career path.

Professor Johannas, Dean of Yale Law School, frequently traveled to Cambridge University to present his recent papers to their prestigious law students and faculty. During a visit to New Haven, and reciprocating the presentations of his research at Yale Law School, Dr. Dunby negotiated a visiting professorship for Richard at Yale's School of Law. He had become quite disturbed upon realizing that his protégé was in such a state of depression, and believed he needed to do something to help him rise above his devastating calamity. Richard agreed with the arrangements and soon found himself leaving behind London, Scotland Yard, and Cambridge University to begin a new chapter in New Haven, Connecticut at the prestigious and conservative Yale University Law School. Dean Johannas believed he would be a welcome addition to their faculty with his impressive, practical experiences and Cambridge credentials, especially in the field of criminology.

Proved correct, the Dean, after Richard's first of a three-year visiting appointment, offered him a full-time tenured position as the newly appointed Chair of Criminology with the goal of updating the criminal law curriculum, drawing new students to enroll in Yale's Law School. It was a strategic move.

Richard soon realized the distance across the ocean did provide a needed distraction from the daily reminders of his devastating losses. Daily student festivities and traditional activities at Yale helped mask his recent memories that still caused many a sleepless night. Yale and its surrounding town reminded him of his youthful, carefree days at Cambridge, which was not surprising since the Yale campus was modeled after Cambridge University. Richard, however, did find

American's historical point of views concerning the fight for their independence from England quite amusing, being that English history believed Americans committed treason, and American history believed they liberated themselves from tyranny.

Professorships, though highly coveted, are not monetarily lucrative, but he did not need the money. His father passed away several years earlier, surprisingly leaving the family fortune to his only son and child, Lord Richard Wikki. Senior Lord Wikki, a respected member of Parliament, House of Lords, disowned Richard fifteen years earlier when he denounced his birthright as Lord Wikki of Foxworthy. One can disown their birthright but not the official title. Richard did not want the restrictions, expectations, or responsibilities of this title to dictate his future. He believed his skilled interest in the intricacies of solving murders would be hampered by tedious aristocratic duties. His only recourse was to deny his birthright, which he did upon entering Cambridge University in 1908, befriending Professor Dunby and acquiring him as his major professor.

Upon graduating, it was Dr. Dunby's recommendation, combined with his innate skills and use of his title—the only time he used 'Lord' since denouncing it—that secured him a position as a Scotland Yard detective.

Soon after arriving at Scotland Yard, he married his college sweetheart, Veronica. Veronica had been a student at Cambridge University majoring in Liberal Arts. At that time, it was one of the few degrees which women could pursue. They met his first year and her second year at Cambridge in a photography class, an elective course. It had been love at first sight "through the rose-colored lens of both of their cameras" was the story they loved to tell.

During the next eight years, life was good for Detective Richard Wikki. He was happily married, respectfully employed, and blessed with a darling little girl, Julianna. The last five years at Scotland Yard were quite productive after a rocky beginning as a rookie. Finally towards the end of his fourth year, Richard earned the respect of his peers and management by demonstrating his loyalty and exceptional use of his uncanny deductive abilities in solving many a difficult case.

Having spent eight years at Scotland Yard, it was the events of the last year that forever changed his life. Now after three years, he could recall portions of the event without breaking down, only a few tears here and there could be found rolling down his face. It was quirky to him how much this singular event impacted all parts of his life.

As the rain shower began and he watched students vacate The Green, he recalled the excitement he felt solving many a case, following bits of clues and putting the pieces together. The adrenaline of the chase while growing closer to the truth was always a source of unparalleled opportunities.

Richard missed that feeling.

Although he found great pleasure in teaching and using his experience to affect young minds, he still found himself wishing to return to the field. But now he was in New Haven, far away from London and Scotland Yard, and carving out a new life.

He did not have the same connections with the local law enforcement and private snitches, but he did have the advantage of his apparent popularity in certain elitist social and political circles of New Haven. Being from Scotland Yard and an English Lord, the Dean had promoted him quite extensively to the local who's who, hoping to attain monetary support for their known-to-be-lofty yearly donation accounts. He hated the attention. He felt like brown shoes with a black suit; he didn't fit. But Detective, Lord, and now Professor Richard Wikki was a team player, and he would do his part to build the new Criminology program within Yale Law School. So off he would go to many a dreadful dinner, ball, parade, and political rally that the Dean requested he attend.

Richard chose to settle near Long Island Sound in close proximity to the historical Five Points Lighthouse across the harbor in East Haven, southeast of the Yale campus. Even though it was somewhat of a commute, he preferred the solitude and serene atmosphere that only water and sand could deliver.

Upon his arrival to New Haven, a colleague mentioned that he knew a Boston family who wished to sell their vacation cottage on The Sound as-is, including all furnishings and household items. It was a little large for Richard, but it provided a place where he could escape from everyone and everything, finding respite near the water. Since he had lost everything in the fire, he only brought his clothes to New Haven. Moving day was not cumbersome. He arrived with only his suitcases stacked in the back of his shiny new, black 1921 Ford Model T.

After two years, he could still remember the first time he walked into the long, narrow entryway that led to the parlor on his immediate left; a dining area was to his right. The largest room in the house was his bedroom, directly above the parlor on the second floor. There were three bedrooms and one bath upstairs, all with windows located in the front of the house, providing a direct view of the Atlantic Ocean. He decided the room next to his bedroom would be made into a study and the smallest of the three a guest room. The guest room gave Richard an uneasy feeling since he did not know anyone who would visit, and he didn't like empty spaces. He had enough of them in his life. There was a large porch off the kitchen on the first floor behind the parlor, covering the entire backside of the house. All three sides of the house were surrounded by nothing but green grass and full-bloomed trees. If there were any cottages close by, the trees would have blocked them, but there were none.

He loved the secluded privacy. In the front of the house, there were four wooden steps leading to a small porch open to the waters on The Sound. The water was some distance, in that a dirt road, a patch of land, and a stretch of beach had to be crossed before one could take a swim. It was perfect!

As time went on, Richard did manage to add a few minor touches to personalize his new home, but mostly he only slept there, spending most of his waking hours at Yale either teaching, advising, carrying out his Chair duties, attending a number of campus-wide committee meetings, researching/publishing (a must for tenured professors), attending Ivy League sports events—mainly football and basketball, or gracing the many events Dean Johannas asked him to attend. But most of all, Richard loved the interaction with the students. These days, he could be found in the student lounge visiting with one or more young men and sometimes a woman or two since Yale's student population included them. However, the male population seriously outnumbered the female gender. The students seemed fascinated with his work as a detective, especially since he was a detective from the renowned Scotland Yard. Students would sit for hours listening to his stories and always probing for more. Richard was not much of a storyteller, but the facts alone seemed to keep students mesmerized. Much to his chagrin, there was always one student in every crowd who wanted to know the unpublished details of the unsolved, exploited case of "Jack the Ripper."

Richard noticed a patch of lightning across The Green, causing a lapse in his thoughts. He once again drew his pipe to his mouth, automatically gnawing on the end.

This was no ordinary pipe; it had been a gift from Dr. Dunby when Richard entered Scotland Yard. Professor Dunby had been like a father to him since his own father had disowned him after Richard denounced his title. Thus, he felt compelled to give Richard something unique and appropriate to commemorate this milestone in his life.

Reminiscing, Richard could still visualize the short, rotund, grey-haired professor presenting him with his triumphant purchase, smiling from ear to ear and waiting for a receptive response while Richard opened the poorly wrapped box. Immediately upon opening the box, he drew out an exact replica of the pipe used by his favorite literary detective, Sherlock Holmes. The large opening at the end with a huge outward curved trunk always reminded Richard of a saxophone. Richard showed great appreciation, but could not bring himself to divulge that he didn't smoke. He graciously accepted the gift gnawing on the end of the pipe which eventually became a habit and a trademark.

Now, as he sat dreaming out his office window while mouthing the end of his pipe and watching the rain storm subside, he realized the pipe always brought to mind warm images of his years at Cambridge University. As he remembered, he smiled and thought to himself, *those were good years*.

The rain storm ended, giving Richard the perfect opportunity to leave campus without being drenched. As he turned away from the window to wrap up any work left on his desk, he noticed Scott Judson's file. Scott Judson was the middle child of the prominent owner of the only newspaper in New Haven. Scott had just left his office on the fourth floor of the Phelps building, a four story, brick structure in the center of a string of Yale buildings that ran from one end to the other on College Street, the street that separated Yale University from The Green.

Scott had been one of Richard's students during his first semester at Yale in his Introduction to Criminology course, which was open as an elective to all students. By the end of the course in December, Scott professed a high interest in preparing for law school his junior year, and asked Professor Wikki to be his major professor, helping him chart his new path. Of course, Richard accepted.

Recently, Scott frequently joined the growing crowd in the student union listening to Professor Detective Wikki's stories and spending hours probing Richard for details. Scott, although highly intelligent, did not focus on his studies as he should, but he had an air of confidence and purpose that set him above many. Professor Wikki noticed his intellect during class one day when Scott asked numerous probing questions which caused Richard to remember details he thought he'd forgotten. Richard hoped this young man would become more than he exhibited at the moment.

During the second semester, Richard and Scott developed a strong mentor/protégé relationship to the point in these last remaining days of the semester, that Scott invited him to dinner at his family's home in New Haven. Richard accepted as Scott left his office stating, "Get back at ya on time and date."

After reviewing Scott's information, Richard filed his folder, reached for his briefcase, turned off the light on his desk and pulled the ceiling fan chain hanging from above while perusing his office for anything he was forgetting. As he closed his office door he lamented, "Tomorrow will be yet another new day."

Chapter 3

Jonathan Judson was a self-made man, paving a path in journalism amidst the thriving metropolis of Boston, Massachusetts. He was determined to build a successful life for himself and his future family. Fortunately, early in his journalism career, Jonathan inherited a small newspaper just outside the Boston city limits from his father, who retired at the age of fifty. During those early bachelor years, he carved out a very comfortable living. Jonathan by no means was an aristocrat, but a part of the up-and-coming upper-middle class gaining respect in society. He worked night and day for years building the paper into a leading news agency in the Boston area.

During the early years of the paper, he met Virginia at an annual high society gala whose guest list included all major business owners in Boston. Virginia was the oldest daughter of a well-known Bostonian lawyer. On that particular night, Virginia was escorted by her father; she was substituting for her mother, Margaret, who was home ill. Upon entering the ballroom, Virginia and her father were announced; Gerald Farmer and his daughter Virginia. As Jonathan and others watched, he thought she was the most beautiful woman he had ever laid eyes on. He fell in love with Virginia the first time he saw her and within a year, they were married.

Soon, they were blessed with their first son, Robert. A few years later came Scott and then Maize. Raising a young family in Boston was not easy when his work demanded long hours away from home, and eventually the family left Boston. The newspaper had grown to one of the leading news agencies in the area and would sell for a good price. With the profit he earned from selling the newspaper, Jonathan purchased a small-town paper—*The New Haven Gazette* in New Haven, Connecticut.

He moved his family—which included Robert, then eleven, eight-year-old Scott, and five-year-old Maize—from the noisy metropolis of Boston to the small, sleepy little town of New Haven. Here, he believed his children would be exposed to a more civilized pace of life, and hopefully his time would be flexible, allowing more quality time with his family.

How the years had flown! Now in 1923, Robert returned three years earlier as a decorated veteran of World War I and became his father's right-hand man at the newspaper. Scott was in his second year at Yale University, and Maize was graduating from high school in a few short weeks.

Jonathan realized and accepted Scott's wish to make his own way in life, but he did hope Maize would fill Scott's shoes at the paper alongside Robert. Grooming her for the future, Jonathan appointed Maize as a part-time assistant after school and weekends under the watchful eye of Ruth Shields, the paper's society editor. Maize seemed to enjoy rubbing elbows with New Haven's finest, finding humor in most social gatherings. Her writing skills were quite proficient, gaining accolades for her youthful and fresh perspective from many a citizen who enjoyed reading her column.

Jonathan learned early in his marriage that patience was indeed a virtue, especially when dealing with the three women in his life. This feminine gender included his mother-in-law, who moved into his home two years prior, his wife, and his daughter. All three spent their formative years in different decades with different values and trends, which at times seemed to compete with each other in 1923. His mother-in-law, Margaret, was from the Victorian "Gibson Girl" era; her daughter and Jonathan's wife, Virginia, was raised in one era and lived her adult life in another—The Progressive Era—and Maize was the product of a new generation, leaving the past behind and forging uncharted territory with new virtues and traditions. Virginia was raised in the "old ways" as Maize at times abruptly pointed out, and was somewhat rebellious in her youth, but grew into a lady of taste and grace. Jonathan admired his wife for breaking old Victorian aristocratic traditions and marrying for love and not her mother's wish for convenience; convenience being a man of taste, prosperity, and a leader in society.

Personally experiencing the pros and cons of both generations, Virginia gained the skills to juggle her mother's Victorian ideals, along with her daughter's headstrong "woman of the twenties" visions of pleasure and grandeur. How she kept sane, Jonathan didn't want to know. What was most important when he stopped to think about it was the superb life that he believed he had built for himself and his family in New Haven. But now there was a glitch, a glitch that made him question the safety of his family.

Maize had discovered a skeleton buried underneath the sand on Long Island Sound beach near the old lighthouse. This was something he couldn't keep a secret. This was the biggest news in this small town in ages and would fill the front page for days. President Harding and his Ohio Gang's political scandal, Mob wars, Ku Klux Klan's cross burnings, the Red Scare investigations, Women's Right's rallies, the latest bootlegging arrests, and Lady Peacock's latest philanthropic "tea" would have to take a back seat.

Jonathan sent Maize home after spending hours at the police station answering question after question. Jonathan had a lot of influence, but none that could keep his only daughter from spending long hours being drilled on every little detail. He sat earnestly beside her the whole time as a confidant, protector, and personal counselor.

As dusk began to darken the skies, he stood up and demanded, "Enough is enough," and sent Maize home.

Robert, who was sitting across the room from his dad and Maize, providing support more for his dad than Maize, graciously offered to drive his little sister home while their father stayed to tie up loose ends. Escorting Maize home was not out of his way, not that he would have minded. Since he returned from overseas, Robert had moved from his folk's home to a nice upper flat just a few blocks southeast.

Maize woke late the next morning, rested from the countless hours of questions by the local police the night before. Although the whole event was at times quite overwhelming, she was thankful her father sat diligently next to her during the whole ordeal.

As her eyes slowly adjusted, squinting from the blinding sunlight through the front bedroom window, she sat up in her bed stretching and rubbing her eyes. She immediately noticed Sandy wasn't in her usual place near the foot of her bed, which meant only one thing— someone came to fetch her earlier. Sandy was her ten-year-old golden retriever who befriended Maize upon her arrival as a young pup.

While looking around the room, she caught a glimpse of a dull glimmer from the rusted, knotted and gritty chain she removed from her pocket and placed on the small table next to her bed upon retiring the night before. She could hardly remember reaching for it yesterday at the beach and removing it from the hand of the skeleton. Everything happened so fast. Why she did that, she'll never know, but now in retrospect, she wasn't sure if it had been a good idea. As she recalled the events surrounding her discovery, she had second thoughts as she removed the chain from the table top and dropped it in the small front drawer. *No one knows it exists … I'll think about this later.*

Once she dismissed the necklace from her mind, she threw on a day dress and a pair of slippers and proceeded downstairs. The house seemed unusually quiet; the only thing she heard was Sandy barking and frolicking in the backyard, enjoying the bright, sunny May morning. As she walked towards the kitchen, she peeked into each room, checking to see if anyone was home. She assumed her dad was at the paper, but where was Mother? Mother had been waiting up for her last night ready with hot tea and cookies.

Virginia's children loved to joke that Mom believed her special brewed hot tea and homemade cookies could cure anything. As she walked to the kitchen to find something to eat, she noticed Julia sitting at their oblong, wooden kitchen table located near the oversized window facing the backyard. She could see Sandy running and barking at the birds causing them to flutter from their respite in the bushes. Julia was busy shaving potatoes and humming a catchy tune. She jumped, startled at Maize's unannounced presence, not hearing her walk through the kitchen door shutters that separated the kitchen from the hallway.

"Oh, Miss Maize, you're awake. Sorry, I was deep in thought enjoying the quiet." Smiling she asked Maize if she was hungry. She was pleased to know that Maize would like some of her famous pancakes and bacon. Julia always enjoyed filling their stomachs like gasoline in a car, telling the Judson children that it would help them run longer. As Julia started rustling the pots and pans Maize sat at the table across from the bowl of potatoes where she had a good view of Sandy and the birds playing cat and mouse.

Realizing Maize probably wondered where her mother had gone, Julia began to explain.

"Lady Peacock's car came around to chauffeur her and your mother to the Central Church on The Green this morning to lend a hand at the Ladies Annual Bazaar. Your father wanted the car left here so you could drive it to the paper when you awoke." Rambling on as if Maize wasn't there, she continued. "He thought it was best you slept until you awoke on your own … you know, because of last night."

Maize heard only half of the conversation as she read the front page headline in the morning paper lying on the kitchen table. "*Debutantes Find Buried Skeleton*," read Maize aloud. "Interesting, I write the news, I don't usually make it." She wondered how Leslie was faring this morning; she'd ring her up later in the day. Curious how Leslie was holding up, she realized there were only a few days left until graduation. A wonderful thought crossed her mind. Maybe she would not have to return at all. Soon Julia proudly announced breakfast was ready to be served as she joined Maize at the kitchen table, continuing to shave the potatoes and smiling while she watched Maize fill her engine.

As Maize drove to the paper, her thoughts revolved around her discovery the day before. She remembered how scared Leslie had been, but she also recalled that later at the precinct during the police questioning, Leslie took the credit, stating, "If it hadn't been for me stretching and leaning back, they would never have uncovered this mystery." She believed, as always, Leslie was overstating the situation to gain attention from her father, who seemed unusually interested in the skeleton, rather than Leslie's welfare.

Maize was one of a handful of classmates who could see through Leslie's dramatic exhibitions, although most thought she was just self-obsessed with an oversized ego. Remembering the questioning from

E.K. Prescott, Ph.D.

the night before, Maize thought she overheard her father and Leslie's father making plans to talk after the girls left for home. *Hmm … I wonder what that was all about*, she thought to herself as she pulled into her parking spot at the paper.

As she entered the newspaper, she realized she hadn't talked to her father since last night at the police station. She had fallen asleep soon after arriving home and hadn't heard him return home. As she walked down the center aisle towards her father's office at the back of the room, she noticed everyone's nose seemed stuck in their typewriters. Everyone wanted a slice of the biggest news story to hit New Haven in years. No one noticed her walk towards her father's office. As she approached Lily's desk, which was positioned in front of his door, Maize noticed Sam on the phone, obviously deep in conversation. Sam was like a grandpa to her; he had befriended her when she arrived, unlike others who turned their backs with envy connecting her with "the boss's daughter" complex. Outside of Ruth Shields, the editor of the social column and her brother Robert whose office was next to their dad's, she didn't usually converse with anyone; not unless someone was fishing for some information not realizing that even if she did know, she wouldn't tell them. Maize disliked transparent people.

"Reporters have been calling from all around the eastern seaboard to extract any information we might divulge concerning the skeleton. I guess they tried us since the police department is definitely not talking," Lily complained, looking at Maize while hanging up the phone. "Good to see you dear. How are you feeling? Rested? My, what an ordeal for such a young lady!" Lily rattled on, not waiting for a reply and motioning to the door behind her. "Your father left strict instructions for you to enter whenever you arrived no matter what was happening."

Lily had been with her father since he bought the paper in 1911. Outside of Robert, many believed that without Lily, the paper would crumble. She not only knew everything that went on in the paper, she protected Jonathan like a lioness, thus earning her the respected title, "The Gatekeeper."

She tapped on her father's glass office door, watching him motion for her to enter as he hung up the phone. He looked up slowly, deep in thought. As she waited for him to finish whatever he was doing, she noticed her dad seemed to be graying around his temples. *Did I put it there*, she wondered. She didn't think it was there yesterday. This was an unexpected observation since he never seemed to age in her eyes; forever being daddy's little girl.

She never noticed the extra pounds that had crept around his middle these last few years or the wrinkles around his eyes; he was perfect to Maize and always would be. But he still had that look in his eyes. It was the same look she saw now, watching him behind his desk across the room. It was the look that said "Let's take 'em on," and that look usually meant trouble for someone. He had a nose for news, and now a local story he could sink his teeth into. He wasn't about to let this story slip through his fingers even if it was tied up in police red tape. He had a daughter to protect, citizens to alert, papers to sell, and favors to call in.

Finally signing the last paper on his desk, which was hard to decipher since he was buried in papers, he smiled ear to ear after seeing his daughter refreshed and looking well. "I see you are rested … good … good … why don't you shut the door and sit down for awhile. I'd like to talk with you."

Realizing Maize had entered their dad's office, Robert appeared just as she was closing the door. Happy to see him, Maize gave him a big hug and both sat down in the chairs in front of their dad's desk.

"Robert, glad you could join us. I was just about to ask Maize how she was feeling."

"Just fine, dad. After a good sleep, I'm ready for whatever the day brings. Looks like a beehive around here. Outside of Lily, no one noticed me; not even Sam. Which on second thought, is a good thing, I really don't want to answer any more questions."

"Nothing like a good news story to get a reporter's blood pumping. You can feel the excitement in the air," added Robert.

"I asked Sam to stay on top of the events, giving him the lead in this story. He's the only one I trust to keep everything below the radar. I also assigned Jake, the junior reporter, to follow up on any leads. The police are extremely tight-lipped about the fungus they lifted from the scene, which in itself causes me to be suspicious."

"Dad," Robert asked, "Did you find anything else last night before you left the precinct?"

"Yes," he answered, looking at Robert and then Maize. "One of my police friends happened to mention they noticed the fungus in the sand first because of its unusual coloring, and then because the fungus showed a distinct greenish hue from other greenery located near the skeleton's head. The forensic team bagged it for further study. Apparently there has been new research studying algae and such called "botanical identification." Sergeant Oleary thought it looked like residue from some sort of plant that was kept alive all these years by moisture pockets under the sand that grew from the incoming tides. Jake is presently reviewing botanical investigation methods."

"That seems weird," questioned Maize. "I didn't read that in the article this morning. Did Sam forget to include that bit of info in his feature?"

"The police asked us not to disclose this piece of information until they have identified what it is, and if it's even relevant to the investigation. There are only a handful of people who know, so you must keep this under wraps, Maize," Jonathan replied, looking straight at his daughter.

"Does Leslie's father know about the fungus?" Maize inquired.

A puzzled look came across Jonathan's face. "Why do you ask?"

"I noticed you two talking last night and thought maybe that's what you were discussing." Maize did not think it prudent to reveal she knew that they had made arrangements to meet later after she and Leslie left the precinct.

"Yes, he is privy to this information. He is an official of this town as chair of the Proprietors of Common and Undivided Grounds; he has access to certain types of information," her father stated matter-of-factly. "And we wanted to collaborate considering both of our daughters are involved in this investigation to some extent."

Maize squirmed in her seat, not liking what she heard.

Jonathan continued. "The police chief knows more than he is telling. It's up to us to uncover the details. That's one of the reasons I appointed Sam as the special investigator, much to the chagrin of other up-and-coming reporters. He's been around a long time and has a lot of connections."

"When will they identify the skeleton?" Robert asked his father.

"Your guess is good as mine. Obviously, it's been there a long time, more than likely the sand eroded a lot of tissue over the years."

"What can I do?" Maize asked, concerned that she might be kept out of the loop by an overprotective father and brother.

"Maize you can help by just doing your job. Why don't you report to Ruth when we've finished here? She mentioned earlier today she has a new assignment for you."

Maize's face must have revealed her disappointment. "Maize, you know I need you around here to be my extra eyes and ears—now more than ever. To give you something special may jeopardize any bits and pieces of information you might uncover. People are more apt to avoid gossiping if they think you are consumed with the society page. They'll think I deliberately kept you out of the loop for your protection."

Maize knew there wasn't any use expending energy to change her father's mind. But, in no way was she going to take a back seat in this investigation. She sighed politely and excused herself while Robert stayed to talk.

Maize looked directly for Sam. She found him where she saw him last, at his desk talking on the phone. Maize plopped down on the chair next to Sam's desk just loud enough to let him know she was there. Sam covered the phone, mouthing he would be with her in a moment. Maize could tell by the conversation that Sam was probably talking to someone at the police station. Putting the phone down, Sam turned his attention to Maize.

"Hi kiddo, glad to see you looking so well," Sam said affectionately. "What's up? Saw you were in talking with your father."

"Yes, dad told me he appointed you as the lead in this investigation." As she moved closer, she whispered, "And … about the fungus."

Sam didn't look surprised as he surmised Jonathan would inform her about some facts concerning the case, he just didn't know which ones until Maize brought them up.

"Sam, I couldn't help overhearing you talking to someone at the police department. May I ask who?"

"The Chief just called to tell me they might have a lead on the identification of the skeleton. It's nice he called, but I think it was more a courtesy in order to hide more important info that they've uncovered. The Chief is not one of your dad's greatest admirers, and would not go out of his way to cough up any info unless he had an ulterior motive."

"Dad said Jake is looking into something called botanical identification?"

Nodding in agreement, Sam continued. "Maize while I have you here, I was wondering if we could talk in a more relaxed, less-intrusive environment about your ... experience?"

Maize trusted Sam and would do most anything for him, thus she didn't see any reason why not. As she rose to leave she replied, "Of course, just name the time and place."

Obviously pleased, Sam replied, "I'll get back with you on that real soon."

"Sounds like a plan to me." And with that, she turned to leave the newspaper, but not before she stopped at Ruth's office to check on her latest assignment.

Chapter 4

Scott realized Maize wanted to talk, but now was not the time. He needed to talk to his father and that was a priority. He knew his dad was returning from a recent business trip to Boston within the next hour; he needed time to collect his thoughts and earn the support of his mother.

Scott was still trying to find his place in the family. To him, Robert was the favored son working in the family business, and Maize was his baby sister who was always treated with tender loving care. Scott never doubted his parents' love, but on the other hand, he never believed that he measured up to his father's expectations. Maybe his lack of maturity or his middle placement in the family or his constant need for his father's approval over-dramatized the situation, but to Scott, this would be one of his defining moments. He wanted to share something that surely would ingratiate himself in his father's eyes and gain his respect, now that he had a specific goal in mind to pave a path for his future.

Jonathan arrived home on schedule as Scott knew he would. Upon returning home from any trip, his dad had a specific routine. He always put his hat, which was his trademark, on the hat hook to the right of the front door where several others rested. If wearing a coat of some type, he hung it on the coat rack, and if carrying an umbrella, he slid it into the umbrella stand. Since the Volstead Act forbade the purchase of liquor, Julia had his illegally acquired—but not illegal to consume—martini chilled and ready with copies of the day's New Haven and Boston newspapers lying on the table next to his favorite worn chair in the study. After relaxing with his martini and perusing the papers, he always slouched in his chair, calling out that he was home.

This was a cue for everyone to come and greet him. It was a well-known fact his children had learned over the years that if you wanted to talk to dad and have a positive outcome, you would wait until you heard the cue. Scott finished the late afternoon snack Julia had prepared for him in the kitchen and was waiting for the cue that signaled father was ready to talk. He had gained his mother's support earlier, and now he and Julia were making small talk to pass the time. He loved his mother's kindness and patience with him, and hoped she would have a few kind words to insert into the upcoming conversation.

Soon came the moment that Scott had been waiting for and planning for days. Julia would go first as usual and see if Jonathan needed anything else, next Virginia would join him in the study discussing events of her day, and then Scott would enter.

Virginia was sitting in the matching chair next to Jonathan, separated by a side table; they were engaged in conversation when Scott entered the room. Scott sat in the half sofa across from his parents. There was one spot open since Sandy had claimed the other side as her space a long time ago. Scott rubbed Sandy in her favorite spot behind the ears as he sat down, catching the end of his parents' conversation.

"Good to see you, Son," his father said.

"Jonathan," Virginia stated, "Scott stopped by a little while ago. He has been in the kitchen devouring Julia's latest batch of homemade sugar cookies. Scott told us about some wonderful news he wanted to share especially with you."

Smiling, Jonathan stated, "That sounds ominous."

Virginia continued before Scott could answer. "He was famished. I don't think he eats enough at school, but he does look so handsome, don't you think?"

Jonathan nodding his head replied. "Yes, Scott always dresses quite nice, Virginia."

"Good to see you Dad, hope you had a pleasant trip," Scott stated as Virginia purposely excused herself.

"Your mother says you have something to discuss." Jonathan was not one to beat around the bush.

Scott could see his father was tired from his trip to Boston; fortunately, however, his demeanor was relaxed and his tone was warm, but fatherly. "Yes Dad, I have been enjoying Yale University this semester. I am taking a class entitled Sherlock Holmes the Great Detective from a real live detective from Scotland Yard. Ya' know, as in London, England." Seeing that he had caught his father's interest like he hoped, he continued. "He arrived in New Haven about three years ago as a visiting professor at Yale's Law School via Cambridge University … ya' know, Cambridge, England. Apparently that is where he earned his degree in criminology before becoming a detective."

"What's his name son?"

"His title is Professor Richard Wikki," Scott announced proudly. Scott noticed his dad nod his head, demonstrating he was interested and listening. *That's a good sign*, he thought to himself. "To make a long story short, Father, I have had some very interesting conversations with him, not only after class but in the student lounge as well as his office. He's a highly respected professor on campus and somewhat of a celebrity with the student body. Students love to hear him recall his

Scotland Yard adventures."

As Jonathan listened, he could see the excitement in his son's eyes and noticed the uplifted tone in his voice. He couldn't help think that maybe Scott was finally interested in something other than golf, parties, and himself. He wasn't sure what it meant, but at least he seemed to have focused on someone and something worthwhile.

"So, Father, I've had so many conversations about the field of criminology to the point that Professor Wikki has agreed to be my mentor."

There was a long pause. Jonathan was filled with mixed emotions from shock to elation to surprise to wondering why his son turned such a corner. Jonathan thought to himself, *I should meet this man*. "Scott, you do seem to be intrigued with this detective professor. He obviously is of good character or he wouldn't be teaching at Yale."

This was going better than Scott had hoped. "Dad, I was wondering if he could be invited for dinner with the whole family."

"Well, Son, I am very busy at the paper with this skeleton story, but I'm sure that would be an interesting evening for all of us. Tell your mother I approve and to make all the arrangements. Just let me know when I need to show up." And with that being said, Jonathan picked up the paper and continued reading.

As Scott rose to leave, elated about the whole conversation, Jonathan made a final statement from behind his paper. "Son, I'm proud of you for taking such an interest in a noble profession. I look forward to meeting your Professor Detective Richard Wikki."

And with that, Scott left the room grinning from ear to ear, knowing that he finally pleased his father.

***

As Maize peered into the Cheval mirror that Grandma had given her when she first arrived—mainly because there wasn't room in her living quarters—she scrutinized her dress and coloring, reviewing her outfit of choice for tonight's dinner. When Maize reported on a social event for New Haven's finest, a woman's dress was an important reading point that must be included in every review.

Realizing dressing for the occasion was a must for any respectable woman, Maize prepared ahead of time for tonight's dinner with Professor Detective Richard Wikki. She was pleased with her reflection from head to toe. Her dark brown hair seemed to enhance the angle of her new bob haircut, and her blushed cheeks highlighted the newest rouge shade by Helena Rubinstein, which, unbeknownst to her mother, she rubbed across her lips as well. Maize had found a gold mine for cosmetics at the new Woolworths store in Wooster Square, east of downtown. It was a treasure chest for a young lady of the twenties— stocking all of the latest cosmetics to the utter dismay of most parents.

The three-quarter length chartreuse green shift with a large, white, lace collar forming a large V-shaped neckline was offset at the hip with the pale pink sash. *It's the perfect accessory*, thought Maize. The shiny rayon stockings which were held up by garter belts had been softened with a few puffs of loose powder. She smiled as she inspected her new Mary Jane shoes with a slight heel that were dyed to match the color of her dress. Maize pondered if she should add a waist length single strand of white pearls. As she put them over her head, she immediately realized it was way too much for a dinner at home. "They'd probably end up in my food anyway," she mumbled to herself as she took them off and placed them on top of her dresser.

Suddenly, a noise from downstairs jolted Maize out of her haze of grandeur. Hearing Scott's voice and someone's she didn't recognize, she thought it must be the famous Professor Detective Wikki.

It was no accident that everyone had arrived before her because she was intentionally waiting to make an entrance. She knew from covering numerous New Haven society parties that a woman must plan and make a gracious entrance. *Just don't trip*, she thought as she began to descend the staircase.

Everyone had gathered in the parlor to enjoy light conversation. Julia had served drinks to all, including Pastor Albert who was known to imbibe once in a while. Maize's family attended the Center Church on The Green where Pastor Albert served. Virginia purposely invited Pastor Albert because the church had quite a history, which would provide interesting conversation if need be, especially if Professor Wikki was not as forthcoming as Scott had alluded.

No one heard her walk down the stairs so Maize was able to pause and take a moment to collect herself. As she stood near the parlor entrance, she noticed Scott and Professor Wikki deep in conversation. It was second nature for Maize to notice how everyone dressed, and he was not at all what she expected. Instead of ruggish looking, he was stylish … almost dapper. His clothes were not of a middle class gentleman but gave an impression of class. He wore a sporty trimmed dress jacket with high and low pockets on each side opened to display a starched white dress shirt and matching tie. His trousers were tailored, not baggy, and ended in a small cuff set off with brown slip-on shoes. His short, light brown hair around his ears was longer on top with a slight wave as it fell naturally on his forehead. Maize's reporting skills caused her imagination to wander; there's more to this man than meets the eye.

Scott was introducing his guest to everyone when Maize entered the parlor. Virginia stood, watching the introductions while waiting for Maize at the parlor door.

"There you are. You look very nice dear," Virginia exclaimed and motioned towards Scott in the middle of the room. "Scott will introduce you to his guest." Virginia gracefully escorted Maize to greet Professor Wikki as Maize's whole body suddenly felt like cement. Panicking, she thought, *I cannot move. Oh gosh, I hope I look as calm and collected as I did in the mirror a few minutes ago.*

She wasn't sure how she was able to walk across the room, but she did. She was glad Scott and the professor were both standing in the middle of the parlor because it meant fewer potential objects for her to stumble over. Scott immediately began the introduction as Maize approached.

"Professor, this is my little sister Maize, whom I've told you about." *Oh no, he told Detective Wikki about ME! What did he say?* She screamed quietly to herself, shooting Scott a stern look. *How embarrassing!* Maize could see her well-planned entrance shatter before her very eyes.

"Maize, it's nice to meet you, your brother is very proud of you. He tells me you are working part-time as a news reporter for the society page at your father's newspaper."

Maize nodded her head in agreement, but before she could answer Professor Wikki, everyone turned to greet Robert who was entering the parlor. Maize watched as the introductions started all over again. Nothing was going the way she had planned. Her visions of grandeur were quickly shattered to the mundane reality of the situation. It was Scott's night, and the family would act accordingly … as would she.

Julia soon announced that dinner was served and everyone filed into the dining room situated next to the parlor. Virginia graciously maneuvered everyone to their assigned seats. Virginia and Jonathan sat at each end of the rectangular table. Scott sat next to Professor Wikki on one side of the dining table and Robert, Pastor Albert, and Maize sat on the other side. Maize felt like the fifth wheel stuck at the end between her father on her right and Robert on her left. She was disturbed. *How in the world am I going to be able to ask all of my questions sitting so far away from the professor at the end of the table hidden by Grandma's hideously large, sterling silver candelabras?*

Everyone was making small talk except Maize, who was in her own world.

Soon Jonathan clanged his crystal glass half full of ice water, signaling it was time for his traditional toast. Grimacing, Maize thought, *I wish he would think of something different to say; he basically says the same thing every time.* Maize watched silently as everyone remained seated and raised their glasses towards Jonathan. *I guess, unless you were invited for dinner more than once, you'd never know.*

"Here's to our two guests who have graced our home this evening. Here's to our special guest Professor Detective Wikki and our beloved Pastor Albert." Then everyone followed decorum and drank to the toast. Next, as usual, Jonathan directed the dinner conversation.

"Professor, Scott seems quite intrigued with your class. What is it called?"

"Mr. Judson, the class Scott is referring to is called Sherlock Holmes the Great Detective. We are studying Sherlock's investigative techniques as well as the fictitious man himself. In London around the 1850s, many citizens believed Conan Doyle's mysteries were about a real live detective."

Everyone began to eat as dinner was served while Professor Wikki continued to discuss the highlights of his course.

Maize, spending more time watching and listening than eating, couldn't help analyze the professor. *He sits so regal, with manners of a gentleman, speaking so eloquently and looking totally calm and at ease, and he's quite the conversationalist.* Maize hadn't expected him to have such finesse. *He should be rougher around the edges*, she deduced.

E.K. Prescott, Ph.D.

Come to think of it, his clothes seem to be made of a finer fabric than worn by most profs. She knew clothes, and especially clothes of the nouveau riche whom she covered in her society column. Maize also seemed puzzled about his age, he had a young, attractive clean-shaven face, but his conversation made one believe he was a man of experience. She found a pause in the chatter and jumped in. "If I may ask a question," she inquired looking at Professor Wikki.

"Of course Maize," he replied with a smile as he looked down the table to his left.

Looking at Professor Wikki around and through the obese candle set in the middle of the table, Maize asked. "Professor Detective Richard Wikki, you have such a long name. How do you prefer to be addressed?"

"That's a good question. First of all, my students at school refer to me as Professor Wikki. Detective refers to my past employment as a detective from Scotland Yard, where I worked for about six years." Richard paused. Maize noticed a flicker of pain flash in his eyes as he quickly continued. "Come to think of it no one actually addresses me as Richard except maybe other professors. What I mean is that personal friends have tagged me with the initials PD for Professor Detective. Some informally call me PD Wikki, and a few of my close friends call me PD."

"Professor, don't forget Doctor," Scott added.

"Oh, yes. Dean Johannas surprised me with an honorary doctoral degree from the Yale School of Law upon acceptance of my present full-time position," replied Richard matter-of-factly. He knew it was just window dressing to keep up appearances. He had noticed in this town that appearances were extremely important. Richard was not about to discuss his title as Lord of Foxworthy, as it was from the past and not relevant. As he relayed all the different compositions of his name, Maize thought all of those names sure seem to give one an air of mystery. *Who are you really, Professor Detective Richard Wikki?*

As dessert was being served, Jonathan maneuvered the dinner conversation towards Pastor Albert and the Center Church. "You know Pastor, I recall the paper did an exposé a few years back about the history of the New Haven Center Church. I don't think Professor Wikki is aware of its unique historic background. Why don't you enlighten the professor about the finer points?"

"That would be a pleasure. I doubt if Scott and Maize are aware of our history. Let's see, where to begin? In 1638 a group of Puritans from London, England landed on Long Island Sound wanting to create a planned colony. They viewed the barrier island as protection and the harbor and surrounding waters deemed lucrative for trade. The new settlers immediately established a protected area of land in the middle of New Haven Colony called The Market which is now referred to as The Green. The original purpose of The Market was to provide an open area of land for 100,000 people to gather in order to be lifted up into Heaven for the Second Coming of Christ. In the meantime, it housed other things including a prison, a cemetery, a school, and an open market. It was mainly used as a general meeting place for political and religious purposes. The Center Church at that time was known as the Congregational Church, and it was also used for religious and secular meetings; it was of Puritan denomination. Seven men—prominent landowners and governing officials—were chosen to oversee The Market. This oversight continues today, but with five Proprietors of The Green instead of seven. The appointment is held until death. When a member dies, the other four go into seclusion until they have chosen the new member."

Richard loved details—especially historical facts which could be seemingly random, but at the right time could be the final piece of the puzzle. He felt at times his mind was like a filing cabinet keeping track of all the little details that came his way only to be retrieved when needed. His gut told him this was one of those times.

Being very fascinated with the historical perspective, Professor Wikki asked, "When did your church receive its name as Center Church?"

The Pastor continued. "The church itself has undergone four separate remodeling projects and some major facelifts on The Green since its conception in 1638. The cemetery was expanding to encompass too much of The Green, mainly because of the deadly Spanish Influenza epidemic, so in 1856, New Haven's cemetery was moved to its present location, Grove Street Cemetery. So I'd say about then."

Maize curiously inquired. "You mean they dug up all the bodies?"

"Well, actually only twelve bodies were unearthed; there is an estimated 5,000 or more still buried there." Pastor Albert continued. "What they actually did was move only the gravestones, and left the bodies buried. The gravestones were placed around the front walls of the Grove Street Cemetery and are still there today."

"You mean we are walking on dead people?" exclaimed Maize.

"Yes, I guess that is one way to look at it. One small portion of the gravesite stayed intact with the headstones in place. About 137 graves and gravestones from 1638 are under our church. We refer to it as The Crypt."

Richard's eyes were full of questions. He thought this was quite a tale the Pastor was weaving.

"When it came time to rebuild our present building, which is the fourth, it was built over that part of the cemetery. The floor of our church provides refuge for the aging gravestones. We are the church in the middle with the United Church on one side and the Trinity Church on the other, but we are the only original church of New Haven since 1639."

Scott asked, "Pastor, did I read or hear somewhere that some very famous people are buried in The Green cemetery?"

"Before we continue," interrupted Jonathan. "Let's all recline to the parlor for drinks. We can continue our discussion while enjoying our preferred night cap."

Once everyone was settled, Jonathan cued Pastor Albert to continue his history lesson. "I believe, Pastor Albert, you were about to answer Scott's question about famous people buried in the cemetery."

"Oh, yes, let's see," the Pastor stumbled as he gathered his thoughts. "Yes, buried in The Green is Benedict Arnold's first wife, one of New Haven's founders, Theopolis Eaton, some of President Rutherford Hayes' early ancestors, and the founder and first President of Yale, Reverend James Pierpont."

"How about the Grove Street Cemetery? Who's buried there?" Maize asked inquisitively.

"Well," the Pastor replied, "Eli Whitney, Noah Webster and another important person, one of the founders of New Haven and the United States, Roger Sherman."

"Wow," Virginia exclaimed, "I don't think even I knew all that information."

"We have a lot of people stop by for tours, so I formed a church council to create a pamphlet to help explain why we have a crypt in our basement," explained Pastor Albert. Looking at his watch, the Pastor noted, "Well my friends I've had yet another delightful evening. I must take my leave."

"Pastor Albert, we thank you for gracing our home with your presence. May we do this again sometime soon?" replied Virginia as she rose to escort the Pastor to the door.

"Always a pleasure my dear," he exclaimed as they both walked out of the room. Turning to pause at the parlor doorway, the Pastor turned to say good night to the rest of the Judson family and Professor Wikki.

Upon taking his own leave, Professor Wikki spoke first. "Scott, thank you for inviting me to your home, it was a delightful evening. I do not have many opportunities to dine with my students' families."

"Professor, I want to personally thank you for taking such interest in my son. He mentioned that you have agreed to be his mentor," Jonathan lamented.

"Professor Wikki," Scott chimed in, "I look forward to learning from a real detective."

"Scott, we'll be seeing a lot of each other, but now I must call it a night as well."

As Virginia entered the parlor, everyone stood to escort Professor Wikki to the front door. As Jonathan opened the door and Virginia handed Professor Wikki his hat that she retrieved from the rack, Jonathan looked pointedly into Professor Wikki's eyes and asked in a serious tone. "Professor, I have a unique situation down at the paper, and I'd like to get your take on it. May I call upon you to join me one afternoon for lunch on The Green?"

Not expecting such a proposal, Richard agreed graciously. "Why, I would be honored, Mr. Judson."

"Please, call me Jonathan. Mr. Judson is for people I don't know," remarked Jonathan. Richard nodded in respectful compliance and all bid good night as the door closed behind him.

As Richard walked to his car, he paused a moment. It occurred to him that Jonathan probably wanted to discuss the skeleton story. A smile crossed his face as he realized that he may soon be using his deductive talents once again. As he drove home east around and down the harbor, Richard could not help but feel he was about to embark on a new adventure; his first investigation in a new country, the United States of America.

Chapter 5

It was difficult to rub the sand out of the small crevices of the necklace, but with a little elbow grease, some more soap, and some good old-fashioned rubbing alcohol, Maize was sure it would be as good as new. After she removed the caked layers of sand from the single medallion attached to the tarnished and rusted chain, Maize noticed a raised, engraved image.

Some of the markings on the medallion and links in the chain still seemed quite gritty, but as she applied more alcohol, a circle appeared like a big, black, solid sun showing four large rays ending with arrow tips protruding outwardly from each side of the circle. As she ran her fingers over the image, she noticed there were smaller rays positioned between each of the four, making four short rays and four large, eight in total.

At first glance, Maize thought the impression seemed unusually raised for a pendant, but she didn't give it a second thought after eyeing something odd. As she held the coarse chain in her left hand while trying to remove all traces of sand link by link with her right, she noticed the necklace was broken from the left of the clasp, revealing an open link. *That's weird*, she thought. It apparently had been closed and then pulled apart.

Finally the necklace was as clean as it was going to be. As Maize held the medallion in her hand allowing it to air-dry, she noticed some scratches in the middle of the raised sun. Looking closer, she tried to decipher the markings, and finally concluded the apparent etchings were just a few random abrasions. She grabbed a soft hand towel and gave it a final rub, soaking up any excess water. As she walked towards her room to dress for her appointment with the Yale admissions advisor, she folded the necklace neatly into the soft hand towel for safe keeping. Once tucked nicely back into the drawer in the table next to her bed, Maize didn't give the necklace a second thought until….

***

It was the middle of June and summer definitely had arrived in New Haven. As Maize drove with the top down on the Touring, she recalled the intense conversation with her mother and father regarding her attending Yale in the fall. She thought it had gone rather well, remembering her mother unconvincingly approved, lamenting that Maize would be the first woman in their family to go to college. Since she was attending part-time and working part-time, Maize knew her mother thought it was just a lark and would pass.

Her father, on the other hand, seemed somewhat pleased to have a daughter attending Yale. He had connections with "Yale people" as he referred to them, and had made arrangements for her to meet with an admissions advisor today. Maize was never really sure who her dad's "Yale people" were, but all she cared about at the moment was arriving at Blair Hall calm, cool, and collected. *I'm a statistic*, she thought to herself as she recalled that less than one fourth of the 300 incoming freshman in 1923 included women.

E.K. Prescott, Ph.D.

She found a parallel parking space one block from Blair Hall near College Street on The Green. Pausing after closing her car door, Maize tugged at the cool marigold sleeveless shift, hoping the wrinkles in her dress that formed from sitting in the car too long in the hot weather wouldn't show. As she crossed The Green, Maize repositioned the new matching wide brimmed cloche hat she ordered from the latest summer Sears catalog, tugging it to cover most of her bob. Maize was so consumed with her appearance, she hardly realized Professor Wikki was walking towards her as she was about to cross College Street to Yale Hall.

"Maize, what a nice surprise! It's nice to see you."

Startled, Maize hoped the blushing on her face didn't give away how embarrassed she was at her apparent absentmindedness.

Professor Wikki continued. "I'm on my way to join your brother for something cool to drink at The Spot."

The Spot, owned by Frank Pepe, was a popular pizza restaurant and hang-out for young and old alike that specialized in their famous white pizza: a thin-crust pizza baked in a brick oven and topped with white sauce, garlic, cheese, and clams.

As she stood listening to him and looking into his eyes, Maize suddenly realized she had never stood this close to Professor Wikki before, not even when he came to dinner a couple of weeks ago. She uneasily took an awkward step backwards while relaying how she was planning to attend Yale in the fall, and that she was on her way to the admissions office to make it official. As she took a deep breath, she noticed that she was speaking rapidly like a star-struck adolescent, she told herself to calm down. *Professor Wikki isn't Rudolf Valentino.*

"I'd love to talk it over with you. Why don't you meet up with us at The Spot? We are going to be sitting outside under one of the umbrella's enjoying the fresh air. You won't have a hard time locating us;

we will have found the coolest spot in the shade."

Maize was flattered with Professor Wikki's invitation, but the feeling was quickly replaced with uneasiness as she thought she must have hesitated too long to respond, because Professor Wikki interrupted her thoughts, assuring her he wouldn't bite. Oh, how embarrassing, she thought.

Quickly recovering, she accepted the invitation. "Of course, I'd be pleased to join you both. I haven't seen Scott since you were our dinner guest. I really don't know how long I will be, but I don't think more than an hour."

Professor Wikki smiled and started to walk away. "Great, we'll see you then."

Maize waved goodbye, refocusing her attention on the mission at hand as she crossed College Street, hoping to be at the top of her game when she met the admissions advisor.

***

As Maize checked her watch upon leaving Dr. Frank's office, she was not surprised that her appointment had taken less than an hour. Not surprised because Dr. Frank seemed to be an extremely precise man who was precisely groomed, spoke in a precise voice, and sat in a precise manner. While he was precisely filling out all the papers, she couldn't help thinking that he must have a precisely boring life. There wasn't much for her to do except nod in agreement as Dr. Frank wrote precisely in each blank. She thought to herself, *Father must have made all the right connections for me to be in his office such a short time. It's done!* She grinned with self-satisfaction, realizing it was official: she was a Yale girl.

Upon crossing The Green to meet Professor Wikki and her brother, she recalled that Dr. Frank precisely stated women entering

E.K. Prescott, Ph.D.

Yale University usually majored in Liberal Arts. That made Maize's blood boil. She knew what she wanted to do and it wasn't earning a petticoat diploma; she wanted to be an investigative reporter majoring in Journalism. Soon Scott came into focus as she crossed Church Street. Scott was watching for her standing and stretching awkwardly, looking above people's heads for the first glimpse of his sister.

When he caught her eye, he waved for her to join them. Upon her arrival, he gave her a loving pat on the shoulder, "Nice to see ya' sis! What a surprise!"

Professor Wikki stood, pulling out the chair next to Scott for her to occupy. As she sat, Maize couldn't help notice Scott was well-dressed as usual wearing a red golf shirt and knickers with high socks, two-toned saddle shoes and a small billed golf hat. Maize thought he looked so gallant with his blond hair and endearing smile. Scott gave her a light kiss on the check. "Let me look at you, aren't you in vogue my dear. You fit right into the college scene."

"Nice to see you again too, Maize," Professor Wikki said as he and Scott sat down. Chuckling he continued. "What an appropriate description. I couldn't have said it better myself. We ordered you a cool glass of lemonade when we first noticed you crossing The Green," he said, motioning to the glass waiting for her. Maize nodded with thanks as she took a cool sip.

"Sis, you really are going to be a Yale girl?"

As Maize nodded affirmatively, Scott continued. "What do you want to major in?" Scott was almost sorry he asked as he listened to Maize work herself into a frenzy relaying how Dr. Frank had the audacity to suggest she major in Liberal Arts because she was a woman.

"Anyway, to make a long story very short, I want to major in Journalism with a focus on investigative reporting," she firmly concluded. "I plan to attend part-time in the fall taking only two courses—a journalism course and literature course—since I'm working part-time at the paper."

"Seems like you are very sure of what you want to do," Professor Wikki observed.

"You ought to be good at journalism sis, lately you have managed to make the front page of most newspapers," Scott smiled, chiding her. "You did uncover quite a mystery. Any news as to who it is?"

"Not as yet, but an approximate time period has been established—somewhere around a hundred years ago, early to mid 1800s."

"I wonder how the skeleton landed near the lighthouse," Scott expressed. "Seems questionable at best. Don't you think?"

Maize continued. "Father said the police thought the erosion of the sand over the years led to the placement of the skeleton near the surface, but that it was definitely buried there from the get-go."

"Well if you ask me," Scott deducted, "something sounds fishy."

"Father has several investigative reporters working on it. Apparently, he's trying to cooperate with the police investigation, but they don't make it easy."

"Well that might be a first. I know there is no love lost between him and Police Chief Sparks," remarked Scott.

Maize noticed Professor Wikki pull from his jacket pocket a funny looking pipe which he began to chew on. To her, it looked like a funny piece of polished black wood in the shape of a saxophone.

Noticing her inquisitive stare, Professor Wikki explained. "I see you noticed my pipe. It was a gift from a dear friend … actually, he was my mentor when I attended Cambridge. It has a special meaning. I never smoke it … I've just developed a funny habit of chewing on the end. I mostly find myself automatically reaching for it when I start to ponder something." Chewing again on the end of his pipe, Professor

Wikki continued. "I find the skeleton case quite intriguing … lots of unanswered questions."

A young waitress approached their table and asked Scott if there would be anything else. She seemed quite enamoured with him, but as usual, Scott didn't notice; he didn't have to.

"Not for me," Scott replied. "I need to run." He finished the rest of his lemonade while looking at his watch, "I'm already late. A couple of my Wolf's Head brothers are racing their cars on the country roads in East Haven."

"You go ahead Scott," replied Richard. "I'll pick up the tab … this time."

"Thanks," Scott replied as he rose and leaned over to kiss Maize on top of her head. "Great seeing you, sis. Can't believe my little sister is going to be a Yale girl. See ya' later Doc." And off he went, not waiting for anyone to reply.

Maize felt sorry for the poor young waitress who was still standing there, obviously disappointed with Scott's untimely departure.

"Well then, can I get either of you another lemonade?"

"No thanks, just the check," replied Richard raising his glass. "We still have some left."

Maize sat somewhat uncomfortable while waiting for the waitress to return with the check. She didn't really know what to say to Professor Wikki.

Sensing her uneasiness, Richard started the conversation. "I'm quite intrigued with your little adventure of late. The newspaper articles I've read have contained few relevant facts about the case." Chewing on the end of his pipe, Richard continued. "I'm sure important facts are intentionally withheld by either the police and/or the newspaper. That was common practice among us at Scotland Yard."

Maize found an opening to contribute. "Yes, I'm sure with your past, Professor, you tend to question all mysterious events."

"It really never leaves you … it's in the blood. That's one of the reasons I love teaching in the criminology area of the law school. My new course, Sherlock Holmes the Great Detective, seems to be very popular with the students."

"Of course it is," Maize blurted out, feeling more comfortable. "You are the real thing. Why, it would more than likely be a class I should take as well."

Richard couldn't help but notice how alive Maize seemed. Her eyes twinkled with excitement as she talked about her work and future goals. *How quickly one forgets the simplicity of youth*, he thought to himself, recalling how students seem to hang on his every word when he described a case. These are young, impressionable minds. But there was a limit to his stories, especially when a case would move him in a direction he did not want to remember. Those stories stayed deeply hidden intentionally, and not to be revisited by anyone, not even him.

"Did you like being a detective for Scotland Yard?" Maize asked.

"Yes, very much so, although at times it was very frustrating and emotional. But, it's very satisfying when you tie together a lot of loose ends to solve a case." He continued as Maize hung on every word. "Of course, every detective has some crimes that are never solved for one reason or another."

"What brought you to America if you loved it so," Maize probed. Noticing a quick flash of pain cross his face Maize continued, "Oh I'm sorry, that's really none of my business. I'm so inquisitive about everything, I sometimes forget my manners."

Richard chose not to reply but instead divert the conversation. "You were having a picnic on the beach when you discovered the skeleton. Didn't you have someone with you?"

"Yes, my friend Leslie Davenport. Her father owns the Taft Hotel across from The Green, and I think four others. I'm not sure, but I think the others are in Boston, Danvers (previously called Salem), Hartford and maybe New York. Leslie's been my best friend since elementary school. She's quite dramatic and skittish. She didn't take well to finding the skeleton, but feeling those bones is quite creepy when you think of it. I mean it was her fingers feeling something unusual protruding out of the sand."

"Did the police find anything else?"

Maize somehow believed she could trust Professor Wikki, rationalizing that he was a respected detective who was used to properly handling sensitive material.

Richard noticed her pause. "I'm sorry if I put you on the spot," he grinned, glancing up at the restaurant's sign. "No pun intended. I just know there is more to this story than meets the eye. This is the first news story in New Haven that has piqued my interest since I arrived. Reading about another Palmer raid or another church burned down by the Ku Klux Klan or the latest Chicago mob blood bath doesn't really appeal to me."

"My father seems really excited about this story. I think he feels as you do. I haven't seen him so excited since the double murder a few years ago, before you came."

"Every good detective worth his salt needs a good investigative reporter on his side. I've had to depend on a few to dig for information which was difficult for me to retrieve. But of course, there is a price; the reporter usually wants me to promise an exclusive to the story when it's solved … if it's solved."

As Richard talked, Maize noticed him chewing his pipe between thoughts. She found it quite humorous that there was never any smoke coming out the other end. She had to laugh to herself. *He's so serious. He's really interested.*

"Your father mentioned at dinner he was going to ring me to discuss something about the skeleton story … maybe I should give him a ring," he said, thinking out loud.

Maize didn't know why she suddenly blurted out that she had picked up a necklace off the skeleton. "It was wound in the skeleton's fingers. In all the confusion, I slipped it into my pocket, not giving it a second thought." As soon as the words came out of her mouth, she regretted every one of them. Lowering her head and looking at her finished glass of lemonade, her voice grew sheepish. "No one knows I have the necklace. It's kinda heavy with a raised image in the middle … I don't know who would wear such a thing."

Richard turned facing her with great concern because it was obvious Maize had withheld evidence in a murder case. Not wanting to alarm her, Richard replied with a calm voice, "No one knows you have it? Not even your father?"

All Maize could do was shake her head. She had a knot in her stomach and a deep sense of regret. *Why did I tell him my secret!* Richard continued while chewing on his pipe. "Some people may not understand that you mistakenly put it in your pocket. Where is it now?"

"It's wrapped in a washcloth in the drawer next to my bed. I cleaned it just this morning before I left the house; it was full of dirt and sand."

Detective Richard Wikki's interest had been sufficiently piqued. "Did you notice anything unusual, I mean outside of the medallion's size and the raised impression?"

"Why, yes." Now that she had opened her big mouth she thought she might as well continue. "I thought there was some kind of engraving in the middle, but on second glance it just seemed like a bunch of scratches from years of erosion."

"Anything else?"

"The chain was broken near the clasp."

Richard did not want to unduly alarm Maize about any miscarriage of justice or have her overreact, which was highly probable, but he needed to see the necklace. "Maize, would you do me a favor?"

"Sure, what?"

"For now, don't tell anyone what you have shared with me, not even your father. I will not tell anyone as well … this will be a special secret just between you and me."

Maize took a deep breath. For some reason, she believed him. She nodded her head in compliance, not knowing what else to say.

"This case intrigues me. Could you bring the necklace to me at my office? I'd love to see it for myself."

"You think it's important?"

"I'm not sure until I examine it. We have three bits of information: a skeleton, its date of death somewhere early to mid-1800s, and the necklace itself."

Maize dared not mention the unusual green algae found in the sand; she had said enough for one day. Maize chose to believe that Professor Wikki was bored and wanted something to do with his time outside of Yale. She would bring him the necklace. She couldn't see how a silly old necklace would be so dang important anyway. It was broken and too rusted to wear. *If nothing else, it gives me an opportunity to see him again.*

"Sure I'll bring it by next week. But now, I must leave as I told Leslie I would visit her by early afternoon. Looking at her watch, Maize realized it was much later than she thought. "Oh my, look at the time," she exclaimed.

Richard stood up as Maize rose. "Maize, you have to trust me, and I will trust you with our secret."

"I trust you, Professor Wikki. I'll be by next week with the necklace."

As she turned to leave, Richard couldn't help but feel a twinge of excitement. The kind of twinge that always told him he was on to something, even though he didn't know what it was. The fun was always in the challenge of the unknown.

Chapter 6

The Davenport's butler directed Maize to the receiving room, as he called it. To Maize, it looked like just another parlor. There, she found Leslie listening to "Second Hand Rose" on the phonograph while poring over an array of magazines which were mostly sprawled over the Oriental rug in the center of the room. Leslie was wearing a soft blue afternoon dress that matched the color of her eyes.

"Miss Leslie," announced the butler. "Miss Judson is here to see you."

Leslie rose, letting the magazines in her lap fall to the floor atop the others. Air kissing Maize on both cheeks, Leslie expressed warmly, "What a nice surprise. I didn't think you were coming."

Both girls retired to the couch. "Sorry. I was drinking a glass of lemonade at The Spot with Scott and Professor Wikki and lost track of time."

"I haven't seen you since the … event," complained Leslie. "Who is Professor Wikki?"

Maize chuckled to herself at the discovery of the skeleton being referred to as an "event," recalling Professor Wikki referring to it as "the skeleton caper." *I wonder what I should call it*, she thought to herself.

"He is one of Scott's professors. He teaches law studies, and he is Scott's mentor." Maize grabbed for a magazine on the floor and continued while flipping through the pages. "Scott apparently has decided to go into law and asked Professor Wikki to be his mentor … I guess you need a mentor."

Leslie wasn't really interested and rose to change the record on the phonograph. "What would you like to listen to—Love Sends a Little Gift of Roses or Hot Lips?"

"The first one sounds good to me," Maize decided.

Leslie returned to the couch, picking up the *Harper's Bazaar* magazine that had fallen from her lap. "Maize, you must look at the new skirt hem lines, they're rising." Leslie thumbed through the magazine finding examples of skirts to show Maize. "Aren't they awesome?" she asked.

Maize looked dutifully at the magazine models while Leslie asked, "How have you been? I mean, since the … event?"

Maize didn't much like calling it an event, but she hadn't come up with a better word as of yet.

"To tell you the truth Maize, I'm having nightmares. Feeling those bones was really creepy. Father says all the publicity keeps it fresh in my mind. He is worried about me and thinks I need to get away from all the commotion."

"Really? Has it been all that bad?"

"Well, I didn't think so at first. But father has made arrangements for me to visit my cousins in New York City. I'm taking the train tomorrow and will not return for a month."

"A month! Why so long?"

"He says I seem to be rattling around here passing time aimlessly until the first of August when I depart for Brussels University

E.K. Prescott, Ph.D

for Women in Belgium. He thought visiting my cousins would help the time pass faster."

"I guess it will. I hope you like your cousins."

Absorbed in herself, Leslie continued. "Father doesn't want me traveling alone and has assigned someone he trusts to escort me there and back, someone named Remy."

Leslie, enjoying hearing herself talk, continued. "I think it's because I'm an only child and a girl. He's always worried I'm going to be kidnapped or even killed."

Maize listened in disbelief as Leslie continued her soliloquy.

"I think he is definitely overreacting, but this has been an ongoing battle since I was very small."

To Maize, Leslie seemed perfectly fine. Leslie was a lot stronger than people gave her credit.

"Leslie, remember our capers?" Maize interjected. Through the years, the girls played a game they called "a caper" on unsuspecting adults. They loved to cunningly play public dramatic scams drawing in others to their stage. Usually Maize created the caper and Leslie pulled it off. Leslie relished her part as leading lady since she was an overly dramatic person anyway. On one occasion, they went to the train station and pretended Leslie had just arrived from California, and was looking for her long lost sister she'd never met. Upon locating Maize in the crowd—always in a crowd—Leslie dramatically conveyed the emotions of an overanxious adolescent, meeting her older sister for the first time. To this day, Maize believed that Leslie should have won an award for that one. To them, it was fun, adolescent games.

Remembering, Maize responded. "I don't recall you being so timid and helpless."

Leslie shrugged her shoulders, choosing not to respond.

"I'd like to think of the trip as a vacation. I've been choosing clothes with Lila, our maid, for at least a week. It will be an adventure to pass the time like Father said."

"I have news," Maize said, changing the subject. "I registered for the fall semester at Yale today."

Leslie wasn't surprised. She knew Maize wanted to go to college, but thought she would prefer a women's private school like Vassar to Yale University.

"Really? You chose Yale?"

"Well, it was somewhat of a compromise with my parents. Much to my mother's chagrin, many women are deciding to attend college these days. So to compromise and keep the waters smooth, I said I would live at home this school year. Father knew someone who knew someone who knew someone to make an appointment for me with the admissions advisor. I think my parents believe since Scott attends Yale, he will look out for me. Boy, are they in for a surprise. Scott is too wrapped up in his own life to keep tabs on his little sister. Plus, he would drive me nuts with all the clinging vines. That's what I call the cooing girls who are always around him. And, since I still want to work at the newspaper part-time, I'm only going to take two courses. I guess it is a win-win proposition for everyone."

Leslie changed the record on the phonograph. "I will be boarding in one of the dorm suites during the school year, and most likely traveling abroad over the summer. When I return from New York City, we'll have to get together."

Bragging, Maize mentioned, "Scott was tapped in May to be one of sixteen juniors recruited by Wolf's Head Junior Secret Society at Yale. He has invited me to a Wolf's Head summer dance around the time you return from your travels. He says there is always an off-campus party somewhere, especially when school draws closer. Maybe you'd like to go? I'd prefer to have someone accompany me since I will know

E.K. Prescott, Ph.D.

absolutely no one."

Leslie was delighted. "Oh, how fun! You'll have to let me know what everyone is wearing so I dress as a 'Yale girl.' I don't want to stick out, of course." Leslie was always consumed with the "proper" whatever. Maize knew her mother probably instilled this in her since childhood. She recalled hearing Leslie's mother say on more than one occasion, "Dear, people in our societal position must always look our best."

"Just look in your magazines for the latest flapper designs," Maize suggested.

"Super! Now I'll have something special to occupy my time during my visit. So, what's new at the paper?"

"Well, Father has assigned several reporters to the skeleton mystery, as he calls it." It seemed to Maize everyone had a term for it but her. "He seems to think there is more to it than meets the eye. He's sure the police know more than they are saying. He seems quite wound up about it. He's even assigned Robert some of his own duties so he can spend more time investigating. So, I figure he will need me to do other things as well. I plan to hang-out just in case."

"You mean your father thinks there is really something to this?"

"Well, he certainly is suspicious. He's really not saying much around me. He obviously doesn't want me involved. I even volunteered to help, and he put me off."

"Interesting. Sounds kinda like my father," Leslie surmised. "Come to think of it, I overheard my father talking to someone on the phone several days ago, telling whomever it was he was sure I didn't see anything. I didn't think anything about his conversation at the time, but … maybe he thinks someone is stalking me, because the next thing I know I'm going to visit my cousins for a month."

Maize was sure Leslie wasn't aware of the clues uncovered thus far, and she wasn't going to be the one to tell her. Leslie could be a loose cannon with secret information. "Leslie, I'm sure you are just imagining things. He's probably just trying to relay his concern for your well-being since the event. He is just being overprotective as usual, sounds like to me."

"Yes, you're right," concluded Leslie. "Mother probably was making such an ordeal over the whole thing that Father felt he had to do something to keep her quiet. She does tend to worry about me so; not that I mind of course."

It was time for Maize to make a graceful exit. She rose from the sofa. "Speaking of mothers, I should leave; mine expected me home hours ago."

Leslie rose, kissing Maize briefly on each cheek. "I'll miss you. Mr. Jim can show you out."

"Likewise, and no thanks, I know the way."

As Maize drove home, she was consumed with thoughts of Yale. She was totally unaware of how the events of the next two months would dramatically impact her life path.

Chapter 7

"Thanks Charlotte, that will be all. Please hold all calls and visitors. This meeting is not to be disturbed." Mr. Davenport sat at the end of a long, shiny, mahogany table in the center of the conference room located next to his office on the top floor of the Taft Hotel. The rectangular conference room was decorated with mahogany trim, dark blue carpet, and portraits of all the Presidents of the United States from Washington to Harding hung on the three inner walls. The outer glass wall facing The Green provided a panoramic view of downtown New Haven.

Waiting quietly for the other four proprietors, Mr. Davenport, the Master Prior, stared out the window and mentally reviewed the safety procedures put in place for his daughter's vacation.

Proprietors of Common and Undivided Lands oversee the mission of The Green, established since its conception in 1641. Originally the Puritan colony assigned seven wealthy landowners and influential Whig-party members to the task of oversight, but as the years passed, the membership changed from seven to five. Being chosen as a Proprietor is a coveted lifetime position drawn from the ranks of prominent New Haven residents. When one of the five members passes away, the other four withdraw into seclusion until a new member is chosen. No one except the five really know what happens behind closed doors. The Green is the only piece of land in the United States which is not under federal, state, or municipal jurisdiction. Since the committee is not accountable to anyone but each other, no minutes of the meetings are required to be posted in city records; they have no accountability to anyone but each other.

George Seymour, who is not a Proprietor but a powerful friend, was included in most of Mr. Davenport's affairs. He was the first to arrive. Upon entering, neither gentleman spoke as the Master Prior nodded, signaling for him to sit in the chair to his immediate right.

When he finished reading the file placed in front of him, Mr. Davenport asked rhetorically, "How are you George? How are the boys at CFR these days?"

"Things are as usual, not what they seem. Hiding things out in the open is a perfect strategy; citizens never suspect a thing. The Breaker Foundation is set to filter monies to overseas banks in London when all is ready at your end."

Chuckling, Davenport emphatically commented, "I like having control over our nation's money, I really don't care who makes the laws."

George grinned, nodding in agreement as the other four members filtered into the conference room, taking their usual seats. Mr. Daggert, a well-known local entrepreneur, sat next to George. Mr. Janseen, a local council member of the Republican party, sat to the immediate left of Mr. Davenport. Mr. Sams, a wealthy landowner and prominent lawyer, sat to Mr. Janseen's left. Mr. Militon, the AIG chairman of the board, sat next to Mr. Daggert's right.

"Looks like we're all here, so let's get started," Davenport announced. "We have several pressing items that need our attention.

Our first order of business is President Harding."

"He is out of control. Not only is he an embarrassment to the Office of President, he has ignored our warnings and is allowing his Ohio Boys to get out of hand," retorted Mr. Sams.

"His indiscretions are public and his deviation of oil funds has been exposed," continued Mr. Janseen.

"The Teapot Dome scandal makes newspaper headlines every week across our nation," George added, shaking his head in disgust.

The Master Prior continued. "He is a runaway train that needs to be stopped before he creates more damage. I'm tired of covering up his messes. Vice-President Calvin Coolidge is a much better risk." The room was silent as everyone nodded their heads in agreement. They all knew what had to be done.

"Good, so we're all agreed, let's move on to the next order of business. Is there anyone who needs to be singled out as a Communist?" asked the Master Prior.

"Mr. Janseen, is there an enemy of the party who needs to be taught a lesson?" Davenport inquired.

"Hollywood celebrities tend to think their position makes them a hands-off target," answered Mr. Janseen. Everyone snickered. "There are a few we are watching at the moment, but none have been targeted as of yet."

"Now to the most pressing matter. As you know, my daughter, along with Maize Judson, Jonathan Judson's daughter, accidentally uncovered a skeleton at the beach when picnicking near the old lighthouse. Do any of you recall the tragic story about the death of Sir Henry Phillips? He was a past Prior; he died about 1889," began Mr. Davenport.

Everyone nodded their heads in acknowledgement.

"As you may recall, at the time it was imperative for our survival that the details of his death be silenced. On his death bed, Sir Henry entrusted me with a truth to ensure our brotherhood. I do not believe it behooves anyone in this room to know anymore at this time. But, I'd like you to know that it will be announced in a few days that the mysterious skeleton has a name. It is Sir Henry's only son, Henry II."

Several of the Priors exchanged quick glances.

Mr. Sams broke the silence. "As I recall, his son had a funeral and was buried in Grove Street Cemetery in their family plot."

"No one is buried in the casket. The reasons why will stay hidden. The cause of death was attributed to the Spanish Influenza epidemic. No one at that time seemed surprised the casket was closed in order to prevent the spreading of germs. It was necessary to circumvent public perception so things could go according to plan," the Master Prior explained, intending to be evasive. Pausing, he continued. "I've sent Leslie to visit my sister in New York City for a month. She is receiving so many phone calls and visits from friends and friends of friends that she wasn't even aware she had. Everyone wants to know the details. As far as I can tell, she is completely oblivious to the meaning of what has been uncovered. By the time she returns, this should all have blown over."

"Good, I'd hate to see your daughter in an unfavorable position," expressed Mr. Daggert.

Davenport's eyes flashed with anger. "No one is to touch her. I have someone watching her night and day. I will handle it!"

Everyone nodded in agreement.

"When the skeleton's identity is revealed, leave the cover story to me. I will take care of everything," Daggert said with conviction.

"Now, on to another matter," the Master Prior continued. "Are you familiar with the new professor in Yale's School of Law, Professor Richard Wikki? He moved here from London, England, a few years back."

Only Mr. Sams seemed to recall who he was other than George, a history professor in The School of Liberal Arts at Yale University and a peer of Richard's, as well as an acquaintance when both attended Cambridge University.

"It has come to my attention that he is an ex-detective from Scotland Yard." Several eyebrows rose as Mr. Davenport continued. "It has also come to my attention that he plans to use the skeleton mystery as a class case study in his Sherlock Holmes the Great Detective course. I can guarantee you, based upon what I have heard about our Professor Wikki, he will be quite intrigued by our little mystery. In fact, if he's the man I've come to believe he is, he will most definitely start asking questions once the name is released. We cannot afford for him to stumble upon the truth, which to my knowledge is hopefully known only by me."

"So what are your thoughts, Ron? You wouldn't have called this meeting if you didn't have a plan." suggested Mr. Daggert.

"You all know I am a member of the Yale Elihu Secret Society," explained the Master Prior.

The Elihu Club is a private Secret Society named after the Elihu Yale who was born in Boston in 1649. Elihu Club, founded in 1903, is the sixth-oldest secret society at Yale and is similar to Skull and Bones, Scroll and Key and Wolf's Head societies in charter and function. Elihu Yale is often but erroneously called the founder of Yale University. His father came to America to escape persecution against Puritans in the time of King Charles I, but the Yale family returned to England while young Elihu was still a toddler, and he never returned to America. In 1718, Cotton Mather contacted the philanthropic Elihu Yale, asking for his monetary help to sustain the college. Mather represented a small institution of learning that had been founded as the Collegiate School of Connecticut, and it needed money for a new building in New Haven. Yale sent Mather a carton of goods that the school subsequently sold, earning them

560 pounds sterling, a substantial sum in the early 1700s. In gratitude, officials named the new building Yale; eventually the entire institution became Yale College, and then Yale University.

"Professor Wikki attended Cambridge University in London during the same time as our beloved George here, who has mentioned their paths have crossed from time to time." Master Prior patted George on his left shoulder. "And since George is a professor of history at Yale, he is one of Wikki's colleagues. I will submit a formal request to the Elihu Membership Council to invite Professor Richard Wikki to be the newest alumni honorary member of the Elihu Secret Society because of his unique and highly respected credentials. It is George's assignment to deliver Wikki as Elihu's newest member. I have also uncovered something very interesting about our Professor Richard Wikki: he supposedly denounced his family title as Lord of Foxworthy many years ago. Thus it seems, he comes from an aristocratic bloodline that Elihu's Membership Council will surely find most agreeable."

"Are you sure he will accept the invitation?" asked one of the Priors.

"That's George's worry. Upon rekindling their acquaintance, he will personally encourage his ole buddy to join him as an upstanding member of the Elihu Secret Society."

"Master Prior, you know we trust you explicitly." Referring to an earlier matter, Prior Sams continued. "Could you promise us if the real story is to be revealed about the skeleton, we are told in a timely manner so we can prepare the Grand Ceremonial Chamber?" All others nodded in agreement as everyone understood the hidden agenda.

"You have my solemn promise." Noticing the lateness of the hour on the wall clock, Master Prior slowly and methodically looked everyone in the eye. "I believe, Gentlemen, the best strategy here is to keep our friends close and our enemies even closer." And with that, Mr. Davenport rose. "Good day, Gentlemen. That is all."

Chapter 8

While waiting for Maize, Richard reread the invitation he received earlier that morning announcing his official appointment as an Honorary Member of the Elihu Secret Society. The reasons given for this appointment highlighted his exemplary service at Yale University, his support of Yale's vision, as Lord of Foxworthy and a detective of Scotland Yard his virtue was without question. In addition, he qualified as an exemplary professor in the School of Law—all of which defined him as an upstanding "Elihu Man."

Although Richard did not officially attend Yale University, which is one of the criteria, he was granted an exception since his degree was from Yale's sister school, Cambridge University in London, England. The more Richard reread the letter of invitation, he knew in his gut there was more to this than met the eye.

He noticed it was signed by the President of the Elihu Club as well as the members of the Membership Board, none of which he knew. Richard had heard of the Elihu Club; you couldn't be part of the University and not have run into it at some point. The Elihu House was located on Yale Street not too far from Richard's office in Phelps Hall on the east side of the campus. It houses fourteen seniors who are tapped at the end of their junior year, announcing the new incoming members of the Elihu Secret Society. Outside of the fourteen bedrooms, there were several guest rooms which provided comfort for the many prestigious alumni who attend various club functions.

He thought it was curious, as he reread an excerpt from the description of the Elihu Club, "A secret society which fosters among its members a desire for earnest work, good fellowship, and a strong affection for Yale University."

Included with the invitation was a RSVP postcard addressed and stamped. This would have been quite an honor for any man attending Yale, and more importantly for someone who didn't. But Richard didn't think so. He did not like how they knew so much about him; he made it a point to confide in no one. Why did he seem to stand out among others, he lamented to himself. He knew the twinge in his stomach was a sure sign; it was always a definite signal something was amiss.

Richard was not one to exactly enjoy brotherhood organizations. He did not revel in belonging to anything, especially something that restricted his movements or called upon trusting in someone or some group. *NOPE*, he thought, *this is not for me.*

But he did believe he should look into this mysterious invitation. Something was going on behind his back; he did not like the feeling, and that feeling was always right. Richard preferred to feel he was in control of a situation, keeping an eye on all people, things, and events; keeping his friends close and his enemies even closer. *Who are these people*, he wondered.

Finally, he decided he would send an acceptance reply mostly for curiosity's sake.

Looking up, he noticed Maize standing in his office doorway. Her big blue eyes were so expressive; it was one of the first things you noticed about her. Her bubbly personality glistened as she asked if she was interrupting. Richard motioned to the chairs next to the far wall. "Maize, good to see you, here sit down," he said, joining her in the adjacent chair. "Did you bring the necklace?"

She grabbed it out of her work satchel. It was still wrapped in the soft wash cloth as she laid it on the small table between them. Richard picked up the cloth gently so the necklace would not slide and began to unwrap it carefully. He felt a sense of self-gratification as his eyes fell upon the trinket. His first instinct was correct; he knew it was something more than a necklace. Maize watched his reaction closely as he meticulously ran his fingers across the engraving she described to him earlier. Richard concluded this was a lot more than a decoration; this was an amulet with a raised symbol of some kind in its center. Richard could feel the blood start moving in his veins; this was a tremendous breakthrough.

He felt Maize's scrutinizing stare as he inspected the necklace; he tried desperately not to give any indication of its importance. Recalling Maize mentioning the broken clasp, he ran his fingers down both sides of the chain stopping where the break appeared. Richard noticed the clasp itself was still closed with the last link opened at the other side of the chain. It was clear to him that the place where the necklace was broken indicated the chain had been pulled apart by force.

Maize sat quietly watching him inspect the necklace. She thought it was exhilarating to watch a professional at work. He looked so enthralled while inspecting the necklace; as if he really missed the action of a practicing detective.

Breaking the silence, Detective Wikki asked with a frowning brow, "Maize, where exactly did you find this on the skeleton?"

"In between the fingers on the right hand of the skeleton; the body was face up."

"How was the arm extended?"

Maize never really thought too much about this. "Hmmm, let me think … when the crime investigators brushed the sand away … let's see … I believe the arm was stretched out raised above the head … like this." Maize raised her right arm out to her right and up near her front as if half reaching for something. As she demonstrated, Richard knew his first instinct was correct—the person had pulled this off someone or something. But who, and why, he asked himself.

Subconsciously reaching for his pipe in his pocket, Richard realized he left it on his desk. Watching him reach for his pipe, Maize decided it was best not to ask any of the many questions swimming around in her brain. She knew the pipe was a signal that he wanted to think, and think he did. *The way the body was found*, he thought to himself, *seems to indicate the person fell backwards while clutching the amulet*. As he wafted lightly on the end of the pipe, holding it in position with his right hand, he once again ran his fingers across the raised engraving with his left hand.

It was obvious to him this was something he needed to investigate. He remembered that Sarah, a colleague in the mathematics department—who had befriended him upon his arrival from London—loved to talk about the power of symbols and numbers. However, he had never thought too much of it at the time.

He recalled how she would talk about numbers and symbols as if they were a language all of their own. He remembered she always said numbers and symbols spoke volumes and were used for coded communication since the beginning of time. Detective Wikki had run across the need to interpret numbers and symbols before, but nothing like this. Nothing like an amulet that suggested a special meaning and purpose. Richard was positive this amulet had a story to tell. He would have to call on Professor Birmingham.

He turned to Maize and asked. "Have you told anyone about this … uh … necklace?

Shaking her head, she said, "No, Professor Wikki, you said not to."

"Good." He didn't want to frighten her but he needed to let her know the facts or at least some of them. Richard smiled and using a caring voice warned, "Maize, no one should ever know—not even your father. It has been some time since you found the skeleton, and this could be viewed by some as withholding evidence."

As he said this, Maize's face turned to one big frown. "It's just an ole necklace, and it's rather ugly if you ask me."

"Maize, I must trust you now, and you must trust me." Looking into her eyes he kindly but specifically stated, "This is not just a necklace. This is what you call an amulet." Maize was still stuck on "withholding evidence" and bypassed any interpretation of the word "amulet."

Richard stopped speaking when he saw the expression on her face. "Maize … what?"

"Withholding evidence is a crime," is all she could say as she looked directly into Richard's eyes with great apprehension.

"Don't worry about that. I know about things … no one will know. The necklace is now going to stay with me. I have it. I am the one with it. I found it."

Maize nodded her head, understanding what he meant. Nothing else needed to be said.

As her fears subsided, she now recalled that Professor Wikki mentioned the necklace was not a necklace but an amulet. "What is an amulet?"

"An amulet is usually worn around the neck like a necklace representing something special. Sometimes it is believed to give the person special protection, or is a symbol representing a specific group, or it could represent some type of key that is used to unlock secrets."

Showing Maize the round sphere, Richard continued. "See this diagram that looks like a sun? I am sure it is a symbol for something, I just don't know what?"

"What are you going to do?"

"I know of a professor who understands these things; I'm going to contact her and hopefully she can shed some light on this mystery."

"Cool." With that, Maize decided it was time to leave. "Professor Wikki, thanks for everything," she said nodding towards the amulet. He knew what she meant.

"Maize, I'm sure I found this lying on the ground somewhere around campus and thought I'd show it to you."

"Thanks, I found it quite interesting," she exclaimed as she grinned. "Good luck with your investigation."

Investigation, he thought to himself. *Yes, that's what I am going to do … investigate … like old times … well … kinda.* Richard rose and walked nonchalantly to his swivel chair behind his old, oddly shaped desk. He was sure it had been hanging around since the beginnings of Yale College in the early 1800s. It creaked every time someone leaned on it as if it was moaning of old age.

Maize rose to say goodbye, silently elated that she seemed to be a small part of a real mystery just like the ones Detective Wikki investigated for Scotland Yard.

"Maize," Richard said. Maize rose and walked towards the front of his desk. Trying to distract Maize from the importance of the amulet, he changed the subject. "Have you heard anything about the identification of our skeleton?"

"No, not a hint. I even looked for any and all missing persons within a ten year radius of the assigned date. No luck." Maize sat down slowly in the chair in front of Richard's desk.

"Hmmm … that is a suspicious piece of information … not sure how it fits. But, it begs the question: if we have a skeleton obviously not buried by normal means, the body had to be reported to missing persons at some point. Why did no one report the person missing? Even if it was from out of town there should be a record somewhere inquiring into its whereabouts."

Before revealing any secrets from the newspaper's investigation, Maize wondered if her father had drawn Detective Wikki into his close circle of confidants.

Maize asked. "Professor, have you talked to my father lately?"

"Why yes, we had a quick but nice talk over the phone. He rang me up a few days ago. He is a very intelligent man with a great nose for news. I offered my services if he would appreciate another pair of eyes and ears."

Curious, Maize asked, "What did he say?"

"He was highly interested, and will take me up on my offer as soon as he returns from his business trip to Boston."

"Oh yes, he goes there quite often. He's supposed to return late this afternoon." Maize continued. "My father has a sneaking suspicion that the police are onto something and only trusting their own. Father is not being advised and he's not real happy about that. Everything seems so secret."

Interesting, Richard thought. He believed Maize was sharp and inquisitive; two attributes of a good investigative reporter. He also realized her independent spirit may precipitate her snooping around in places that could cause unwarranted trouble. He knew she wanted to know the truth and would do what she could to uncover it. In that way she reminded him of a young Richard so many years ago at Cambridge University.

As she sat in the single chair in front of Richard's desk, Maize said, "Professor, this seems like a good time to mention something

I learned regarding the skeleton from my grandmother. I thought it might be of interest to you. I'm not sure how relevant it might be, but recently, one evening during dinner, my grandmother was talking about a newspaper article concerning the unnamed skeleton." Since Richard looked interested, Maize continued. "Mother happened to make a side comment about Mrs. Marion Teal and that she and Grandmother should have been young girls about the time the paper dated the skeleton. I'm not sure what Mrs. Teal had to do with anything, but anyway, Grandma didn't remember anyone missing. She thought surely someone would have known because New Haven was such a small town at the time; it would have been difficult to keep that a secret. I recall her exact words, 'That would have been fuel for juicy gossip.' I loved seeing the youthful sparkle in Grandma's eyes as she recalled the past."

Richard watched her intently as she dramatically recounted the incident using as many facial and hand gestures as possible. She was on such a roll; it was entertaining just to watch. "Well, anyway, I made a point to ask her about it again when we were alone. Often, she is more forthcoming when just the two of us are casually chitchatting in her room about whatever we please." Maize all of a sudden felt she was talking way too much, and that maybe Professor Wikki wasn't really interested in what she had to say. She paused, blushing.

"Please, go on. What did you find out?" Richard had learned a long time ago that women seemed to need a lot of room to tell their whole story and the main point would surface eventually. He found patience was usually the best course of action during these times.

"Well, the opportune time came just a few days ago when I visited my Grandma in her room. She likes her quiet time; mostly in the afternoons several hours before dinner. Whenever I come to visit, she always greets me with a loving smile and 'there's my little tender flower.' As a child I found that expression very endearing, but as a young adult I

78   *E.K. Prescott, Ph.D.*

just go with it. It's her nickname for me. Never figured out why … just is. Anyway, she was quietly absorbed with her needlepoint when I asked if she could remember something unusual around that time period. She thought a little while, complaining her memory was not as good as it used to be. Then all of a sudden, like a memory sparked her neurons, she gasped, 'Why, yes!' Well, I knew I was in for a story and better just sit back and listen for the duration or I'd never find out what she had remembered."

Richard couldn't help but grin, thinking Maize was more like her grandmother than she'd like to admit. But in Maize's case, her animation kept one quite involved. He nodded his head signaling that he was following her and to continue. He didn't want to interrupt her flow. It was entertaining.

So she began again. "She said they called him HP. Not sure of his full name, she spurted out different forms of his name trying to remember and finally came out with Henry Phi, Philipson, Philand … she couldn't recall; she knew his first name started with 'H' and his last began with a 'P' and that he had some numbers attached at the end like first, second, or third. Thinking this information might be important, I immediately went to my room and wrote a few notes about our conversation."

Maize dug into her satchel, retrieving her reporter's notebook she kept with her at all times.

Richard took this time to interject a thought to circumvent another soliloquy.

"Maize, why don't you think of yourself as an investigative reporter and relay just the facts to me … kinda like if you were helping me with an investigation."

"No problem," she said, oblivious to his underlying reason. Rereading her notes she began. "As I said, he was referred to as HP and the H stood for Henry and the P, well, maybe Phil, Philip, Philand … she wasn't sure … and that there were numbers attached to his name. She recalled he was not a very nice boy, always getting into trouble in and out of school, and that his father was some type of important person in New Haven." Maize looked up. "But she didn't remember his name or occupation."

Richard encouraged her to continue with a smile and nod. "Grandma thought she recalled rumors that his father sent him away to an Ivy League prep school, but was expelled within a few months. She rambled some, but recalled he was not well-liked anywhere." Maize continued reading her notes. "She didn't find it strange his father shipped him off to Boston to work in some hotel after he was expelled. She surmised his father thought hard work would straighten him out, but it didn't. I asked her why she thought that. The last she remembered, he returned a while later, and then was found dead."

Richard flinched at such an odd and unexpected turn of events. "Just like that?" he asked.

Nodding her head, Maize added, "She seemed low-key about the whole idea. But, it seemed quite mysterious to me."

Richard asked. "Are there any newspaper articles we can review about this?"

"I'm sure there are, but this happened before my father bought the paper, and I don't know how well the papers were archived."

Time was ticking by and Richard hated to ask if there was anything else, but he did. Looking at her notes she said. "Nope. That's it." Raising her head to look at Richard, she asked, "Do you think there could be a connection?"

Reaching for his pipe, he said, "Don't know, but all leads need to be investigated."

Maize was suddenly awestruck. She sat straight in her chair as she realized Richard thought her notes might be a lead. *WOW!* She told herself to settle down and not overreact. She didn't want Professor Detective Wikki to think she was an immature, ditsy, female Yale freshman. She said his name over and over again to herself. *Professor Detective Wikki.* She thought it had a nice ring to it. *How about PD for short … yeah PD Wikki. That sounds awesome! What a silly girl I am,* she lamented. She was glad Professor Wikki was staring out the window and didn't notice any outward gestures while she lapsed into childishness. Maize knew she really wasn't, and that was the demeanor she wanted to convey. She waited silently as Richard stared out the window gnawing on his pipe. Suddenly he slowly turned his chair around to face Maize who was still silently sitting in the chair in front of his desk. Maize wondered what he had been thinking.

"Tell you what, Maize." Richard had formulated a plan and wanted to verbally pitch it properly. Richard continued thinking as he spoke. "You have access to the archives, correct?" She nodded. "It would look suspicious if I started asking questions, and as of right now, your father has not entrusted me with any information to ask any questions, so…."

Maize could tell he was trying to find the correct words to relay his ideas. She listened intently, not wanting him to realize she was hanging on his every word.

Richard continued. "So, I was thinking … why don't you try to find out more about this young man? You might even check his school records as well as old newspaper articles. Hopefully they will identify the skeleton soon and make our search a lot easier. Maize, let's keep this strictly between us. That means not mentioning anything said here to a friend or any relative. We don't want to arouse suspicion."

"No problem." Maize was elated Professor Detective Wikki thought she was capable of handling such a task.

As Maize rose, she thanked Professor Wikki and said she would let him know what she uncovered. As she turned towards the door she noticed someone standing outside. She slowly turned and mouthed to Richard that someone was out there.

In a loud voice Richard asked. "Excuse me, can I help you?" A casually dressed young man popped his head in the door. He had the appearance of a student, but his aging face showed otherwise.

Seemingly startled, the young man replied. "Oh, yes, sir … um … I am looking for Professor … ah … Gallard's office."

Richard responded matter-of-factly. "There is no Professor Gallard in Phelps Hall that I am aware of."

"Well I was told to go to 456 Phelps Hall."

"Sorry. Right office, wrong person. You might try the next building."

After the young man left, Richard told Maize. "This happens frequently; students looking for a certain professor in the wrong place."

Maize nodded. She was ready to leave and start her assignment, even though it wasn't official. It was for Professor Detective Wikki and that was official enough.

Richard reminded Maize as she was about to exit the door. "Be sure to ring me next week to give me an update, or you could stop by. But there is no guarantee I will be in my office." Maize nodded and left.

As Richard returned to dive into the papers piled on his desk, he tried to think of anything but the grading which sat before him. He enjoyed teaching but abhorred grading. He believed it would be a great profession if he didn't have to assign a letter grade to students' work. As he thumbed aimlessly through the first stack of papers, he thought it was a stroke of genius to elicit Maize to be his arms and legs. She seemed to enjoy the possibility. *Just like having my own student assistant*, he thought to himself. Then his mind wandered to the young man hanging around his door supposedly waiting for Maize to leave. *How long had he been there? Was he eavesdropping? If so, why? Was he really looking for someone named Professor Gallard?* As he pondered these questions, he remembered how the young man was dressed, or more importantly, how he wasn't dressed. He did not appear to be groomed as a typical Ivy League student. Come to think of it, he recalled his hair was somewhat disheveled, and his dress was a little too casual. He shook his head as if to wake himself out of this inquisitive state and decided, *I am being way too suspicious … or am I?*

Chapter 9

As Richard walked slowly down the four flights of stairs from his office on the fourth floor of the Phelps building, he couldn't help but think how much easier it was to walk down four flights than to walk up four flights. Outside of acquiring an office with his colleagues in the school of law, he much preferred the view out of his window overlooking The Green than being anywhere else on campus. The only other office he thought even compared to his was the one across the hall; it overlooked the inside of the main campus which was fortified on all four sides by Gothic designed buildings in a variety of shapes and sizes. Either office provided a bird's eye view, allowing one to keep involved with the every day life of the Yale student body. There wasn't much you didn't see happen on either piece of land.

Richard enjoyed walking the inner campus courtyard; it reminded him of his college years long ago at Cambridge. The Yale main campus was one long city block adjacent to the east side of The Green which was separated only by College Street. At both ends of the rectangular-shaped campus lie Chapel and Elm Streets which bordered The Green as well; both The Green and Yale University shared the bordering streets of College, Elm and Chapel. On the far side of the campus across from Phelps Hall ran High Street, where the infamous Skull and Bones Senior Society house and the Harkness Tower reside. Large Gothic buildings fortified every inch of the college's rectangular perimeter, providing numerous entrances from the street as well as from the inner courtyard. These buildings of all shapes and sizes with an array of unusual rooftops were used as dorms, chapels, classrooms and offices; they provided a continuous border protecting anyone in the inner courtyard from the city life of New Haven. Even though Yale buildings were also placed sporadically in every direction in a two city block range, this area was used as the main campus.

Richard paused as he exited the first floor onto the left side of Phelps Gate, a large rotund entrance located in the middle of the Phelps building, which provided passage from College Street to the inner courtyard. As he turned to his left, he took note how quiet the campus seemed during the summer months, even though summer school was in session for another five weeks, the buzz of the school year would not compare.

As he crossed the courtyard, he paused on the connecting sidewalk under a large maple tree. Richard noticed the grass was green, trees were blooming, birds were chirping, and all seemed right with the world for one moment in time. He stared towards the end of the recently manicured courtyard near Church Street eyeing the newly constructed dorm, Connecticut Hall, which was separated by a crosswalk from Osborn Hall located near College Street. It was a colonial looking three-story building with a bell tower on the side facing Osborn Hall. Richard was amused at the obvious architectural interest in bell towers; they were all over the campus. One could set his watch to the infamous Harkness Tower bells that rang at midnight, noon and 5 p.m. every day.

Richard was on his way to meet Professor Sarah Birmingham of the Mathematics Department, whose area of interest was symbology and numerology. Professor Birmingham had been a part of Yale's mathematics department for over ten years, earning her tenured position within the first five years of her appointment. Sarah literally ran into the back of Professor Richard Wikki upon his first day at the university while both were walking across campus to attend the President's 1921 "Welcome Back" message to all staff in Battell Chapel. Her nose was unfortunately buried deep in a magazine article which was embarrassingly revealed later as the newest gossip about Mary Pickford and Douglas Fairbanks instead of something scholarly, like the mathematical analysis of the Second Law of Thermodynamics.

Their chance meeting provided a new and exciting friendship for Richard and a disappointing prospect for Sarah. She had been smitten with Richard since she first laid eyes on him that day; though she was embarrassed beyond belief. He on the other hand, had come to New Haven to heal the past which did not include a relationship with the opposite sex any time soon. It became increasingly evident that their friendship was becoming uncomfortable; her wanting to be closer and Richard backing away. Thus, each in their own way decided it was best to drift apart and just be friends. Richard believed being friends with the opposite sex, devoid of an intimate relationship was a very difficult position to maintain unless friendly sex was mutually agreed upon. He wasn't one for trysts, so it had to end, even though the free-spirited youth of the day might differ with his point of view.

Sarah had earned several honors and accolades for her research in symbology and numerology to the point of accepting requests to lecture in other countries. He knew she would know what the amulet symbolized and if she didn't, she would know where to look. He needed her expertise. It had been several months since Richard had last seen her. When he rang her up to set a meeting date, he could tell she was both surprised and elated to hear his voice. He was intentionally vague about the amulet and in doing so, he hoped he did not give her any reason to think he wanted to pick up their relationship from where it had left off.

Awakening from his pause of paradise, Richard looked at his watch and noticed time had gotten away from him once again; he was late. As he began to cross the courtyard to the library in Dreyfus Hall, Richard thought he noticed someone move about the same time in the same direction. Always on alert, especially since he had the questionable amulet on his person, he was suspicious.

Not wanting to give this person any reason for hiding or running, Richard walked nonchalantly to the steps entering Dreyfus Hall. He turned around slowly and sat on the fourth step, pretending to pause and read the papers he held in his hands. It was quite common anywhere on campus to see a professor reading or grading something. He took this moment to scan the area. Apparently, as he was turning to sit, the person he tagged as following him had stopped to seemingly gaze at the courtyard under the same tree Richard had just vacated.

Since he had perfected the task of pretending to do something while he scanned his perimeter many years ago, Richard was able to deduct that no one else seemed to be in the vicinity, thus this young man was alone and apparently not planning on meeting anyone. It is quite unusual for someone to be standing in the exact position he just vacated; Richard was sure this person was following him.

He isn't very good at looking inconspicuous, he thought to himself. Why someone was following him was concerning because of the latest developments, but by whom? He would find out. Richard decided to play this scenario out and see what transpired. Once he believed this person did not seem to be of any immediate threat, Richard slowly rose and entered Dreyfus Hall, turning right towards the library. He would see how far this chap was prepared to go.

The door to the library was composed of heavy, antique wood planks with a black, horizontal, metal door handle and matching hinges that creaked slightly when pulled open. Upon entering, one noticed the high, scalloped domed ceiling with various miniature figures etched here and there, as well as the many ceiling fans that were running full force this hot summer day in early June.

The main room of the library in Dreyfus Hall was quite open and large with a long, narrow counter not too far from the entrance which was usually manned by student volunteers. The young Ivy League student at the counter with his nose stuck in the latest student newspaper publication of *The Yale Daily News* appeared drained from a long, hot summer afternoon manning a sparsely attended library, due to the low summer student population and the popularity of the new library. Precisely why Richard chose this spot; privacy from unwanted ears and eyes. The Chattenden Library—donated by Mrs. Chattenden in honor of her son—was the newest building and preferred library on the main campus just south of Dreyfus Hall—would be buzzing.

The long, narrow windows were covered with ember-looking shades that caused the sun to cast a yellowish hue throughout the library. The stained-glass pictures above the windows cast a colorful spectrum as well, causing a blinding light that prevented anyone entering to quickly find their bearings. Richard stood motionless for a few moments near the front counter trying to focus his eyes through the sunny glare. It was nearly 5 p.m. and the clock tower would chime any second; quite loudly since it was located behind them across High Street.

As Richard looked from right to left, he noticed the walls displayed what seemed to be from a distance, historical pictures of Yale

University, rows and rows of bookshelves with desks, and various types of chairs scattered throughout. To the right of the library, he found Sarah. She was reading comfortably in an area decorated to resemble someone's living room in hopes to promote casual reading. Her shoulder length auburn hair glistened in the light shining through the shaded windows. Her face seemed at peace as she sat comfortably involved in whatever she was reading. As Richard walked closer he noticed she wore his favorite color—yellow—and her legs were slanted to the side with a hint of ankle showing. Upon setting eyes on her, he was reminded of her last words which still echoed in his mind. *"I can't compete with the past, and I don't even know what it is. You have an unfair advantage."* Richard had buried the past so deep it was even locked from him, and not to be revisited any time soon.

As Sarah checked the time, she noticed Richard walking towards her. *On time as usual*, she thought to herself. *Late.* She smiled at the sight of him; her beautiful green eyes sparkling. He couldn't help feel a sense of warmth recalling the good times they had together. He wouldn't have blamed her if she didn't want to see him, but when she smiled at him as he walked towards her, he was glad she did.

Sarah was thankful at this moment in time she was not an overly excitable person and thus able to keep her emotions at bay. She hoped her eyes did not betray the feelings erupting within; she would have loved to run into his arms and give him a big hug. As Richard walked towards her, he began to think maybe this was a mistake. He hoped they could establish a middle ground; not a romantic relationship but more of a collegian friendship.

"It's nice to see you," Sarah said calmly and politely as she rose to greet him face to face. "I see you are right on time."

Deciding not to explain his tardiness, Richard nodded his head in agreement and smiled. "Nice to see you again too, Sarah." Fumbling

E.K. Prescott, Ph.D.

with the medallion he placed earlier in his front lower left jacket pocket, Richard looked directly at Sarah and asked if there was somewhere they could go so they would not be overheard.

"I need to show you something important that is best not discussed out in the open," Richard stated matter-of-factly as he glanced quickly around the room for signs of his new best friend.

Both puzzled and aware that Richard did not play games, Sarah realized that this was more than an informal "nice to see you again" meeting.

"Why, yes." Sarah turned toward her far right where closed glassed study rooms lined the wall. Pointing in that direction, she exclaimed. "We can use one of those rooms. They are for studying and thus somewhat soundproof." Sarah led the way as Richard followed making sure no one was moving in tandem behind them.

Even though he saw no unusual movements, his infamous gut told him someone was watching.

Upon entering the study room. Richard realized it was decorated to serve its purpose. It was a small sterile room with one table, several hard-backed chairs, and no pictures hanging from the non-descriptive bland walls. He motioned for Sarah to sit at the table with her back to the window that faced the library; he then sat beside her. As they sat for a moment in awkward silence, he realized that he hadn't been this close to her since the night they parted. She still wore that perfume. What was the name of it? He remembered it was expensive for a professor's salary, but Sarah never questioned him about his ability to afford such a gift. That was one of the things he liked about her, she didn't probe into his personal life.

As they faced the blank, cream-colored wall in front of them, Sarah spoke first. "Richard, why all the secrecy?"

He turned to his left just enough so he could see her but not enough so anyone could read his lips. "I have something I need your expertise to decipher."

Sarah knew of Richard's Scotland Yard past and how much he enjoyed a good mystery. With all this secrecy, she had already concluded he had fallen into something that could keep his imaginative mind busy.

"This sounds so ominous, Richard. What is it? Why the need for such measures?"

"I'm not sure what this is," he said as he pulled the amulet from his jacket pocket. "It was given to me by a friend who had nothing better to do with it but pawn it off on someone who might enjoy its history, but the more I look at it, the more I believe there might be something to this."

Sarah knew as usual, he was not telling her the whole truth. And, she knew as usual, he would not unless he wanted too.

Richard held it gently in his left hand purposefully in front of his body using his index finger on his other hand to feel, once again, the unread indentions. Prior to this meeting, Richard removed the rusted broken chain knowing its appearance would only add to more questions about his true intentions.

"The shape is trying to tell me something. And, there is a figure in the middle that I'm sure gives a clue to its purpose." Richard hid the amulet in his hands as he gently laid it on the table directly in front of Sarah. She took a moment to analyze it from that position.

"May I?" she asked.

He nodded, "Of course."

Sarah reached for the amulet and held it in her hands, running her fingers over all the indentions of its shape and body. Richard sat quietly, watching her organize her thoughts.

"Richard," Sarah spoke as she continued to analyze the amulet, "You are correct in your initial assumption that this amulet is a representation of something." Sarah was very careful with her words; she knew Richard had come to her for the truth and her expert truth is what she would tell him. "This amulet represents something that looks like a chaosphere or a circle representing a chaos star. In a chaosphere, all the spikes protruding are of equal length." Speaking as she outlined the sphere with her index finger. "This has four large spikes represented as if they were placed in east, west, south and north positions. In some cultures, north represents air, south: wind, east: fire, and west: water. These are the four basic elements of balance in the universe. I am not sure about the smaller protrusions that are equally placed between each larger one … counting eight total. The figure 8 is symbolic in itself, it represents infinity."

"Can you explain what chaosphere means," he asked.

"Well it is basically a mathematical concept that studies the behavior of a certain dynamic system called Chaos Theory. The conditions of this theory basically state that small actions produce rather large consequences, creating a chaotic atmosphere."

"How is this theory used?"

"For example, when it relates to business, you have a goal or target and then a means that influences the behavior to meet that target."

"And this behavior is chaotic?"

"Well, yes because there is not a mediate direction, but an underlying controlled, intended goal and inputs. The surface is a chaotic system and the foundation is a controlled system of intentions."

"I'm almost afraid to ask, but tell me more about this mathematic model the amulet symbolizes."

Sarah took a deep breath, once again gathering her thoughts. "Okay."

"I can keep up with you … I think." Richard grinned. He was quite intrigued.

She continued. "Theoretically speaking, chaotic behavior is best observed in a natural system such as weather. This may be explained by analysis of a chaotic mathematics model which represents such a system. Quantum Physics provides such a model; the quantum model which investigates the relationship between chaos and quantum mechanics."

"I hate to admit it, but now you've lost me."

"Researchers are presently studying in quantum physics something called the Butterfly Effect. It basically is the belief that butterfly wings create tiny changes in the atmosphere that may ultimately alter an existing weather condition such as a tornado. The flapping of the wings represents a small change in the initial condition of a system which causes a change of events leading to a large scale alteration of events." Sarah paused to let Richard soak all this in.

"Okay, let's see if I have this straight in plain English." Richard slyly reached for the amulet and laid it in his hands directly in front of him with the etched symbol face up. "This amulet represents a belief that energy can be manipulated, by having a solid goal, and providing stimulus to let it chaotically take its own shape. When combining chaotic systems and the butterfly explanation, one could reasonably concur that this amulet is a symbol that represents a system, people, or organization that has a goal or intention of using chaos to achieve its purpose … or uses chaos to hide its purpose."

"Well said, Professor Detective Richard Wikki. I'll give you a better example. Let's say you had thoughts of moving back to London. If these thoughts became an intentional wish, energy would form your first chaotic thoughts to a more controlled manifestation of the end result or goal. Your chaotic thoughts of moving home would eventually become controlled energy which then make it possible for you to manifest your move back to London. Thus the old adage … be careful what you wish for."

"Hmmmmm."

"One more thing—I mentioned the use of Quantum Physics which is a good example of how math and science connect. You might be interested in the work of Professor Gibbs in the science department. He is tinkering with the Second Law of Thermodynamics. He believes there are numerous probable states of a system; each being assigned a certain probability … thus predictable."

Not really sure how this information fit, Richard replied. "Interesting, I'll look into it."

Richard ran his finger gently over the etching in the middle of the amulet. "Now to this, what do you think this means?"

Sarah explained. "From what I can tell, it is a shield … like a Coat of Arms of some kind."

Richard pulled out a small magnifying glass from inside his upper left coat pocket. Grinning and quite pleased with himself, he said, "I thought we might need this."

"It looks as if there is a banner with three words in Latin and the word 'Sherman' underneath; it's really tiny."

Sarah reached for the amulet and the magnifying glass and translated the three Latin words in the tiny banner below the Coat of Arms. "Mortem … the living have a task to do; Vince … conquer, win, overcome; and Virtue means bravery or courage. Interesting."

Richard quickly wrote this down on one of the papers he had brought with him. He also took a moment to scribble some notes from their earlier discussion. He knew instinctively that this was all connected, but he had no clue how.

"Do you know what this shield means?"

"More likely it represents the Sherman clan. I can easily look it up in the library."

Richard asked her to do just that and he and Sarah then rose and left the room. He followed her to the archive section in the very back of the library. Richard waited patiently while Sarah searched. He thought to himself, *Someone could be killed back here and no one would know it for quite some time.* He took this opportunity to see if anyone noticed them leaving the study as if watching their moves. But he saw nothing.

Opening the book she retrieved from the resource library, Sarah showed Richard the picture of the Sherman Coat of Arms. It looked exactly like the etching.

"I believe it represents the Shermans from Yaxley, England. It looks like a Templar's warrior shield with a lion is in the middle and three leaves placed around it; one in each upper corner and one underneath. See here… it states that these Shermans were tradesman in the shearing business." Sarah continued to read silently trying to find anything else of importance. "Well, well, what do you know about that!"

"What … what is it?"

"It says basically that this is the Coat of Arms of our historic first mayor of New Haven, the Honorable Roger Sherman."

This didn't mean much to Richard, even though Sarah found it quite intriguing. He had not been in New Haven long enough to connect with its historical past. Sarah closed the book and looked at Richard. Laying the book on the nearest table she said, "That's about all I can tell you."

"Sarah, I can't tell you how much I appreciate you taking the time to help me."

Looking at the amulet, she stated, "Well, this is an interesting piece to analyze. I had fun doing it." It occurred to her that there was something in the back of her mind she had wanted to relay about the amulet. "Oh, I know what else. I also know that this chaosphere without the coat of arms etched in the middle is a symbol representing something called Chaos Magick, magic with a 'k' at the end."

Richard frowned. "Chaos Magick?"

"It is not widely known. It is more of a movement that believes you can use the stuff we talked about … you know the use of intentions and energy … to change both your subjective and objective reality. This supposedly leads to the use of what some call magical practices that manipulate the universal energy force."

To Richard this seemed a little far fetched, but he recalled there were strange cases while he was at Scotland Yard that begged a logical conclusion as well.

He sensed that Sarah wished to talk further, but he needed time to process all of this information alone. He was glad to see Sarah again and he did not want to seem unappreciative.

"I know that look," she stated matter-of-factly. "The look that says I'm focused on something and my blinders are on."

Richard didn't know what to say. He was embarrassed to some degree and at the same time in agreement as well. So he said nothing. The pregnant pause spoke volumes to Sarah.

"Richard, it was great to see you. I know you needed this information for something you are working on and I can see it is consuming you at this moment. So, I am going to take my leave in hopes that we can meet again soon continuing our cordial conversation under different circumstances."

Richard didn't want to stumble awkwardly over his words, so he paused. "You know me too well, Sarah. I am really glad we were able to meet again. I too hope we can meet again soon."

As Sarah was leaving through the front door of the library, she sadly realized he didn't say when.

As Richard left Dreyfus Hall, following the identical path back to his office, he noticed from a distance someone was standing in the

Phelps Gate rotunda next to the door he would use to enter Phelps Hall. As he walked closer, he realized it was the chap following him on the way to meet Sarah. Upon closer scrutiny, he recognized it was the student who had stopped by his office earlier looking for Professor Gallagher. Richard thought quickly. If this man had actually been following him, why would he be standing there nonchalantly as if he was passing time? Richard walked calmly but directly to the young man. Speaking first, he said, "I remember you from this morning. Did you find Professor … let's see what was his name? Ah yes … Gallagher … Professor Gallagher?" Richard noticed the young student didn't seem shaken or the least bit nervous. He put out his hand to shake Richard's which was not reciprocated.

"Professor Wikki, I would like to first apologize for this morning. You caught me off guard. Dr. Seymour asked me to relay a personal message … I was strictly instructed to NOT let anyone see us talking. So, obviously, when you noticed me, and there was another student in your office, I had to think of something quick."

Richard was not impressed. He stood perfectly still waiting for a credible explanation. "Go on. Why were you following me?"

"I could not return to Dr. Seymour's office without delivering his message. I was waiting for a good time to approach you. I noticed you leaving the library and acted on a hunch that you would return to your office. I'm sorry for any inconvenience."

Richard stood passively, waiting for more information.

The young man continued. "Dr. Seymour said he was an old acquaintance and now a colleague of yours. He wanted me to find out if you received your honorary invitation to become a member of the Elihu Secret Society. He wishes to extend an invite to speak with you personally concerning this prestigious appointment over dinner one evening soon."

By this point, Richard was becoming annoyed. *These people work fast. I just got it today*, he thought to himself. "Why?" he asked, without much emotion.

"Dr. Seymour would like to discuss the benefits of becoming an Honorary Elihu Society member."

"That sounds like something he would say."

"He wanted you to know how happy they are to have a man of your caliber joining the brotherhood."

"Why all the secrecy?"

"Dr. Seymour said if you asked, I should tell you he would explain everything over a nice leisurely dinner at the Taft Hotel."

None of this sat well with Richard. He wondered why George didn't just ring him up instead of all this hocus pocus; there were far too many secrets in this town. He didn't really buy the whole story but decided to play the game. Too many things were all happening at the same time.

"Please give my ole buddy Dr. Seymour my regards, and extend my appreciation for his invitation. I will gladly meet with him some evening of his choice, as long as it doesn't interfere with my schedule. We can catch up on old times," he replied, tongue-in-cheek.

The young man started to leave, walking in the direction of College Street. "Thank you, sir. I will relay your acceptance. Dr. Seymour's secretary will call you in the near future to set up the appointment." And then he was gone.

Richard just shook his head in disbelief as he walked up the four flights of stairs to his office on the fourth floor. It was going to be dark soon and he wanted to pick up some papers to grade later. As he entered his office, he couldn't help think this whole thing was quite bizarre. An amulet that has something to do with Chaos Theory, an Honorary membership to the Elihu Secret Society, and now a secretive invitation to meet a so-called old friend, Dr. Seymour. None of this made sense. *Does this all fit together somehow*, he thought to himself, *or are they all separate events?*

Just as he was about to pick up the stack of papers waiting for him on his desk, the phone rang. "Hello, Wikki here."

"Richard … Jonathan Judson."

"Hi, I see you have returned from Boston."

"Boston is just what I want to discuss with you. Can you meet me at Sophie's restaurant across The Green from Yale on Church Street tomorrow? Let's say about 11:30 for lunch? I'd like to take you up on your offer to help me."

"That can easily be arranged. I don't teach tomorrow and as of right now, there are no boring meetings to attend."

Jonathan chuckled. "Good, I'll see you tomorrow."

Richard hung up the phone, grabbed his pipe, shoved it in his coat pocket, and patted his upper inside left pocket to verify the safety of the amulet. It was becoming almost a ritual to keep track of both his pipe and the amulet. As he turned out the lights and shut his office door, something struck him as odd. His old friend wants something more than a membership; this was out of character and above his station to pursue anybody for anything. Richard had no intention of meeting George for dinner any time soon.

Chapter 10

Richard loved the morning—the time of day when the world wasn't fully awake yet. One could sit for hours soaking in the quiet serene solitude. It was one of those mornings perfect for sleeping in and having a leisurely cup of coffee on the front porch, while slowly beginning the day tranquilized with the picturesque scenery: a bright, sunny day, with cloudless, blue skies, and deep, emerald blue water glistening from the sun. Thus, Professor Detective Richard Wikki made a conscious decision not to go to the University. There wasn't anything pressing. After all, he had papers at home to grade if he was so inclined, no classes to teach, and no boring meetings to waste his time. He would enjoy the morning relaxing and reading today's newspaper while savoring his traditional strong large cup of coffee with no sugar, no cream.

Richard lounged on his front porch under the cover of the shaded roof, enjoying the soft, warm ocean breeze, connecting with the world while sipping his coffee. There was no one in sight for miles. His house was separated from his neighbors on both sides by at least one acre. His neighbors on his left were vacationers from New York

City. To Richard, they seemed to come and go without much notice. Most of the time, his home was just his own little slice of beach—quiet, serene, secluded, away from any and all prying eyes and ears—just like he wanted it.

His mind wandered back to his meeting the day before with Sarah. Sarah was a woman of every man's dreams: beautiful, smart, fun, and kind. But she wanted more than he had to offer. Richard wanted nothing but friendship. It suddenly occurred to him that he never brought her here to his home. To Richard, his home was a sanctuary; a very private place. He recalled they were always busy going somewhere or relaxing at her place; they always had a great time in whatever they decided to do. There was no reason to come here. Hmmm, maybe because he never shared his personal space, it caused her to feel estranged. Richard did feel some remorse in that things could not be the way she wished. The problem was not her; the problem was him. Richard understood this and went on with his life and hoped she'd done the same. Recalling yesterday, Richard felt it had been good to see her late in the afternoon in the library at Dreyfus Hall. He knew she would know what the amulet represented and she did not disappoint.

As he took a sip of coffee and continued his line of thought, Richard quickly flip-flopped from romance to the investigation—both evoked passion deep within him. Holding the amulet loosely in his hand, he couldn't help thinking about how much he had learned about this little ole necklace. He spoke aloud, "So you belong to someone who is a member of a group that apparently pays homage to the Sherman family dynasty, is involved in controlling outcomes, and believes in mysticism. Who are you?" His mind began to wander. *I wonder if the body holding the necklace was involved with the person who was wearing it. Did he know his killer? Why did someone want him dead?*

This new information gave Richard a direct route to pursue, but added a lot more questions than answers. He was hoping his lunch with Jonathan today would provide him with possible leads as well as shed some light on some of his unanswered questions.

Taking the last sip of his coffee and placing his cup on the table next to his lounge chair, Richard noticed the front page headline of today's New Haven Gazette:

HARDING LOSES WHITE HOUSE CHINA IN GAMBLING BET

He thought President Harding was quite a character; he had only been in office a little over two years and had managed to draw a lot of unwanted publicity.

Richard had not yet entertained the idea of becoming a U.S. citizen, although he did feel loyalty to this country. *At least loyalty to the office of the Presidency as much as the next man*, he said to himself.

Richard was not quite sure how long he would be living in the United States or if he would just end up making it his home. He intentionally made no long-term plans. With that, he rose to take his coffee cup to the kitchen and proceed to his room to dress for the day. He was looking forward to meeting Jonathan. He liked him and that alone spoke volumes. Richard couldn't help wonder, *What does Jonathan want from me? How does his trip to Boston fit into this?* He also wanted to know who this Mr. Davenport of the Elihu Secret Society was besides Maize's best friend's father.

As he dressed for another hot day in New Haven, he pondered the thought of leaving the amulet at home in a safe place while he dined with Jonathan. On second thought, he was sure it should never leave his person. Even if he rationally knew he should be the only one who had a clue of its existence, deep down he felt someone else was aware of it too, even after one hundred years. And, that someone knew of its special properties and was determined to recover it no matter what the costs.

***

Sophie's was a popular upscale lunch and supper club in New Haven on The Green that reorganized to become a "private" club, in order to circumvent the law.

The Volstead Act was passed in 1919, which made it illegal to import, export, transport, sell, and manufacture intoxicating liquor; anything more than 0.5 percent alcohol content was illegal. Speakeasies were a great way to get around the everyday hassle of law enforcement. For every legitimate saloon that closed a half dozen underground places sprang up. Many speakeasies invented elaborate rites-of-passage such as rooms only reachable through certain doors, secret passwords, and handshakes in order to keep hidden from the ever-watching eyes of the law.

Sophie's was different; it didn't need all these elaborate disguises. Numerous local, state, and federal officials were paid off to look the other way. Thus Sophie's, like many other speakeasies, thrived during these turbulent times.

Since 0.5 percent beer (called near beer) was the only so-called alcohol legal to purchase, many citizens started drinking liquor instead. Drinking liquor was not illegal, but purchasing it was. Drinking to get drunk became a popular pastime; as popular as eating out and socializing. Many Americans became quite innovative in ways to conceal liquor: hip flasks, false books, coconut shells, hot water bottles and garden hoses were used to transport liquor.

Richard was quite amused by all the hubbub about alcohol; until it affected him. He found himself missing his nightcap (bourbon and water) he so enjoyed while living in England. He looked forward

E.K. Prescott, Ph.D.

to his bourbon at night, and planned to continue his nightly tradition before retiring each evening. Having the Dean of the Yale School of Law as a friend and colleague was an advantage once in awhile. Thus the problem was solved soon after his arrival.

Even though he was circumventing the law himself, it was such a common practice of society that no one seemed to think much about it. The only objective was not to get caught. As a detective and man of the law, Richard was deeply chagrined at all the crime that transpired because of the Volstead Act: it was creating an illegal industry in the United States—bootlegging, gang violence, and the rise of an organization known as the Mafia. But, there was nothing he could do about it, it just was what it was, he told himself numerous times. He would not get involved.

As Richard entered the restaurant, he noticed all the tables near the large rectangular front window were filled. Those always filled first because of the shaded scenic birds-eye view of The Green. But today, Richard wanted to be in the back where he could keep any eye on everything and everybody; secluded so no one could overhear them.

Sophie's was built like most buildings of the day, taking advantage of architecture to keep everyone as cool as possible during the hot summer months with large high domed ceilings and lots of ventilation. The new cooling invention called "air conditioning" was only available in the two movie theaters in New Haven and the Shubert Theater. Plans were being made to air condition as many businesses as possible, but that was going to take time and money. Most believed Sophie's would be one of the buildings renovated sooner than later, outside of the Taft Hotel of course.

While Richard waited to be greeted by the hostess checking memberships, he took the opportunity to case the restaurant; it was second nature to him as well as something to do to pass the time.

Sophie's was tastefully decorated; tables were dressed in white linens, glassware, and silverware garnished each place setting. In the middle of every table was a tasteful decorative vase full of fresh flowers placed so you could see the person across from you. Waitresses and waiters looked crisp in their white and black uniforms proudly displaying the Sophie's logo on their shirt pockets. It was hot but bearable because of numerous large ceiling fans going full force, large floor-length standing fans in each corner of the building, and the windows facing the sun were covered with ornate drapes, providing shade from the heat. There was a "social center" which was used as a liquor bar at one time; and actually still is, but now renamed for appearances. It ran across that back right of the restaurant. The social center was quite elaborate with neon signs, its own ceiling fan, glasses hanging upside down from a large cupboard, and a long, shiny, mahogany bar with matching stools outlining its perimeter; at Sophie's, details and ambiance was as important as the food.

"May I help you?" the hostess pleasantly asked with a big smile, interrupting Richard's train of thought.

"Oh, yes. I am a guest of Jonathan Judson. I am here to meet him for lunch."

"Yes, you must be Professor Wikki. Mr. Judson just called to say he was running late, and to seat you wherever you prefer."

"Well in that case I prefer that table," Richard said, pointing to a table slightly to the left in the back of the restaurant. Since most customers were seated front and center, there were several empty tables in that area of the room. It met his needs.

"That will be fine. Follow me please." After he was seated, a woman sitting at the bar caught Richard's eye.

"While you wait for Mr. Judson, Sam will be by to take your drink order," the hostess mentioned as she laid the lunch menu to his right and quickly returned to her post to greet and seat the next customers waiting in line.

Richard barely heard her as he was fixated on the silhouette of this woman. She looked as if she was posing for a photo shoot as she sat fashionably dressed with her legs crossed at the knee, slightly leaning forward with her right elbow resting on the bar tabletop while she held a cigarette with an elongated plastic holder. He watched her femininely take slow puffs of her cigarette; her chin held up high as if looking at the fan in the center of the bar. Richard thought to himself, *How odd to set such a pose. She could not be from around here; not New Haven elite style. Probably from New York City*, he deducted, as many people came to New Haven to see a matinee or evening show at Shubert Theater. He noticed her style of clothing and material gave the appearance of a very well-to-do young woman; one that traveled abroad. She was dressed quite fashionably from head to toe with dark brown, short hair with four large perm waves falling in four distinct layers all the way around her head. Her fair skin was accented with rouge and a red shade of lipstick. She wore a sheer pink low square-neck dress with the bodice forming a V just below the waist. The mint green skirt, made of the same material, fell straight under the V bodice to maybe just at her knees. Richard couldn't tell for sure, since she was sitting the length of her skirt, but he definitely noticed her long, slim legs and matching pumps. He found her quite striking. In fact, he noticed several tables seemed to be aware of her presence; women were acting catty and men were gawking.

"May I take your drink order, Professor Wikki," asked the young waiter. Richard asked himself, *How does everyone seem to know who I am?*

"My name is Sam," said the waiter in a friendly manner. "I would suggest some of our specialties such as the Mary Pickford or Sidecar." Most establishments created highly unusual names for liquored drinks in order to please their customers, while staying out of the eyes of the law. It was kind of a tongue-in-cheek gesture though, because everyone knew this was done, even the law.

Richard ordered French 75 which he knew would have bourbon in it.

"Fine choice, sir. I will bring it straight away."

With that, Richard quickly glanced back to the bar to continue his investigation, but she was gone. "Where did she go?" he mumbled. He wondered if she left her purse. No. It had been sitting on the stool to her right, seeming to keep a place for someone or to keep someone from sitting next to her. Her half-finished drink was still where she had left it. Maybe she went to the restroom. He couldn't find her anywhere.

Tearing him from his train of thought, Jonathon Judson bellowed as he approached their table, "Hello, Professor." Jonathan seated himself to the left of Richard. Just then the waiter brought Richard's French 75.

"Can I get you something, Mr. Judson?"

"Yes Sam, my usual."

"That would be a Mary Pickford, sir," the waiter stated proudly, and Jonathan nodded in agreement.

"I see you found a table in the rear of the restaurant where you could sit with your back to the wall and peruse the whole restaurant; not to mention it's nicely secluded."

"Yes, Mr. Judson, I thought it would be best that our discussion was not overheard," Richard explained.

"Good idea. By the way, Mr. Judson is my father's name, my name is Jonathan."

"Very well, Jonathan," Richard stated raising his glass to him. "Since you brought up names … these people seem to know me by name. I'm curious why? I've only been here a handful of times since I moved to New Haven three years ago."

Jonathan quickly explained. "As you can tell, I am a regular, a member, and somewhat of a high profile figure in New Haven. I called and told them to treat you with the same respect they afford me."

Richard nodded, affirming Jonathan's explanation, took a sip of his drink and scanned the room to see if his mystery woman might have been seated at a table, but he could not find her. She seemed to have vanished into thin air.

"So how is Yale treating you these days," Jonathan politely asked.

Richard had already decided to let Jonathan take the lead in the conversation. He had set this lunch meeting with a definite agenda; Richard was going to let it play out. "This time of year is slower because of a shortened summer school schedule. It has been nice to spend time at home reading and relaxing," he replied.

"Oh, yes, I remember you mentioned that when you were over for dinner. You bought a place on Long Island Sound down the road a little way from Five Mile Point Lighthouse. By the way, did you know its nickname is The Skeleton? Interesting, given the current circumstances."

"Outside of its untimely nickname, I like it. The few homes in rural east New Haven are quite scattered along the beach area; nice and private."

"New Haven has a rich history. Since you have the time, you should look into it."

"As I recall, Reverend Albert told a wonderful historic story about the cemetery underneath his church. The history surrounding the cemetery was quite fascinating in itself." Richard thought this was as good a time as any to pose his question. "I was talking with a colleague of mine the other day, and the Sherman family tree came up; too long of a story to explain how. She mentioned it was connected to someone named Roger Sherman who was the first mayor of New Haven. Do you know anything about him?"

Jonathan and Richard paused as Sam set Jonathan's drink down in front of him. "A Mary Pickford; just as you like it," Sam proudly proclaimed.

Jonathan nodded in affirmation, noting the hidden meaning.

After Sam left, Jonathan quietly turned to Richard, explaining, "They always put a little extra liquor in it for me. If I can have a stiff drink here during the day, it beats taking time to see the doctor to get another liquor prescription." Raising his glass, Jonathan continued. "Now the Shermans … they are from England where Roger Sherman's ancestors were sheep shearers—thus the name. His family tree is walking all over New Haven, much less the whole state of Connecticut. His lineage can be traced through such names as the Days, Seymours, Baldwins, and Whites, just to name a few. He was a very powerful man during his time. While serving as New Haven's first mayor, he served on the Committee of Five who drafted the Declaration of Independence. He was also a senator and a representative of the new United States, not to mention the patriarch of one of America's oldest and prolific political families— Baldwin, Hoar and Sherman families. He was married twice. After his first wife died, he married a preacher's daughter Rebecca Prescott from Danvers, as in Salem Massachusetts. Between the two wives, he had fifteen children."

"No wonder they are spread all over the state," chided Richard.

Jonathan grinned and took a drink before continuing. "Did you know Roger Sherman was the only man to sign all four documents of the new United States of America—Articles of Association, Declaration of Independence, Articles of Confederation, and the Constitution. He was more powerful than President Washington, Ben Franklin and the lot of them."

"Really? That is interesting! History books only talk about the names you just mentioned. Makes one wonder why his name is left out?"

"Yes it does." Jonathan knew much more than he was saying, but felt it was not the time to divulge unknown facts of American history; the information was of no consequence at the moment. He needed to attend to his agenda.

"Let's order," Jonathan suggested as he picked up the menu. "There are a few dishes I recommend, but one of my favorites is the Crème Vichyssoise à la Maramor; most think it is better than the Vichyssoise at the famous Waldorf Hotel. Besides, it's a cool delicacy on a hot day like this."

"Sounds good, I'll try that as well," exclaimed Richard. Jonathan signaled Sam, who had been waiting for the sign that it was time to order. "We will both have your Vichyssoise."

"Should I refill your drinks?" Sam asked.

"Why not, we still have some business to discuss," answered Jonathan.

As soon as Sam turned to submit their orders, Jonathan began again. "I don't have a lot of time so let's get down to business."

"I'm all ears and my time is yours," replied Richard.

Before Jonathan could begin, he noticed the mayor and his new trophy wife walking towards their table. "Good afternoon Mayor," greeted Jonathan. Jonathan started to rise to shake his hand.

"Oh, please stay seated. We just finished lunch and noticed you sitting here. We wanted to be sure and say hello, didn't we dear," said the mayor as he patted his wife's hand that was loosely hanging through his right arm. As Richard quietly looked on, Jonathan thought to himself, *The mayor never just says "hello." I wonder what he wants?*

"Oh, yes," Shirley chimed. "Please thank your daughter Maize for the wonderful article she wrote about my tea party in Sunday's Society page."

Playing along, Jonathan politely replied, "Yes, Maize sat in my office and told me what a fine afternoon you prepared for the wives of the Lawn and Garden Club members." Shirley smiled ear to ear, rather pleased with all the attention.

"By the way," Jonathan continued, "I'd like to introduce you to Professor Wikki. He teaches criminal law at Yale."

Mayor Garfield looked and nodded at Richard in recognition of the introduction. "Professor Wikki, how nice to meet you. My friend, Dean Johannas, speaks very highly of you."

Richard said nothing, but smiled, acknowledging the introduction. With no verbal response from Professor Wikki, the mayor turned back to Jonathan. "Well, nice to see you Jonathan. Please give Maize and your wife our best." And with that, they turned and left.

"Richard, now that's an interesting story. The mayor divorced his wife a few years back and married his long-time mistress. It didn't seem to hurt him politically. But then, not much can hurt you if you are a Republican who was born and raised here, attended Yale, are a member of Skull and Bones and the Center Church Congregationalist and you are of course, the mayor."

Richard thought to himself. *We haven't even started the main course or the main topic of conversation and I've already learned a lot.*

"I have not had the opportunity to be formally introduced to the mayor. Although, I have been at many affairs in which he has attended. The Dean loves to drag me out and show me off when he can."

With that, a cute, young waitress brought them their meal.

"Well, I sure hope that is all of the interruptions for today. I need to get back to the paper. I want to cut to the chase." Looking around for unwanted ears, Jonathan began. "It concerns the skeleton discovered several weeks ago on the beach near where you live. As you well know, I need to work closely with the police department to keep open

E.K. Prescott, Ph.D.

communications flowing, but at times they make impossible demands. The Chief and I barely tolerate each other. But nonetheless, there is some information I have agreed to withhold for a short time."

Richard kept silent, sipping on his second French 75 as Jonathan continued.

"They want me to keep the skeleton's identity secret for a while. Why, I am not sure. But, my guess is, the name of this skeleton would open a lot of secrets locked behind closed doors. Anyway, his name is Henry Phillips II. He was in his twenties, they think. My son Robert whom you have met is picking up a lot of my responsibilities to give me time to follow leads and forge ahead with my own investigation. I have a lead investigative reporter who I trust explicitly doing some footwork for me here in the New Haven area. Not a single employee has the big picture, not even Robert. Everyone has a piece of the puzzle to investigate and reports directly to me. There is to be no collaboration for fear of losing their jobs. My years in the newspaper business tell me there is something very important buried here; more than a skeleton in the sand."

"So, the skeleton has been identified … that is certainly interesting," Richard exclaimed. His mind was racing. He thought about the amulet. *So the amulet was found in young Henry Phillips' right hand. Who did he pull it off of?* He knew this was a big lead, but to where or to whom? He was not going to tell anyone about the amulet; but if he did, it would be Jonathan. He trusted him. No, the amulet was best kept from everyone. Richard too was sure there was something sinister about this whole case.

Jonathan turned slowly towards Richard, lowering his voice. "Henry Phillips' father was a wealthy merchant and land owner, as well as a highly respected citizen of New Haven and a Proprietor of The Green. It seems he died a few years after his son, in 1889."

"Why are the police so secretive about the identity of the skeleton?"

"Because Henry Phillips II was supposed to have died of tuberculosis, and was buried in Grove Cemetery," Jonathan replied.

"Who is buried in the coffin if he's not in it?" asked Richard.

Jonathan answered. "The police are in the process of obtaining an order to exhume the coffin before this information hits the news. They are worried that some citizens will try to dig up the grave themselves. That would cause quite a stir in our little town."

Richard's eyes grew wide. He thought to himself, *This must be the same person Maize told me about in my office. The one her grandmother remembered. The name fits.* Covering his thoughts, Richard muttered, "I can understand that problem from my days at Scotland Yard. The police will try to contain the situation as much as possible." Richard paused for a moment and then continued. "It is always important, especially in those situations, to have a good investigative reporter on your side."

"Exactly," Jonathan said, and turned to finish his meal. Richard had already finished his Vichyssoise, since Jonathan had been doing most of the talking and he was doing most of the listening.

Jonathan continued. "Anyway, I discovered Henry Phillips II was sent to Boston to work at the Boston Congressional Hotel, which by the way, is owned by John Davenport. That's why I went there; I wanted to follow young Henry's tracks. I discovered his father, Henry Phillips I, was a member of the first Boston Masonic Lodge of the United States; the first Grand Masonic Lodge in North America began during Sherman's time. In 1733, about eighteen men met at Bunch of Grapes Tavern on King Street in Boston to organize the first fraternal society based loosely on medieval stonemasons' guilds in Europe. Many of our esteemed forefathers were members—George Washington, John Hancock, Paul Revere, Ben Franklin and Roger Sherman, to name a few. I was able to uncover through some connections that young Henry was only in Boston for about two months. I am not sure where he went from there. I couldn't stay more than a few days for fear of people becoming suspicious by my long absence. My gut tells me we need to continue this line of investigation. I'm sure the police are already worried what I might be up to and that is why I have asked you here. I would like to hire you to continue this lead."

"You would like me to go to Boston and see what I can uncover?" retorted Richard.

"My plan is that you go undercover. Since it's still your summer vacation, so to speak, you could take a trip to Boston for a … how do you Brits say it … a holiday," suggested Jonathan.

Richard was quite interested in the whole scenario. He was delighted to have the unexpected opportunity to follow his own investigation and hopefully uncover how the amulet fit into all of this. "To tell you the truth, I've missed the thrill of the chase. I would love to work on this. Plus, it's very intriguing."

"I thought that I would call upon you to use your Lord title, and your cover would be that you are vacationing in the States; wanting to take in our perspective of history. I'm sure it would be highly unusual if anyone would recognize the famous Professor Detective Richard Wikki from Scotland Yard and Yale University all the way in Boston," chided Jonathan.

"Sounds like a plan to me," Richard agreed, smiling at Jonathan's reference. He tried not to show the shock on his face when Jonathan acknowledged he was a Lord. He quickly surmised he had conducted a background check like any good journalist. No big deal.

"Good, I must get back to my office," Jonathan stated as he looked at his watch. "It seems since the major newspapers have exposed the Teapot Dome Scandal, the news doesn't stop. Now President Harding and his Ohio Boys are making the headlines daily; they seem to be up to their necks in a major cover-up, and I need to polish the next article with the editor."

As Richard pulled out his wallet to pay the bill, Jonathan stated, "Oh no you don't, Lord Wikki, this is on your expense account."

As Jonathan laid money down to pay the bill, he slipped a large envelope of cash to support Richard's upcoming investigation. "I have arranged a train ticket for you tomorrow morning at 7 a.m., and you have an open-ended reservation at the Boston Congressional Hotel."

As Jonathan rose, he said in a low, serious tone, "In my business, you have to be a good judge of character. With your background, which I investigated by the way, I trust you explicitly. Do what you know needs to be done, and report only to me." Richard nodded, confirming Jonathan's wishes. With that, Jonathan rose, and said goodbye.

Richard stayed seated for a few minutes. He wanted to recap their conversation before he returned home to pack. As he sat sipping the rest of his drink and watching Jonathan leave the restaurant, he thought he was seeing things. There she was! The same woman at the bar. She seemed to come out of nowhere. It looked as if she was following Jonathan out of the restaurant. Why? To what end? It just seemed all too coincidental to Richard. Shaking his head in disbelief, he knew somehow, somewhere, he would see her again.

Chapter 11

Maize wasn't really looking forward to this assignment, although she did find Lady Peacock to be quite a fascinating person with all her peculiar and eccentric gestures, which were overtly excused by the pompous, politically correct elitist women in New Haven. But, behind closed doors, the lack of political etiquette was a topic of conversation only topped by jealousy over Lady Peacock's high status among the powerful, the rich and the famous, all the way to Washington, D.C.

She was no stranger to Maize since she and her mother were friends. Maize had come to appreciate her outlook on life and also to expect the unexpected. Maize liked her, not only because she could get away with such frivolousness, but mostly because she didn't care; she didn't have to, being the richest and most politically connected woman in New Haven. Maize was positive if Lady Peacock was born in her generation, she would have been a flaming flapper, forging a path for women's freedoms. Now at age sixty, Maize thought Lady Peacock was a tremendous example for any woman, much to the chagrin of her best friend, Leslie, who was raised to be a polished and politically correct debutante.

Being overly fashion-conscious because of the high-end story she was covering today—one of Lady Peacock's famous tea parties—Maize decided to wear her most flattering outfit: a calf-high, pale green, hourglass dress hosting a tasteful scoop neck accented with a pale yellow sash hanging from her waist and angled to the right, knotted loosely at her left hip. *Now for accessories*, Maize thought to herself. *This is the part I hate. Everyone will be fashionably attired, and if I'm not somewhat acceptably put-together, I will stand out like a sore thumb. And more importantly, it would be a major faux pas for a New Haven society reporter to be unfashionably correct.* She turned to her full-size standing mirror and planned her accessories; she added a long string of white pearls, a small glitter purse with a chain strap, and a pair of casual, tan Mary Jane shoes. Maize tried on a few decorative headbands, but decided none of them matched her dress.

As always, Maize was very critical of how she looked. Whispering to herself, she gave one final once-over in the mirror. "This will have to do," she said aloud, tugging at her dress. "I have applied just enough makeup so I don't look like Betty Boop and have powdered my stockings so not to be embarrassed from the glare of the rayon." She had recently purchased them at the new Woolworths in town. Woolworths was the newest, trendy, middle class 5 & Dime General Store, which she knew her friend Leslie wouldn't be caught dead entering. And finally, before turning to leave, Maize sparingly sprayed herself with Coco Chanel's newest fragrance, Chanel #5 which Leslie purchased at Macy's in New York City for her birthday last year. *If I can't dress high-class, at least I can smell high-class*, she chided to herself as she left for Lady Peacock's residence.

It was a beautiful summer day; not too hot, mostly warm and breezy. As she meandered from street to street, Maize remembered she needed to get in touch with Professor Wikki. She recalled from their last meeting he had asked her to look in the Gazette's archives to see what she could find relating to the skeleton story. She had done so, but mostly found a few names, places and events that seemed to be disconnected. To Maize, the facts were random and unimportant, but her gut told her it would make sense to Professor Detective Wikki. She made a mental note to contact him for a one-on-one meeting, believing this information was too delicate for a party line telephone conversation.

It was imperative that she make a good impression as an investigative reporter. *Who knows where it could lead*, she fantasized. Plus, she had been eavesdropping on her father's and her brother's conversations as of late, and overheard them discussing the forensic report on the green fungus found next to the skeleton's head, saying that it should be available any day. She was sure the fungus was an important clue. Why, she didn't know, but Professor Detective Richard Wikki would. Her thoughts quickly focused on the present as she turned left onto Prospect Street.

Lady Peacock lived in the most exclusive and elegant neighborhood in New Haven, 616 Prospect Street, only a mile from the Yale Campus. There sat a gorgeous, large Gregorian brick home set away from the road on a half-acre of land surrounded by a lush landscaped lawn with myriads of greenery and colorful flowers. Lady Peacock's late husband Samuel, a graduate of Yale, had made his money in railroads; she was well taken care of and would be for the rest of her life.

Maize moaned as she recalled Charles would be waiting for her at Lady Peacock's. Charles was Maize's admiring photographer. He was more than admiring. He was annoyingly doting. But, he was great at what he did and he made Maize look good, so she just tried to discourage any unwanted actions.

As she inched closer to Lady Peacock's house, Maize noticed

someone in the middle of the road. "Who in the world is that waving," Maize said out loud in astonishment. As she moved closer, she came to a complete stop in the middle of the road so she didn't kill this person; all she could do was shake her head in disbelief. Raising her voice, Maize yelled out the driver's window. "What are you doing in the middle of the road, acting like a lunatic?"

Charles walked up to her and politely explained between breaths. "I was early ... finished setting up my equipment ... decided to wait for you ... didn't want you to miss the house."

Exasperated, Maize politely replied. "Charles, please back away, I'm going to turn into the driveway now." Once parked, Charles was johnny-on-the-spot, ready to open her car door, asking if she needed help carrying anything. In order not to be rude and to avoid becoming flustered before a big story, Maize calmly shook her head while silently grabbing her things. Charles closed the car door behind her. Maize turned briskly without speaking and followed the decorative stone path to Lady Peacock's front door as Charles was still talking, seemingly to no one, and following dutifully behind her.

Lady Peacock's butler, Jason, was waiting for her at the door. "Good day Miss Judson. Lady Peacock is in the backyard reviewing final instructions with the staff." Jason was the exact opposite of his employer. He stood erect and poised, expertly groomed from head to toe with nothing out of order. Even his manners and expressions were deliberate and proper. He was one of New Haven's most coveted butlers. Over the years, many a woman had tried to persuade Jason to leave Lady Peacock's employment. But Jason, even though seemingly annoyed with Lady Peacock's flamboyant manner from time to time, was extremely loyal to his employer. If truth be known, most of the time he actually enjoyed her free-spirited personality.

"This way, miss." Jason led Maize down a long corridor perfectly decorated with oil paintings, mirrors, and flowers. A large, pecan wood staircase to the immediate left of the hallway proudly displayed a white hand railing which spiraled upwards into an open hallway outlining the upstairs rooms. The parlor was a large, decorative room on the other side of the wall behind the staircase. In the center of the parlor on the far wall gallantly stood a beautiful oversized brick fireplace topped with a decorative white painted-wood mantel; a large, antique gold framed mirror accented the wall above it. The hardwood floor was covered with a room-sized powder blue floral oriental rug which accented the wedgewood painted walls. Chippendale sofas and wing-backed chairs with a lyre wood card table set between them filled the room. Extra chairs had been scattered here and there to meet the demands of the guest list.

As Maize turned left to walk out the opened parlor doors to the picture perfect backyard, she thought to herself, *No woman in her right mind would miss this social event*. To her left was a large, rectangular tent providing shade, beverages of all kinds, plus comfortable, cushioned outdoor lounge chairs for the weary. To her right, Maize noticed Lady Peacock's staff setting up the newest popular outdoor game, croquet. *This was going to be quite a story*, she thought. *I'm going to make Lady Peacock very happy.*

"Over here, dear!" Maize looked around and noticed Lady Peacock waving her hands with great excitement in order to get her attention. Maize quickly walked towards her. There would be some instructions for her, of that she was sure. Maize knew Lady Peacock would be dressed to the nines. Her fair skin and bright red hair always provided a wonderful background for her elaborate style. And today her guests would not be disappointed.

Lady Peacock was dressed more for a night out on the town than an afternoon tea, but that was to be expected. She wore a straight turquoise silk shift with rows and rows of loose fringe tassels from bodice to hem, which was just below her knees. It was the perfect "shimmy" dress, adorned with a matching band headdress accessorized with a cluster of glimmering tassels falling to the right of her head.

"How good to see you, and how nice you look," Lady Peacock announced, holding out her arms to greet Maize as she scanned the yard for anything out of sorts. Running all her sentences together as usual, Lady Peacock welcomed her. "I'm so glad you are the one covering the party … your mother will be here … I don't think she knows it's your story … I'm sure she will be pleasantly surprised." Without taking a breath, Lady Peacock lovingly took Maize by her arm and continued. "I'd like to introduce you to our very special guest; she is from New Delhi, India. Walk with me, dear, to the dining hall."

The dining hall had been transformed into a large sitting room with small tables exquisitely dressed for afternoon dining. Tables were scattered here and there to accompany small groups of guests. The dining hall was across the hallway from the parlor. It was adorned in much the same fashion, but with the addition of a Parisian crystal chandelier positioned in the middle of the room. To the back right, Maize noticed a striking young, dark-skinned woman who seemed to be sitting all alone in a deliberately secluded area.

As Lady Peacock weaved Maize around numerous small tables sporadically filled with guests, she pointed to this young woman. "My dear, a party would not be a party unless we had a psychic for entertainment."

Maize noticed this special area was decorated with unique spiritualistic artifacts, which created a mystical ambiance. There were two comfy high-back chairs in between a lyre card table on which several types of tarot cards were placed. The area was adorned with purple satin drapes, eloquently fluttering as the warm summer breeze

E.K. Prescott, Ph.D

blew across the dining hall from the opened floor-to-ceiling windows framing the luscious backyard landscape. On the long decorated table against the wall lay several pamphlets and books for casual reading if anyone was interested, as well as an array of scented candles of various sizes and shapes surrounding what looked like a large crystal ball. Maize thought to herself, *I should have known … leave it to Lady Peacock to have the most fashionable entertainment to date: a psychic.* These days, psychics were a must at any elitist party, and Lady Peacock was not about to be outdone.

As Lady Peacock and Maize approached, Innocent stood to greet them. She was dressed in her native Indian traditional attire. Her long, dark hair was parted in the middle and adorned with a decorative jewel chain ending with a round purple gem in the middle of her forehead. Her hair was straight and pulled back from her face and shoulders, flowing down her back. She wore a decorative turquoise and gold salwar kameez—a long tunic hanging below the knees with drawstring pajama-type pants worn underneath. Her accessories included a matching silk scarf flowing gracefully around her neck and falling toward her back, and clear sandals highlighting her small feet.

Lady Peacock introduced Maize to Innocent, speaking as if the world was her stage. "I want you to know, dear … I met Innocent while attending a spiritual retreat in Australia … you know, wanting to get in touch with the real me kind of stuff. Well, anyway, Innocent is an assistant to Charles Leadbeater, the President of Madame Blavatsky's Foundation in Australia. Our dear Innocent was one of my teachers; I fell instantly in love with her. Thus, she is here. I planned this tea party around her schedule; she's touring America for the Foundation."

Maize had no clue as to what Lady Peacock was referring, but she nodded her head in compliance.

As Lady Peacock turned towards Innocent, obviously desiring to address her duties one-on-one, Maize quietly stepped back and busied herself reading some of the pamphlets lying on the table to her left. As she fumbled through the brochures, Maize noticed a large picture of Edger Casey near the left end of the table. She noted that there was an oversized announcement promoting his upcoming lecture on the first of August at Shubert Theater titled, *Atlantis: Fact or Fiction*. Looking to the far right end of the table, Maize noticed posters highlighting *The White Witchcraft Book of Shadows*. She questioned, *What is a White Witch? And what is a Book of Shadows?*

As Maize walked to the other end of the table to investigate, her eyes caught the mountainous stack of pamphlets in the middle of the table: Theosophy Society membership applications. She picked up a pamphlet entitled *Madame Blavatsky's Principles of Theosophy*. As she opened the brochure, she noticed the colorful commercial picture of Charles Leadbeater and the Theosophical Society Mansion. *Quite impressive*, she thought to herself. Maize continued to read: *The Principles of Theosophy … religions of the world are branches on the tree who is one ancient trunk … mythology often transmits some knowledge in symbolic form … the soul gets involved in the world of matter; it experiences and learns.* Her eyes dropped to the bottom of the page: *Theosophy is the portion of ancient knowledge brought to us by H. P. Blavatsky toward the end of the 19th century, as taught to her by her Teachers in Tibet.* Little did Maize realize that her recent past, present, and near future would be a living testament to Madame Blavatsky's spiritualistic world, melding with the scientific realities of the early twentieth century.

Breaking her train of thought, Maize heard Lady Peacock speak her name.

"And Maize should receive a special reading, Innocent. She is a very special person."

Oh, boy, just what I need … a trip to the other side, thought Maize. But, not to disappoint Lady Peacock, she nodded with a smile, accepting the generous gesture. "Thank you, but at the moment I need to find my assistant, Charles," she exclaimed while looking around the dining hall.

"Oh, you mean the good-looking young man I met earlier. He mentioned he helped you with your assignments," noted Innocent.

"Good looking? Never thought of him that way, but a competent assistant, yes." Maize took this opening to make a graceful exit from an uneasy situation. "Thank you, Innocent. I will stop by later for a reading. Lady Peacock, I must excuse myself. I have facts to gather and a story to write." And with that, Maize politely turned, crossing the dining room to the parlor where she hoped she would find Charles.

The rooms were beginning to fill with guests. Maize found herself trying to maneuver around small gatherings of women. She loved walking slowly while eavesdropping on interesting conversations; it always gave her an edge on what was really happening. Any society reporter worth her salt had an edge.

As she entered the parlor, Maize noticed the mayor's trophy wife commanding a young crowd near the fireplace. Maize chuckled to herself. It was all so superficial. She intentionally strolled by to hear the latest gossip. Shirley Garfield, the mayor's wife, was showing a picture on the front page of a Chicago paper; it read: INTIMATE CHAT AT THE WHITE HOUSE. Shirley was pointing to the picture of President Harding's mistress Nan Britton and their love child, Elizabeth. Apparently, Nan had been smuggled into the White House for many a tryst. Maize didn't want to look like she was gawking, so she kept moving; she didn't need to hear anymore about their illustrious president.

Near the parlor doors that opened to the backyard, Maize noticed her mother visiting with some ladies from their church, The Center Church, the most prominent on The Green. Virginia noticed her daughter as Maize approached. Giving her a soft kiss on the cheek, Virginia greeted her. "Why dear, I didn't know you were going to be covering this event." Virginia looked at her two friends. "You'd think living in the same house, and my husband owner of the Gazette, I would know these things. Mrs. Jordon and Ms. Graham, this is my daughter, Maize. She works at the paper as a part-time society reporter. And my Maize has been accepted at Yale University, starting the fall semester. She has aspirations of becoming a journalist, much to the disappointment of her grandmother who thinks she should marry above her station."

The women both nodded, acknowledging their introduction, while Virginia continued. "My dear, you look fabulous."

"Thanks. You know, Mother, how persuasive Lady Peacock can be," Maize retorted. "She told Father she would have no one else covering her tea party."

Virginia chuckled. "She does have her way, doesn't she?"

Maize looked around the room. "You can definitely say that there is an extreme sense of fashion here, from Gibson Girl to Flaming Flapper and everything in between. This is definitely the who's who of New Haven women. I think she pulled out all the stops on this one."

"Maize, both Mrs. Jordon and Ms. Graham are going to be hosting a Women's Rights Seminar next month at the Winchester building in downtown New Haven, mainly to encourage more women to vote locally as well as nationally. It hasn't been that long since women received the right to vote, and they want to attract women of your generation. You might like to attend, and maybe even cover the story."

Maize gave a thoughtful nod.

"You know, Maize, you could embellish the story as it is being held at the Winchester building, especially since Sarah Winchester has been making such a big name for herself upon her move to California after her husband's death. I remember reading her husband died at an early age from tuberculosis in 1881," noted Virginia.

Ms. Graham's eyes widened. "That's right. It is said she grieved so much from her husband's death that she sought out a medium to find answers. The medium told her to move west to build a new home, and that she was paying for the millions of lives her husband's invention had taken. You know, the Winchester Rifle, among others. Apparently, when channeling her husband, he told Sarah to continue building their home in the West as long as she lives or her life will be cut short. Supposedly, she's had twenty-two carpenters working on her house around the clock since 1884."

Mrs. Jordon added. "I think she is in her early eighties by now. They say the mansion is a maze with no rhyme or reason; it's full of twists and turns, dead-ends, and secret passageways."

Maize's interest was piqued. "I thought that was just a rumor?"

"No dear, it's more fact than fiction." Virginia chimed in. "It is believed that the spirits of those killed by her husband's guns roam freely day and night in their new home."

"Well, I definitely think that angle has a society interest storyline somewhere. I'll talk to Ruth, the society editor."

All three women nodded, elated for the potential exposure.

With that said, Maize changed the subject. "I need to talk to Father later. Mother, do you know if he is at the paper?"

"Well dear, I think he said something about meeting Professor Wikki this morning at the train station before he left on vacation. Not sure what time that would be though."

Maize was surprised. Professor Wikki was leaving town without telling her. "Where is he going?"

"Your Father said something about Boston. You'll have to get the details from him. Why are you so interested?"

Before Maize answered, Charles caught her eye setting up the

camera outside near the main tent. *What is he doing*, she wondered.
"Excuse me Mother." Nodding to the others, "I have to rescue Charles.
Looks like he's being mobbed by groupies … not that I think he really
minds … but he has work to do." *What a timely excuse to get away*, Maize
thought. She didn't want to tell her mother a little white lie; no one
knew she was helping Professor Detective Richard Wikki. It was their
secret. Maize wondered, *Hmmm … how long is he going to be gone?*
Where is he staying in Boston? No worry, she thought to herself, *I'll find out*
from Father. It was well-known in her family that whenever Maize was on
a mission, not much could stop her; she was like a bull in a china shop.
She decided as she walked across the east side of the lawn to meet
Charles. *I need to talk to Professor Wikki … in person … but how?*

Maize tapped Charles on the shoulder, abruptly interrupting his
social life. "Charles, we are about finished here. You need to take a few
more group photos and we'll be off. You made quite an impression on
Innocent, you know … the psychic."

Charles was spinning from testosterone overload. He turned
slowly towards Maize. "What? Oh yeah?"

Maize asked. "Did you take some photos of her?"

Charles nodded.

"Did you take some with Innocent and so-called important
women?"

Charles nodded again. He was trying to answer Maize and pay
attention to his fan club at the same time while trying not to offend
either.

"Run along girls," Maize politely ordered, somewhat annoyed.
"Charles has work to do. You can talk to him later."

As the girls walked away giggling and chattering, Charles
proclaimed. "You didn't have to be so abrupt. I was enjoying the
attention, even if I was robbing the cradle." Charles slowly began

packing his equipment.

Maize began to lend a hand and asked, "Did you happen to hear anything of importance for our story while you were milling around today?"

"Not really." Charles stopped and pointed to an elderly woman sitting with another across the lawn. "See ole Lady Mizzer across the way … the one sitting in the chair wearing an old-fashioned, long hoop skirt and high-collared blouse?"

Maize followed his finger as it pointed to Mrs. Winthrop. "You can't miss her with those gargantuan yellow and turquoise peacock feathers sticking out of her hat."

"Yes, I see Mrs. Winthrop," she answered.

"Yeah that's her … ole Lady Mizzer. Look at the person sitting next to her. She seems bored to tears with Lady Mizzer's unrelenting stories."

"Boy, aren't we fashion-conscious these days, and what's with this dumping on Mrs. Winthrop?" Maize really didn't want an answer, so she continued. "What did you overhear that was so unimportant?"

"Oh, she was whining that someone sat in Eli Whitney's seat, number sixty-three, during Sunday morning church service … you know the one who invented the Cotton Gin … he's buried in Grove Street Cemetery."

"Yes, I know," Maize said with some disgust.

Charles continued, "I guess it has a plaque or something commemorating where he sat every Sunday. She was appalled, as if saying it was saved every week for his ghostly presence."

Recalling Pastor Albert's history lesson at dinner several weeks ago about buried people in The Green, Maize blurted, "Don't tell me he's one of those still buried in The Green and his stone was moved to decorate the rear walls of Grove Street Cemetery … in alphabetical order."

Charles looked at her funny. "No I think he died in 1825 and the last burial on The Green was in 1812; the stones were moved shortly after."

"How on earth do you remember something like that?" asked Maize.

Charles shrugged his shoulders. "I don't know. I guess I have always been interested in unusual facts about our little town. And, for some reason I can remember numbers and dates … I know, it's weird."

"There you are!" Lady Peacock declared. "It is very hard to keep up with you, my dear. It's time for your reading."

Maize jumped, startled by her unexpected presence. "Why Mrs. Peacock, I've been so busy making you look good." Maize smiled.

Mrs. Peacock once again politely took Maize arm in arm and escorted her towards Innocent's corner. Maize, hooked like a fish, turned to Charles. "Charles, please pack and take everything back to the newspaper. I will meet you there. I won't be long!"

"Here she is!" Lady Peacock proudly announced to Innocent. "I finally was able to corral her … more like reel her in … so to speak. Anyway, Maize needs to experience your gift."

Maize smiled and reluctantly sat in the open chair, obviously vacant just for her.

Noticing Jason out of the corner of her eye, Lady Peacock snapped her fingers. "I'll have Jason move the room divider so you will have ultimate privacy and quiet."

As Jason moved the divider, Lady Peacock began a short soliloquy on how she had acquired this precious artifact during one of her trips to the Middle East. But no one was paying much attention to her story. Maize was deep in thought, wishing she was anywhere but here as Innocent prepared the table for her reading.

"Well my dears, I'll leave you two alone. Have fun!" Lady Peacock left the room with the same exuberance as she entered it. Innocent, sensing Maize's reluctance and skepticism, decided to sit back and chat in hopes of easing the negative energy hovering over her.

Innocent began the conversation. "I do so love Lady Peacock's energy."

Maize did not want to be rude and disappoint Lady Peacock, so she decided to jump in and play the game. "Yes, she is a dear friend of our family."

Changing the subject, Maize inquired, "I see you have a very unique display with a variety of information. I was wondering if you could tell me a little more about Edgar Cayce. I see he is going to deliver a speech here in New Haven the end of July and I might like to cover it."

Innocent replied, "Edgar Cayce is a clairvoyant, sought out by many elite business owners and common citizens. At the moment, he resides in the state of Texas, doing readings and such. Unfortunately as of late, it has been reported that he's being exploited by greedy humans who want him to channel where hidden treasures are buried, but he will not do so."

"What can you tell me about his speech topic, *Atlantis: Fact or Fiction*," probed Maize.

"In the metaphysical world, many of us believe that Atlantis was a legendary continent in the Atlantic Ocean that sank because of their selfish need to be God-like. The Atlanteans were a highly evolved society. According to Cayce, the Atlantean Society was divided into two political factions: a positive and good faction, called the 'Sons of the Law of One,' and a negative, evil faction called 'Belial.' They were advanced technologically to the point that their advancements destroyed the whole continent. It is believed some escaped by boats, and found refuge in Egypt. Fortunately, they took their secrets with them and passed them on to the Egyptians. We believe these secret mysteries have been secretly passed down from one generation to the next, protecting its truth in order to keep mankind from exploiting this information for selfish gain."

Maize really didn't want to know any more than that, so she changed the subject. "I see you have brochures about the Society you are affiliated with."

"Yes, I work with the Theosophical Society. We opened a center called The Manor in Sydney, Australia, a few months ago; that's where I met Lady Peacock. The original Theosophical Society was founded in New York City in 1875 by Madame Blavatsky. She opened the center to study mediumistic phenomena. By the way, Madame Blavatsky believes, as does Edgar Cayce, in Atlantis; and that the inhabitants were an Indo-European language group called Aryans."

Maize sat still, not knowing what to say, or if she should say anything at all. It all seemed quite bizarre to her.

"To make a long story short, we have many centers established around the United States as well. Unfortunately, we recently have had to deal with some dissension ending with splinter groups starting their own organizations."

Maize looked at her watch. "I'm so sorry to rush you, Innocent, but I need to get back to the paper to write the society column for tomorrow's paper. Lady Peacock would be quite unhappy if she was not highlighted in tomorrow's Society Event section.

"In that case, would you please pick one of the tarot decks laid out on the table."

Maize didn't know one from the other, and just grabbed the one closest to her.

"Ah, this is the Egyptian tarot deck, very nice!"

Maize was in too much of a hurry to ask her what that meant, though she was curious.

"Please shuffle the deck and when you are done, split it in two piles; it does not have to be even. Now, put one deck on top of the other. Good."

Maize noticed Innocent took a quiet moment closing her eyes seeming to collect her thoughts.

"Well let's see what your cards say."

As Maize watched her lay down the cards, she thought Innocent had a rhyme and reason for each placement; they seemed to flow in threes. There were nine cards in all with the tenth one put aside. Innocent began to carefully turn each one over one at a time; not saying a word.

Maize sat still and watched.

Suddenly, Innocent began, "Looks like you are going to start a journey, but it's not a vacation. It will take you to several cities."

Maize just nodded. She did not want to reveal any information that would give her any clues what to say next. But, Maize was sure she had no plans to travel anytime soon.

"In this journey, you are searching for something specific in each city. My guides are telling me what you seek are signs to reveal the sins of man."

"Whoa!" Maize coughed.

Innocent paused a moment. "Would you like to ask a question?"

Maize was somewhat entertained but also feeling very uneasy. "Me? Reveal the sins of man? That's a little heavy, don't you think?"

"Let's turn over the tenth card I placed to the side and see what it says."

Maize wasn't sure she wanted to hear what she had to say; even if she did think this was all bogus.

Innocent suddenly looked very serious. *Not good*, Maize thought to herself.

"Maize, I want you to be very careful. There seems to be some danger around you. The card says you started a chain of events that will drop the veil for decades to come."

Maize stood up, quite startled. *This is getting a little spooky*, she thought to herself. "Thank you, Innocent. I really appreciate you taking your time to do this reading for me. I think I need some time to digest all of this. Maybe I can catch you the next time you are in town."

Innocent slowly nodded her head, implying thank you and good day. She watched Maize as she left the dining hall. She knew a lot more than she told Maize. Innocent shivered, and bowed her head in prayer. She was afraid for Maize.

Chapter 12

The world is mine, everything is working as planned. I am in control. Davenport stood, looking out the floor-to-ceiling window that filled his office wall overlooking The Green from the top floor of the Taft Hotel. It was 5 a.m., Davenport's favorite time of the day. The world was just waking up; only the birds were up and about, chirping their morning hellos. It was beautiful. It resembled the calm in the world that was hidden by the chaos he had created. That was where the real power existed. All other was just a means to an end, his end. As it has been since the beginning, the force's anonymity is paramount. It had been preserved through the ages; it could not be unveiled. The secrets from the ancients must stay hidden from mankind until the preordained time. Fortunately, their plans to change the power in the U.S. would circumvent attention away from this untimely find—a discovery that if revealed, would ruin centuries of work.

In the back of his mind hid an uneasy feeling that the recent discovery of young Henry Phillips' skeleton, as well as his empty casket, somehow threatened this unwanted disclosure and would be a thorn in his side for some time.

However tedious, these recent events were just a pebble in the sand. They had bigger problems than a skeleton, an empty casket and Professor Detective Richard Wikki; they must keep Teddy Roosevelt Jr. out of jail! Teddy's political career was probably already ruined—now it was mainly about keeping the Roosevelt name from being dragged through the mud; especially since Franklin, Teddy's first cousin, was being groomed for the Presidency.

That was of utmost importance to the overall plan—a plan that must not and will not fail.

A little over a year ago, on April 14, 1922, the Wall Street Journal reported a secretive government arrangement; leasing of government petroleum reserves to a private oil company without competitive bidding. These oil leases that President Harding signed over to Harry Sinclair as a concession to become President of the United States were now making headlines across America and dubbed by the media as The Teapot Dome Scandal. For the first time in American history, greed and corruption stemming from the White House was about to be exposed, and Teddy Jr. was caught with his hands in the cookie jar.

Going into the 1920 presidential elections, the major oil companies had compiled a list of concessions they wanted from Washington if the Republicans were to regain power. Collectively and individually, there had been lobbying for these measures with little success throughout the eight years Democratic President Woodrow Wilson was in the White House. Wilson, along with Presidents Theodore Roosevelt and William Taft, all worked during their time in office to establish and maintain a naval oil reserve in Wyoming for emergency reserves. This program was overseen by the Navy and at the moment, specifically by Edwin Denby, the Secretary of the Navy. Many politicians and private oil interests opposed the restrictions placed on the oil fields, claiming that the reserves were unnecessary, and the American oil

E.K. Prescott, Ph.D.

companies could provide for the U.S. Navy.

Harry Ford Sinclair, oil giant of Mammoth Oil since 1916, wanted the Republicans to handpick a presidential candidate who would put a compliant interior man in office. When Warren Harding became the Republican candidate, the game was set. As a United States Senator of Ohio, he was virtually ineffective, his womanizing, drinking, and gambling were well-known among his peers; he was corruptible. Sinclair's money enticed Harding and the Republican Party, as they wanted to regain control of the White House, but there was one major flaw in their plan; even if the President did appoint Sinclair's man as the head of the Department of the Interior, the Teapot, Buena Vista, and Elk Hills oil reserve rigs would remain in control of the U.S. Navy. Before their plan could happen for exploitation, the oil program would have to be transferred to the Department of the Interior; a move that could be made only with the approval of the President on recommendation of the U.S. Attorney General.

Upon being elected the twenty-ninth president of the United States, Harding and his Ohio Gang, as the press dubbed them, decided who would serve in Harding's cabinet. They created a cabinet that could by law, move the control of the Navy oil reserve to the Department of the Interior. Albert Fall would be the Director of the Interior, and Harry Daugherty would be the new Attorney General, as he was the brains. Once Harding assumed office, his administration became a collection of swindlers, sharpies, con men, and extortionists, descending on Washington like a pestilence, securing just about every job in the new administration that provided opportunity for corruption. Even Daugherty's brother had a role; he acted as the gang's money launderer and banker.

Albert Fall, knowing he had the Attorney General's blessing, moved decisively to take control of the nation's resources, putting the naval oil reserves at the head of his list. He quickly transferred the oversight of the oil reserves by the Navy to the Interior. The Secretary of the Navy, Edwin Denby, wanted nothing to do with this plan, saying it was "full of dynamite." Denby then designated the Assistant Secretary of the Navy, Theodore Roosevelt Jr., to serve as intermediary between the Navy and the Interior. Before joining Harding's presidential campaign, Roosevelt had been a director of one of Harry Sinclair's oil companies, and counted him as a personal friend. Thus, he was appointed to President Harding's cabal as Assistant Secretary of the Navy. He would be useful.

There was only one more piece to the puzzle for the Ohio Gang to make millions from the reserve oil leases: the President's approval. Fall immediately drafted an executive order stating President Harding approved, moving the oversight and control of the Navy's oil reserves under the Navy to the Department of the Interior. The President signed the order. Now everything was ready to sell "oil leases" to Sinclair for the Teapot, Wyoming oil field, and to Edward Doheny for the Elk Hills, California oil field. It was done. The leasing rights would make everyone filthy rich.

Unfortunately, Fall didn't count on the execution of this transfer of oversight to make national headlines. Colonel James G. Darden, an old friend and political backer of President Harding, held claim to part of the Teapot field that predated Harry Sinclair's lease. President Harding was busy contending with the railroad and mining strike and did not want to be involved against his friend. Fall was furious, and sent Ted Roosevelt Jr. a note apprising him of the situation. Fall expected the acting Secretary of the Navy to remove James Darden's crew by military force. Teddy wavered at such an unusual and unlawful request, but soon was persuaded by Fall, noting there was a precedent for such an undertaking, which was a colossal lie.

E.K. Prescott, Ph.D.

The following morning, Captain Shuler, four young marines and Arthur Ambrose, a geologist, left Washington for Wyoming. In Casper, they were met by several Interior Department officials and a couple of newsmen from the Denver Post. After a long stare-down, Darden's foreman conceded, knowing they meant business, and the Marines posted "No Trespassing" signs. It was over, and the damage had been done. These actions gave the Denver Post a hammer with which to pound the government, Mammoth Oil Company, and Harry Sinclair. The unraveling began.

As Davenport continued to stare out the window from behind the bar waiting for Remy, he was amazed at how well the Ohio Gang was keeping the citizens at bay. Even the Senate wasn't all that fired up about investigating this scandal until now; late summer of 1923.

A knock at the door broke his train of thought.

"Remy, incoming."

"It's about time you got here," Davenport grumbled. "There has been a change of plans."

As Remy entered, Davenport motioned for him to sit with him across the room where several leather sofas and matching chairs surrounded one big shiny, mahogany coffee table. The coffee table was designed to give Davenport a substantial distance from anyone in that area of the room. He motioned to Remy to sit in the sofa directly across from him, so they would be separated by the center table.

Davenport was dressed in a New York Kuppenheimer navy blue streamlined suit created by the Leyendecker brothers in New York City. He only wore the best. Remy was just as handsome and charismatic as Davenport in his own style. He did not march to the fashion conscious elite of New Haven. He was Remy, no need to follow status quo. He wore a long, tattered maroon and gray kurta churidar which resembled an American night shirt, and baggy gray cotton pants with canvas shoes.

Remy sat as instructed and waited silently for Davenport to begin the conversation. It was never really a conversation anyway—more like a listen and comment once in a while type of conversation. Even if it was only an agreeing nod of the head, the emphasis was always on agreeing. No one ever disagreed with Mr. Davenport except maybe the other four, and only in a respectful questioning manner. Everyone in this circle knew who had the power, and Davenport's power came from the top—the Rockefellers (United States) and the Rothschilds (England). This partnership was based upon the premise that the five would develop a sustainable infrastructure within the United States that would help them reach their overall goal: a World Government.

In 1913, President Woodrow Wilson signed The Federal Reserve Act. The Federal Reserve System was created as a private central United States banking system which is able to dominate the United States political system. Although called Federal, The Federal Reserve System is privately owned by member banks, makes its own policies, and is not subject to oversight by Congress or the President.

In 1921, David Rockefeller helped fund a new department in the United States government; the Council of Foreign Relations, which is related to its sister organization in England, The Institute of International Affairs. Both were at one time known as "Rothschild's Round Table" and comprised of advocates of a world government, orchestrated by Lord Alfred Milner of London, England. In 1921, Colonel House, an advisor to President Woodrow Wilson when he was in office and who had the support of the House of Rockefellers, presided over the creation of The Council of Foreign Relations, and its control over the Federal Banking System, created by Colonel House. The intentional illusionary marketed definition of The Council of Foreign Relations is as follows: A non-partisan and non-profit organization dedicated to improving the understanding of U.S. foreign policy and international affairs.

The Rothschilds came to power in Europe after the Neapolitan Era. The Rothschild brothers—five in all—are a banking dynasty, founding banking houses in Frankfurt, London, Paris, Vienna, and Naples, holding financial control of Europe. These families are the modern keepers—known as the negative elite in some circles —and protectors of the ancient mysteries.

Adding to their power moving towards global domination, the Rothschilds developed their interests on the Atlantic side of the world, becoming the financial administrator behind Rockefeller control of the largest oil company in the United States, Standard Oil. By 1870, John David Rockefeller owned at least 95 percent of the oil industry.

However, as the years progressed, David's reputation was blemished by a scandal between the refiners and the railroads, and total unscrupulous domination of the oil business. In 1888, the New York Senate Committee launched an investigation and lawsuit into Standard Oil's questionable business practices. In 1896, Standard Oil contributed $250,000 to Republican William McKinley's campaign for President against anti-trust legislation supporter and Democrat, William Jennings Bryan. By 1907, there were seven different lawsuits pending against Standard Oil, arguing amongst other things, contempt of court for disobeying an 1892 suit to dissolve the trust. The final ruling of the Supreme Court was stated in the Wall Street Journal: U.S. Supreme Court on May 15, 1911, couched its decision in these clear terms: "Seven men and a corporate machine have conspired against their fellow citizens. For the safety of the Republic, we now decree that this dangerous conspiracy must be ended by November 15th."

In the dissolution, Standard Oil broke into eight other companies, which have since consolidated right back as Amoco, Chevron, and Exxon/Mobil.

By 1921, The House of Rockefeller, supported by the House of

Rothschild, recouped their global power when they redistributed and renamed the power of Rothschild's Round Table: The Council of Foreign Relations in the U.S. and in England, The Institute of International Affairs. In 1922, a little over a year after their combined governance, the New York City Mayor John F. Hylan was reported saying during a public speech, "The real menace of our republic is this invisible government which, like giant octopus, sprawls its slimy length over city, state, and nation. Like the octopus of real life, it operates under cover of a self-created screen … At the head of this octopus are the Rockefeller Standard Oil interests and a small group of powerful banking houses generally referred to as international bankers. The little coterie of powerful international bankers virtually run the United States government for their own selfish purposes. They practically control both political parties."

No one listened.

"I assume you know what will happen to you and your replacement if anything happens to my daughter." Davenport sat leisurely with the eyes of a tiger ready to pounce at any moment. No one mistook his charismatic demeanor as a sign of weakness.

Keeping eye contact, Remy nodded his head in agreement. "I have our finest and most trustworthy member guarding her with his life, just as I would."

"Good." With that said, it was time to return to business. "I have brought you here to discuss your next assignment. I want you to follow Richard Wikki. He is taking a most unusual vacation to Boston. I want you to find out what he is really up to. I do not for one minute think this is by accident." Davenport very seldom shared the details with Remy; he knew not even to ask.

"I will find out, sir." Remy rose as he assumed he was dismissed.

"One more thing. Contact HIM and set a meeting for tonight

at our usual time and place." No one ever spoke HIS name. HE was an enigma, not seen, not heard; an illusion. HE did not exist in any database, HE was a non-entity; created for a purpose. HE was the master illusionist. HE kept reality in the shadows and life an illusion.

***

The Harkness Tower clock across the street from the north side of the Yale Campus was loudly striking midnight. It was a clear summer night, nearing the end of June. It was quite comfortable, unlike the many unusually humid nights a week ago. Still dressed in his business best, Davenport parked his Cadillac in his usual hotel parking spot and walked across The Green to meet HIM. When at all possible, even to Davenport and company, HE preferred to stay in the shadows, unseen at all times. Davenport knew HE would be waiting in the usual spot around the corner in order to be heard and not seen. He was used to these games, knowing that occasionally HE had to physically appear reporting to the five Proprietors. He was not an enigma to them; he was a weapon.

Upon approaching their designated rendezvous, Davenport heard his deep, froggy voice. "What can I do for you Davenport?" Only HE would dare address Mr. Davenport in such a manner. It was only in private, not in front of the five where he gave him his due. And, it was not because HE was being polite; he knew the boundaries playing the game HIS way. Even though Mr. Davenport liked to threaten him that he was not irreplaceable, HE knew that he was. It would take years to develop another HIM, and things were moving too fast, to the point of spinning out of control financially and politically.

Davenport moved towards the voice, moving out of the bright lights of the street lamps, answering, "I have an assignment for you. I want you to follow Richard Wikki. I am sure he is looking for something, and may even know something about the recent skeleton discovery. I do not want his investigation to lead to us in any way. You will create an illusion for him to follow, thus creating plausible answers to any and all his questions. He will see what we want him to see and nothing else. Do you understand?"

"Yes." HE was a man of few words and lots of action; he provided results.

"Follow Professor Wikki until he returns to New Haven. I will take over then. You do not need to report to me. Just create the illusion."

"It is good as done." With that HE swiftly left, leaving Davenport to finish the conversation; talking to himself.

"Damn HIM!"

Chapter 13

The recently renovated Charles Street Jail never looked so glorious. Once the home of many notorious criminals, now proudly stood the Boston Congressional Hotel, resonating the Bostonian elitist strength and dignity. Located on Beacon Hill adjacent to the Charles River on Charles Street, the converted jail stood eight stories high, and hosted 114 rooms which were comprised of half-floor suites for long-term tenants, smaller suites that included a bath, and two or three even smaller suites sharing one bath. Its original jailhouse granite, iron beams, bared windows, and floor plan were combined with geometric Gothic, Romanesque, and Renaissance structures to express the trendy spirit of the twenties.

Lord Wikki stood outside the front of the hotel soaking in all the intricacies of the booming metropolitan town of Boston. The streets were full of irritating city noises; the chiming of trolley car bells, automobile horns honking to hurry lazy motorists along, bicycle bells warning pedestrians to move over, and even an occasional clopping and baying from a horse pulling a carriage full of citizens who still weren't ready to move into the next century. Telephone poles and wires obscured the view of the beautiful downtown skyline from the Bostonian vacationers and townspeople enjoying an outdoor stroll.

As Richard took a moment to view the obstructed city skyline and the original historical edifice of the cruciform-shaped building, he noticed the ornately chiseled Bostonian granite that provided an exquisite border for the oversized hotel entrance. While in awe of the immense masculine outside structure of the one-time city jail, something small, however, caught Richard's eye. It was a minute etching outlining a family shield with a triangle etched in the middle facing towards the East.

What would cause someone to intentionally carve this unusual design … and there above the front entrance? It must mean something to the owner, Mr. Davenport, Richard thought to himself as he motioned for the cab driver to unload his luggage. He couldn't help take note that Mr. Ron Davenport's name seemed to pop up a lot these days.

"Whoa, young man!" Richard shouted as a young bellboy flew past him to assist the cabby with his bags.

Abruptly stopping in his tracks, Marcus replied. "I'm so sorry, sir. It's so exciting to meet someone of your stature." And then he was off to finish the job.

Before Richard could process what the young lad had said, he heard the beckoning of the Concierge. "Ah, Lord Wikki, we have been expecting you. Please excuse Marcus. At times he is a little overzealous in reaching to be an excellent example of our five star service."

Richard's mind started spinning to search for a reasonable answer for all this unwanted fuss. He finally concluded that Jonathan must have made him out to be quite a celebrity. Irritated by the closed, claustrophobic feeling of his high-class clothes he wore to match his title, Richard was painfully aware of a sinking feeling in his gut. *Geez,* he said to himself. *These were only a few of the many reasons I denounced*

E.K. Prescott, Ph.D

my title: these awful stodgy clothes, as well as the embarrassing notoriety everywhere I went—and they hit me square in the face as soon as I stepped out of the cab.

But before he could muster a pout the concierge was bustling him off the busy sidewalk and into the hotel.

"Lord Wikki," he said with eloquence and style which had been perfected through his years of service, "My name is Rufus. I am at your service." Rufus snapped his fingers, alerting Marcus to put Lord Wikki's baggage on a cart, which Marcus would soon push as he escorted Lord Wikki to his private suite.

Rufus, talking in a continual stream of consciousness, did not allow Richard to get a word in edgewise. "We have your suite all ready for you just as you ordered. Marcus will escort you to the eighth floor. We have especially prepared for you, Lord Wikki, the large half-floor suite at the east end of the hall with a view overseeing the Charles River. I'm sure you will not be disappointed in your accommodations. And, please feel free to call upon me personally for anything. I will personally arrange any of your travel needs as well. Every effort has been made to make your stay with us as pleasurable as possible. Do you know how long you will be staying with us?"

Richard almost missed the question as he had consciously tuned out his fake high-end accent and attitude, soaking in the exquisite historical jailhouse ambiance. Richard stood near the north end of the ninety-foot-high central rotunda, illuminating eight floors of rooms that highlighted eight floors of open hallways and circling the entire opened area. The architects artistically married the original 1850 jailhouse decor with the high standards of a modern luxury hotel, accenting the eating establishment, suite doors, and handrail moldings with the original jailhouse granite and steel bars. The original lighting was also kept, giving one the constant sense of evening, even though it was three o'clock in the afternoon. The large grayish marble columns and multi-colored marble floors, mammoth chandeliers, shiny brass, and gold moldings framed most every structure in sight. Large gold framed mirrors as well as original paintings provided the luxury high end clients demanded.

One instantly felt the eeriness of being inside the original jail, and the here and now of a five star hotel. Across the rotunda were shops, restaurants, a grand ballroom, a private reading area, game and cigar rooms, a beauty parlor, a barber shop, and a door to the outdoor leisure lounge, replacing the one time outdoor jail exercise yard, not to mention an illuminated sign pointing downstairs to a cellar private club named "The Liberty Club." The name seemed quite comical to Richard as the hotel was a major city jail not so long ago.

Rufus politely repeated. "How long do you plan to stay with us, Lord Wikki?"

Jarred to the present upon hearing his name, Richard replied. "I'm not sure Rufus, it could be a few days; it could be a few weeks."

"No matter sir, your room will be available for as long as you need it."

"Good, Rufus," Richard replied. "I do have a question or two."

Rufus nodded.

"What time does the café across the common room open for dinner?"

"About five o'clock sir, but if you call ahead and arrange a place for yourself, Lord Wikki, they will be happy to accommodate you any time. Of course, I would be more than happy to make you a private reservation." Rufus added. "We also have something new that we provide for our special guests: excellent room service. Just call us and your order will be brought to your room. There is also a private elevator on the eighth floor that will take you one floor below us to our private gym and pool area for special guests like yourself. You will find elaborate separate accommodations for both men and women, including a hot tub and a eucalyptus room. This key provides access to the private elevator on your floor—"

Reaching for the key, Richard cut Rufus off, annoyed at his continual overachieving chatter. "Thanks, but I will make my own reservation." Rufus nodded in compliance.

As Richard moved toward the open foyer, Rufus snapped his fingers alerting Marcus to hop-to and follow Lord Wikki with his cart of luggage. Richard thought this whole scene could be quite comical if he was in a better frame of mind. But as it was, he had a lot more to think about than putting up with all the pomp and circumstance he eagerly left behind so long ago. He silently prayed this wasn't going to be a pattern of things to come. Turning unexpectedly, almost bumping into the luggage cart that Marcus was hauling at his heals, Richard thought of one more question.

"Rufus, my good man. Tell me, when does the Liberty Club start serving … if you know what I mean?"

"Oh yes, yes sir, Lord Wikki. As a Gold Member guest of our hotel, the cover charge is dropped, and you are entitled to the benefits of the Liberty Club at any time." Leaning closer using a low voice, Rufus added. "Our guests have been known to be quite inventive when bringing their own libations." Rufus gave him a wink.

Not impressed, Richard took a step back from Rufus.

Marcus interjected. "Sir, Lord Wikki, if I might interrupt … the elevator operator is holding the elevator for us."

Saved by the bell, and hoping Rufus would not follow, Richard stated matter-of-factly, "Well then young Marcus, let's not keep the man waiting."

All was neat and ready for Lord Wikki upon entering his suite.

As Richard scouted his room, it brought back memories of the luxuries of his youth. He instantly felt the summer breeze from half-opened windows and ceiling fans, blowing from the back bedroom down the hall and out the front room door which Marcus had propped open with the luggage cart.

Upon entering, Marcus unloaded the luggage cart and checked every room to be sure all was prepared as instructed. Fresh bouquets of flowers had been put in each room to provide color and freshness. The suite included a tastefully hidden serving pantry, replete with refrigerator, electric plate warmer, cupboard, and sink.

The left side of the room was arrayed with windows, highlighting the picturesque view of the Charles River, the Boston Common's park, and downtown. The living room, decorated in eighteenth century English style, included a wood-burning fireplace with an antique mantel and an oversized hanging mirror. Off the living room was a small dining area continuing the English décor. It included a small ornate table and chairs with a crystal chandelier hanging over the center of the table. A small matching hutch displayed a row of ornate bottles which secretly housed an array of illegal liquors. The oversized bath was down the hall between the dining area and bedroom. The bedroom was designed to be a mix of luxury and comfort, accentuating the two outside walls of windows, inviting the outside in.

Richard pulled a large sum of money from his pocket and gave Marcus a hefty tip which was expected from a man of his stature.

"Thank you, Lord Wikki. You are quite generous. Please feel free to ask for me if you need anything." Marcus left, pushing the luggage cart down the hall. As soon as Marcus closed the door to his suite, Richard decided to pour a libation from one of the decorated decanters. Taking time to enjoy the view, he sat in the lounge chair nearest the window in the living area, slowly sipping a much needed drink.

E.K. Prescott, Ph.D.

As Richard began to relax, he unconsciously, as so many times before, felt for the amulet in his left inside pocket, and then automatically reached for his special pipe from his right jacket pocket. He had a general plan of action, but that required befriending a lot of people, extracting information from people who knew people. He was very good at this; it was like a game to him with one challenge after another. At times even exhilarating; it was the thrill of the hunt. He didn't need a well-designed plan, because his gut instinctively led him.

Tired from the long day, Richard slowly slouched down into the soft, pillowy chair. Closing his eyes, he finally succumbed to a well-deserved nap, but not before mentally preparing himself for the task at hand. For to him, portraying Lord Wikki was the biggest task he faced.

***

"Good evening, Lord Wikki," greeted the friendly elevator operator.

"Thank you … Frank. It is Frank, correct?" inquired Richard.

"Yes Sir, hasn't changed since the first time we met. Where can I take you?"

"The first floor, I think I'm going to get a quick bite to eat." Richard pulled his pocket watch out of his vest. Checking the time, Richard commented, "Hopefully it's still early before the heavy dinner crowd arrives; I'm not really one for crowds."

"You never know in a hotel, but usually it fills up later in the evening, You know, the Liberty Club is as popular with our Bostonian citizens as with our hotel guests."

"Is that a fact?" Richard had decided upon arrival that Frank was a man of many answers, information he didn't even know he possessed. He would make an effort to gain his trust, which he didn't think would be too difficult since he already surmised Frank had the gift of gab.

Richard decided to let out a little fishing line to see what he could pull in. "Frank, you seem to really enjoy your work. It's so nice to run into a happy hotel elevator operator. These days, people seem to be so grumpy. I bet you enjoy getting to know your guests. In fact, I bet at times, some of them enjoy opening up to you."

"Well, I don't want to brag, but I am very good at what I do. Sometimes, though, some people are quite closed, and I have to keep to myself. Take for example, there was a gentleman a few weeks ago who seemed to be quite to himself until he wanted to know something about one of our guests. I need to be as accommodating as I can, because that brings the big tips, you know. So I did answer a few of his questions, though I don't like telling on people."

I'll bet, thought Richard. Without a diversion, this job could be quite boring. Testing to see if Frank would be forthcoming, he continued. "About whom did this man inquire?"

"Let's see, we had a guest who owned his own newspaper in New Haven visiting for a few days. He frequents our hotel when he travels to Boston; that's how come I know him off the top of my head. Come to think of it, the gentleman inquiring stayed with us just about as long as Mr. Judson … uh … I didn't mean to say his name. I do try to keep our guests' anonymity."

Richard tried desperately not to show the surprise on his face; not so much his remembering Jonathan, but that someone was inquiring about Jonathan. Noticing the first floor was fast approaching, Richard quickly asked. "What did this man want to know? Did he have a name?"

"Come to think of it, I could not get his name for the life of me, and I'm pretty good at that. He obviously didn't want me to know who he was … I didn't think to inquire at the desk … didn't matter at the time…."

Interrupting, Richard asked again. "What did he want to know?"

Working the elevator knobs to bring the elevator to a stop at

E.K. Prescott, Ph.D

the first floor, Frank responded matter-of-factly. "He was really curious about where Mr. Judson went everyday, and at what times … and, if Mr. Judson mentioned why he was in Boston." After a small jolt, Frank opened the iron rod gated elevator door to the first floor. "Here we are, safe and sound."

Richard had a lot more questions, but now was not the time. Thus, he decided to tip Frank well every time he rode the elevator to insure forthcoming conversations. "Thanks for the ride and the conversation and don't spend it all in one place."

"Yes, sir … see you on the way up."

As Richard entered the dining room, he couldn't help wonder who was following Jonathan and why. He was sure Jonathan had no clue, or he would have said something.

"Good evening, Lord Wikki. Welcome to The Clink. Do you have a seating preference?" asked the maitre d'. As if reading Richard's mind, he continued. "Oh, we are briefed daily about new guests arriving, especially those of your stature."

Richard just nodded his head, choosing to ignore its implications. He noticed two tables unoccupied near the right rear of the restaurant. He pointed to the table where he could sit with his back to the wall. "That one will be fine."

"Good. Nicole will escort you to your table." As he followed her to the table, Richard noticed the occupants in the room; it was second nature to be aware of his surroundings. He quickly scanned the room as he walked behind the hostess. One table stuck out among the others; it was a table with one woman. Not only because she was quite striking, as it was her rich, deep auburn hair that caught his eye, but mainly because it was highly unusual for a woman to be in a public place without an escort. High-end elitist etiquette would never allow a well-bred, respectable woman to be seen in public alone. Richard thought maybe she was traveling from abroad, and didn't realize the rules of the land, or maybe, she just didn't really care.

As he passed her table, which was only two tables from where he had selected to sit, he tried to act nonchalant. It would be an act quite below his station to be caught staring and it wasn't his nature. As he seated himself in the chair against the wall, Richard noticed two waiters whispering and looking in his direction. Richard lamented. *I hoped I could keep a low profile, but thanks to Jonathan it doesn't seem possible.* He seemed to be quite the celebrity, but he still didn't know why. Surely, being a Lord from England was not that big a deal.

Dinner was every bit as exquisite as Rufus told him it would be. He hoped the Liberty Club would be a pleasant experience as well, mostly because Richard had a craving for his favorite bourbon. During dinner, trying not to be obvious, Richard noted the striking woman sitting two tables up looked at him briefly every time she took a drink. He found her quite intriguing, and he wasn't sure why.

After he paid his bill and thanked everyone for a wonderful dinner, Richard decided to walk slowly past her table. As he did, she raised her head and nodded a polite hello. He smiled as he passed, noticing she did not have a wedding ring on her left hand. He was not good at this kind of thing and decided to continue walking out of the restaurant. Usually, he would be in a social situation that would lend to having a natural conversation with a beautiful woman. This was too awkward for him. More than likely, since she was alone, Richard surmised she was a guest of the hotel and he would probably run into her later. Anyway, he reminded himself, he was not ready for any kind of relationship. *But*, he continued, *I am here to meet as many people as possible; no telling what I might uncover. Just take the elevator operator for example.*

As he entered the rotunda, he noticed a small group of

musicians playing to his left near one of the many lounging areas and decided it would be a great opportunity to people watch and think about his next step.

Richard soon noticed the auburn-haired woman from the restaurant cross the rotunda. He watched her while she lazily window shopped from one trinket store to the next. He couldn't shake the feeling that there was something familiar about her; maybe he had seen her before, or maybe it was because she resembled his colleague and friend Sarah. He noticed she obviously knew some of the shop clerks, spending time in short conversations. To Richard, that meant she had been a guest of the hotel for some time. Since she seemed so interested in him at the restaurant, Richard was surprised she was not aware he was sitting in the center lounge area listening to the small quartet. Again, she did not hide the fact that she was unescorted. Thus, it did not surprise him when she walked past the Liberty Club sign and down the steps to the cellar dwelling alone.

Chapter 14

Richard paused on the shiny oak wooden balcony that served as a foyer with an attached descending staircase to the main cellar. The Liberty Club, at one time a torture chamber, had been transformed into a lively jazz club. Where once there was fear and death, now stood a concave celebrating life. The original granite walls, iron bars, and bricks once used to keep humans accosted, now were used to celebrate the virtue of freedom. The large, colorful replica of America's Statue of Liberty stood at the right of the large, highly polished, original wooden plank bar. The bar was constructed in a U-shape, parallel to the two far original bricked walls. Numerous round tables covered in fine linen filled the room, leaving only space for a large dance floor and a stage for a live band. There were three, arched wooden doors with black iron moldings to the right of the dance floor, leading to rooms used for business meetings and private dinners. The ceiling was right out of a page from Michelangelo, chiseled with colorful baroque images. The granite walls provided a damp coolness, which was moved by large ceiling fans and vented to the outside. Richard noticed a large sign advertising the band of the week; a large blown up picture highlighting each member of the all male band, The Four Knights.

As Richard perused the main floor, the club gatekeeper inquired about his pass. All speakeasies generally required an admittance token of some kind; many times it was just a password, money, or even a trinket.

"Oh excuse me Lord Wikki, you have carte blanche anywhere in our hotel."

"Oh no, not you too," Richard muttered under his breath. He gave the gatekeeper a nod and walked down the stairs, only to be greeted once again by the host of the Liberty Club. Disgusted, Richard grumbled to himself. "This is really getting old. Wait until I talk to Mr. Jonathan Judson. What did he tell them?"

"Please follow me, sir."

Richard, pointed and said, "I'd prefer to sit on that side of the room at the empty table next to the wall."

"That sounds perfect, sir."

There were only a few empty tables, and most of the stools and chairs at the bar were occupied. The women were dressed as if they had just stepped out of Vogue magazine, and the men were not far behind them. The eclectic styles from Victorian to Flapper provided a unique picture of fashion. To Richard, it was fun to people watch. *Not the kind of scenery you see in New Haven*, he thought to himself.

Patrons were now milling about while the band was taking a break; conversing, flirting, refilling libations, visiting the powder room, and mingling. It all seemed quite superficial to Richard. As he took in his environment, he noticed the auburn-haired woman from the restaurant standing alone at the top of the stairs near the Liberty Club's entrance. She was dressed to kill. Her wavy auburn hair was loosely pulled back in a bun at the base of her neck. Wisps of curls were falling freely, accentuating her pale face with bright red lips, and dark outlined eyes.

E.K. Prescott, Ph.D

The straight, black, knee-high shimmy dress, with black silk stockings and Mary Jane heels tied with black ribbon bows highlighted her natural beauty. Richard had noticed her walk down the Liberty Club entrance stairs earlier. He thought to himself, *I didn't notice her cross the foyer to her room to change her clothes. When did she double back? I'm usually more aware of these things.* To Richard, she seemed to be looking for someone, or maybe he thought, somewhere to sit as an unescorted woman. Without putting much thought to it, he moved across the room and up the stairs to rescue a woman in distress. Whether she actually was or not was beside the point; Richard believed she was in need of saving.

"Excuse me for intruding, but I noticed you were in the restaurant earlier this evening, sitting alone. If I may presume that you are unescorted, I would like to invite you to sit with me at my table," Richard said with much suavity and confidence.

"I'm flattered you noticed." Hesitating, she continued. "Well, you are correct, I am alone this evening," she said politely with a wide smile. Looking around the main dining area, she commented, "It seems as if there are very few places for a lady to sit. This is not something I would usually do, but given the circumstances, I accept your chivalrous offer."

Richard nodded and pointed, motioning for her to walk down the stairs ahead of him. Arriving at his table, Richard politely pulled out a chair to seat her across from him, and then he sat in his chair against the wall. She wasn't very forthcoming with conversation as she watched the band starting to tune up their instruments for the next show. So, he decided to break the silence. "I'm Richard. Are you vacationing here in Boston?" He was a little appalled he couldn't think of something more interesting to say, but that was the best he could think of off the top of his head.

"My name is Helena Longworth. I'm traveling alone on holiday from England. I have met a lot of the hotel staff, but do not know any of the Boston citizens."

Richard wouldn't confess to it, but he was relieved that they had a common background to ease into a conversation. "My roots are from England as well; Cambridge, as a matter of fact."

Helena smiled, happy to have a connection with someone in the States. "I overheard the staff in the restaurant refer to you as Lord Wikki. I was wondering where you were a Lord."

Here goes … time to create my identity. "Yes, my family title is from the House of Foxworthy. I'm originally from Cambridge, but have lived the last three years in New Haven, Connecticut." Intentionally redirecting the conversation away from himself, Richard asked, holding up his drink. "May I order you one of these? It's called the Liberty Special."

"I've been told there is quite a commotion about buying liquor here in the United States."

"But not about drinking it," added Richard. "The political machine has figured out how to skim money off the citizens and create a whole new criminal power structure at the same time," Richard remarked cynically. "But, never underestimate the ingenuity of the American people," he stated with a smile on his face as he raised his glass.

While he signaled for another drink, Helena asked. "How do you like it here compared to living in England?"

"Actually, the weather in New Haven is similar to Cambridge, and of course a lot less damp." As Helena's drink was served, Richard asked. "And what about you, how do you like Boston?"

"I've only been here a few days. It seems to be a busy city like London. I find it peculiar that people drive on the other side of the street. It looks a little confusing, especially since the steering wheel is on the left side of the car instead of right. Glad I'm not driving around the city." Taking a sip, she continued. "People seem nice enough, especially the hotel staff."

Richard sat back in his chair. He could not get a read on Helena, and that made him feel uncomfortable. She seemed at ease sitting with a stranger, and her etiquette and ability to converse intelligently led him to believe she was from a well-mannered and educated environment. He was intrigued by her; he knew there was more to her than met the eye.

While Richard was in his own world, Helena held the conversation, noticing Lord Wikki didn't seem to be much of a conversationalist. "Recently, I have visited a couple of historical sites. I went to see the Old North Church where the church sexton in 1775 climbed the steeple to signal by lantern to Paul Revere that we, I mean, the British were coming. I want to go to the Boston Museum of History tomorrow. In a few days, I plan to go to a city that was once named Salem, Massachusetts. We've had witches in Europe since before the 1500s, but they seemed to have taken America by surprise."

As Helena continued to talk, many guests walked towards the dance floor as the band began its next session with a lively song: Black Bottom. Richard sat forward as he was beginning to have a hard time hearing her with the energetic loud music in the background. With all the commotion in the dining area and on the dance floor, as well as the loud band music, Richard tried to stay focused on Helena and nothing else.

Suddenly, breaking his concentration, he heard someone come up behind him. "Hi Unc! Man this sure is a cool big house, took me awhile to locate the bees knees gum chew," she said, as she gently put her hand on Richard's right shoulder.

As he jerked, turning in her direction, she continued. "I wonder what bit the jailbirds did to be cooped in this rattrap."

Richard was dumbfounded; stunned with his mouth held wide

open. Trying to collect his composure, he could hardly believe his eyes. In front of him stood a modern day flapper with all the trimmings: short, curly brown hair adorned with a glittered headband, wide blue eyes outlined with eyeliner and black mascara, pink cheeks and ruby red lips, a black silk shift with three rows of beads framing the short hemline, black net stockings, and shiny, buckled black heels. Speechless, Richard watched Maize, or a facsimile of Maize, slide uninvited into the empty chair between him and Helena.

"Nice rags Unc. I see you two are sipping some forbidden hooch. Who's the song bird sitting across from you?"

Not willing to admit he did not know what was transpiring, Richard introduced Maize to Helena. "Maize, this is Miss Helena Longwood. She is vacationing here from England." Taking time to get a grip on the situation, Richard continued his rambled introduction. "Helena has been in Boston for just a few days. She's been sightseeing mostly."

"Nice to meet ya'. I'm Maize Judson," she responded, putting out her hand to shake Helena's. "I don't always throw the flapper slang around like that… I thought I'd surprise him."

"Looks like you succeeded," Helena said, trying to hide the laughter she was holding deep inside. "Lord Wikki was just telling me a little, very little in fact, about New Haven."

"Uncle Wikki isn't my real uncle, it's kind of a pet name," Maize added, quite animated and smiling at Richard. "Since his arrival to New Haven about three years ago, my family kind of adopted him. My father owns the only newspaper in New Haven—the New Haven Gazette. Did Unc tell you that he once was a detective for Scotland Yard? My father, Jonathan Judson, was quite intrigued with Lord Wikki's background."

Helena looked at Richard, who just raised his hands, signaling defeat. Helena grinned as Maize continued. "He left the Yard and came to New Haven to teach at Yale University in the School of Law. It was quite the news for our little town, and big kudos for Yale."

Richard sat in disbelief. He wondered what Maize was up to. *How did she know where I went? How did she get here, and more importantly, why is she here? There's got to be a great story behind this charade*, he thought to himself. *I can't wait to hear this one.* For lack of something to say, Richard commented. "Helena visited the Old North Church and plans to visit the Bostonian Museum of History tomorrow."

Looking at both Richard and Maize, Helena added. "Yes, it's been quite interesting to see America's take on the revolution."

"I like her Unc, can we join her tomorrow? It sounds like fun … the three of us."

Richard tried to softly nudge her under the table, but missed. Noticing the missed kick, Maize added. "Oops, pardon my manners. I should have asked if you would enjoy our company."

Finding the whole idea quite agreeable and amusing, Helena thought this might be fun. "Sure, what time would you like to meet?"

Richard blurted, "We'll meet you around 11:00 outside of the museum." He was going to take control of this conversation before Maize got totally out of control.

"That sounds wonderful. I look forward to it. It's nice to know a few people."

"Well, my darling Maize," directing his eyes towards her and her alone. "It's time to take our leave." Maize knew she was walking on thin ice; but she knew everything would smooth over, eventually.

All three mingled their way through the maze of tables, chairs, and people seeking quiet refuge in the hotel foyer. As they walked silently to the elevator, Maize thought Richard seemed stiff and aggravated. She was sure when he heard the dirt she had dug up, he'd feel better. As they walked, she thought the deafening silence would never end.

"Hello Lord Wikki," greeted the elevator operator. What floors?"

"You working late?" inquired Richard.

"My relief is sick. I need the extra dough, so here I am. Floors?"

"Ladies first," replied Richard.

"Fourth floor for me," said Helena.

"Second, please," added Maize

As Frank worked the elevator to the second floor, Richard instructed. "We have a lot to talk about before tomorrow, Maize. I'll be down to see you in a half an hour."

Maize noticed it wasn't a question, or even an invitation; it was an order.

As the doors opened at the second floor, Maize concluded. "Nice to meet you Helena, see you tomorrow." Looking at Richard she continued cheerfully. "Room 221, see you in thirty minutes, Unc."

Chapter 15

"It's me," Richard said as he knocked at Maize's hotel room door. As she opened the door, he noticed the room was decorated with the same elegant features as his, but a lot smaller in size. The small parlor was adorned in Victorian-style furniture which included a fireplace with one simple flower vase painting hanging above its plain, white mantel. Maize had reserved the hotel package encompassing three rooms that shared one bath located down the hall, unlike Lord Wikki, who had the best suite money could buy.

"How good to see you Professor Wikki," Maize greeted Richard as she invited him to enter and sit. Richard happily noticed she had changed into a normal day dress from her outlandish flapper attire, and removed all the paint on her face.

"So now its Professor Wikki, is it?"

Maize could not tell his mood by his demeanor. He was good at that, she said to herself. She thought if he was upset, she surely should be able to tell. Richard sat in the chair to the right of the couch in the center of the parlor facing the fireplace.

"So, you were saying?" Richard inquired. He was not in the mood for small talk, and wanted to hear the explanation for her unparalleled, dramatic exhibition. "What is your creative mind up to? And for God's sake, why are you here?" Richard continued questioning her with a straight face.

Maize took a deep breath, thinking she shouldn't beat around the bush and get right to the point. She realized he was in no mood for her wonderful elaborations in which she prided herself. She took a seat at the end of the couch nearest Richard. Looking directly at him and meeting his gaze, she politely answered. "Well, first I'm here because we had an appointment yesterday to go over what I've uncovered." It was very difficult for her not to embellish. She paused to gather her thoughts. "I knew you would not show up without a message of some kind. So, I did a little digging and found out you went to Boston on a well-needed vacation. But that didn't add up, since we had an appointment, so it had to be at the last minute."

Richard smiled inwardly, noting Maize was trying to be as succinct as possible, but her unique style still showed through.

"I decided you would need what I had to tell you, so I made the decision to follow you to Boston."

"But I'm on vacation. Why would I need to know what you dug up?'

There was a pause as she decided not to answer him verbally; she didn't trust what might come out of her mouth. Instead, she tilted her head and stared at him for a moment before rolling her eyes, letting him know that she didn't buy it.

"Before you say anything else," Maize continued, lowering her voice and holding up her index finger, politely signaling for Richard to wait a minute. "I've heard of phones being bugged and wires being intercepted. I didn't want someone overhearing *our secret.*"

Richard decided to sit back in his chair, because he knew a long story was coming whether he wanted to hear it or not. Maize couldn't be close-mouthed any longer; her usual animated storytelling style took over.

"So, when I arrived at the hotel and asked for Professor Wikki, that Rufus guy ... what a dope. He said, 'Oh you mean Lord Wikki.' Of course I thought that was strange, but I just went with it. At that point, it occurred to me Lord Wikki was some kind of disguise, or you would have used Professor Richard Wikki. And, good ole Rufus said he saw you enter the Liberty Club a little while ago. Since I happened to mention that I am your niece, and since for some reason you walk on water around here, he personally escorted me to the club's entrance. It was all quite easy." She paused. "Now that I actually think of it, being your niece is quite believable," she said with great satisfaction.

Being a man of few words, Richard asked, "And you are here because of a missed appointment?"

"No, not exactly ... more on the ... need to know."

"What?" Richard looked at her, quite puzzled.

"Well, if you were following some kind of lead, you'd probably need to know this information."

Richard put his hand out like a stop sign. "Whoa, little Miss Flapper, do your parents know you're here?'

Without much thought, Maize answered. "Mother does. She is aware I'm in Boston ..." Trailing off to a whisper, she finished. "... to visit family and some friends."

Not wanting Richard to jump in just yet, Maize continued. "She wasn't too keen on the idea at first, but she said I'd be on my own in college soon, and she'd have to get used to the idea sooner or later."

"And your father?" Richard did not like the implications that could be made by some. It wasn't so much the professor-student questionable relationship, but the idea Jonathan had sent him here to follow a lead; it was too dangerous for a young girl. Not to mention the fact that there is a lot of secrecy surrounding his visit; the probability of more people involved threatened his anonymity.

"My father has been working night and day at the paper. Seems like besides our skeleton caper, the King Tut craze and the awful hangings of blacks in the South by the Ku Klux Klan are keeping him quite occupied. Neither Mom nor I have seen him much. That happens periodically in the newspaper business." Thinking she needed a break, she rose. "I think I'm going to get a glass of ice water. Would you like some? And if you'd like to use the water closet, as you Brits call it, it's down the hall to the right." Maize had prepared a pitcher of ice water for his visit; her throat was dry from all her explaining.

"No, thank you, not at this time anyway," Richard replied.

As Maize poured herself a glass of water, Richard continued. "So let me get this straight—you are here visiting family, but staying at the same hotel as me—"

"But Mom doesn't know that," Maize abruptly added, cutting Richard off in midstream.

"Now just let me finish. So that was just a cover story to relay some kind of important information you thought I needed to know immediately?"

As Maize resumed her seat at the end of the couch, she nodded. She didn't want to interrupt him because she thought he was handling this extremely well.

Richard continued his point. "It never occurred to you that I may not want you here in Boston no matter if the information is as important as you seem to think it is?"

Maize looked wide-eyed with a girlish smile on her face, and slowly shook her head. She was sure he'd get used to the idea.

"And somehow, you came to the conclusion that I used to be

a Lord instead of a professor, thus I was disguising my true identity for some reason?"

Maize thought he expected a response, so opened her mouth to reply.

Shaking his finger, Richard replied. "Not yet. And, the reason I'm incognito is to follow up on clues about the skeleton you and Leslie mistakenly discovered. Have I summed it up correctly?" Richard was sure he would get to the truth a lot faster if he took control of the conversation.

Maize took a deep breath. She could see he wasn't getting the total picture. "Okay Professor, please let me continue."

Sitting back in his chair, Richard replied. "Please do. I am definitely intrigued to understand how your mind works." He thought as he watched her, *how could anyone be upset with her? Look at her … she seems so innocent sitting there …* but he knew better.

"Well, to begin with, I thought we were kinda, like sorta, maybe some type of partners. You know, because I'm investigating the background information about our secret."

Richard chuckled. "Don't worry Maize. I'm sure you are not bugged, and no one is lurking over you shoulder, unless it's me."

"Well then, ya' know, the necklace."

Richard hoped she'd forgotten about the necklace as he nonchalantly patted his inner coat pocket for reassurance.

"By the way, the last time we chatted, you were going to talk to your professor friend about it."

Richard realized he had to lie; a little white lie. If not only to keep Maize contained, but also for her safety. Someone had followed her father and was probably following him. He needed her trust, but now was not the time.

"Yes, I met with Professor Birmingham. After she examined the necklace, she believed it had no particular significance. It's a dead end. Usually you run into quite a few dead ends before the truth is revealed. Actually, I don't remember where I put it. I probably left it in one of my pants pockets hanging in my bedroom closet at home." Richard breathed a sigh of relief as Maize seemed to accept his description of events. Intentionally changing the subject, he asked, "Now Maize, tell me what is so important that you had to follow me all the way from New Haven to Boston."

As she rose to retrieve her notes from her suitcase in the bedroom, she replied. "Just a minute, I want to be sure I relay the facts correctly."

Richard took this opportunity to stretch his legs and roam around the room. He noticed the air seemed cooler as night began to fall; it was a welcome cool after a sticky, hot day. As he retook his seat, he couldn't help thinking how seriously Maize was taking the little bit of work he asked her to do. Upon returning, he watched her flip pages of notes, apparently gathering her thoughts. She seemed so intent on what she had to say. Amidst his rambling thoughts, it occurred to him, *what am I going to do with her*? He felt as if he needed to protect her, especially since someone was following him, and now probably her as well. *This is not going to be good. She has to return to New Haven tomorrow.*

"Well, first of all Henry Phillips II was the only son of Henry Phillips I, a wealthy merchant in New Haven. Apparently, his father was a Proprietor of The Green until his death. Henry I served on almost every committee or board in town. He was survived by his wife and only daughter Francine, named after his sister Francis. His daughter, Francine Cunningham, resides in New Haven, a widow of a wealthy merchant. Anyway, it seems Henry II attended private elementary and secondary schools in New Haven." She took a breath and looked up at Richard. "I looked into each school's records as far back as I could, and it seems like little Henry II was a big troublemaker year after year. Apparently, he was politely asked to leave school. You had to read between the lines on that one. It stated he should find a more suitable environment for his educational needs." She returned to her notes. "Anyway, it was about that time he came here to the Boston Congressional Hotel to work. The newspaper article made it sound like his father sent him on a business trip." Maize then sat her notebook in her lap, pausing to look at Richard.

Richard took this moment to interject his thoughts. "Well Maize, you haven't said anything that would cause anyone to come all the way to Boston to relay firsthand."

"There's more."

"I certainly hope so."

Maize continued with her report. "I decided to go visit my grandma again to see if she recalled anything else; remember you strictly told me not to talk to any of the Phillips' living relatives. Long story short, Grandma remembered a rumor about a bunch of kids getting involved with what she called 'dark spirits.' She was very young and really didn't pay much attention to kids' idle gossip. She told me someone named Sarah Greensworth was still alive and might know a little more. So Grandma set up an appointment, cause that's how ladies call on someone, she said, not like the younger generation dropping in on a whim, it's not respectable. Grandma insisted on going with me. She had set it at a respectable hour—10:30 a.m.—when women of taste receive callers. Oh, she was dressed in her Sunday finest. She actually looked quite nice."

Richard was growing tired of her background color. *Why can't she just get to the point?* Interrupting, he asked. "And what did she say, Mrs. Green … er … whatever?"

"Basically, she remembered it was rumored that some of the kids were having 'witch meetings' out on the beach near Five Points by the old lighthouse. The kids' names involved were kept a secret, but she said all of them knew Henry Phillips II was one of them. She mentioned it was a well-known fact among the kids that Henry was not a person you could trust. She said he was always looking for trouble, and he usually found it."

Richard was just about to interrupt her, hoping to speed up her verbal exposé when Maize interrupted. "One more thing, I decided to return to the newspaper after I dropped Grandma at the house. I had a hunch. I wanted to search the archives for any news about supernatural events or dark arts activities reported during this time. It took a little digging, but this is what I found." Maize pulled out a copy of a newspaper article and read:

DARK ARTS – DARK YOUTH

New Haven has recently seen a rash of mischievous acts by some of our more adventurous youth. Students have been spotted running across lawns at night with dark capes screaming, "Beware of the times!" Dark Arts emblems such as the crossbones have been painted on downtown store windows. As of late, it is feared a group of youths are holding bonfire rituals of some kind on the beach near the light house. Is this the antics of our beloved Yale brotherhood societies or has this debauchery filtered down to our young people? As conscientious Christian members of New Haven, we need to stop looking the other way and save our youth from the hands of the Devil. There will be a town meeting at the Presbyterian Church at 7:00 this Wednesday. I wonder, did the witches of Salem arrive here with our Puritan founders?

Submitted by
Pastor George Brown
Presbyterian Church,
New Haven, June 1880

After she finished reading the article, Maize gave the paper to Richard. As he reviewed what she had just read, his mind began racing. Maize continued. "What was really strange is that I could not find a single follow-up article, not even one about the meeting. It's like it didn't happen. That's like, highly improbable from a news reporter's perspective. Maybe some elite members of our society at that time squashed the whole story, not wanting their children to be implicated, or there is a cult of the dark arts thriving in New Haven under our very noses."

As he reached for his pipe in his coat pocket, Richard gave the paper back to Maize and sat back in his chair. It was time to think. Maize grinned as she watched Richard contemplate what she had just read. It seemed at times like this that he mentally went somewhere else—not even realizing Maize was still in the room. She decided to wait on him. As Maize watched, she gleamed with pride. She had obviously uncovered something important. She relaxed, laying the notes next to her on the couch. Maize was proud of herself, and she hoped Professor Wikki was as well.

Richard was silently contemplating if he was more astonished at the information, or Maize's ability to uncover the information, or her tenacity to take the train alone to Boston to deliver the information in person. He noticed how good Maize felt about this news, but he needed time to think alone in his room. It astonished him how pleased he was to see her genuinely interested in following lead after lead. Most young people would have stopped at just reviewing the archives like he had originally asked. He believed she would make a very good investigative reporter some day; if she didn't get herself killed in the process.

Breaking his silence, he turned to Maize, gnawing his pipe between words. "Maize, I do have to say you did a good job following leads and uncovering this information. I assume you told no one."

She nodded her head in affirmation.

"Good girl. Let's keep it that way for now. I hate to admit it, but you were right on two accounts: I needed to get the information, and in person. But, that does not alleviate the fact that you are a young girl traveling alone in a big city, unaware of the dangers that might exist."

Richard moved to the end of his chair and looked into her eyes and calmly stated. "I would like to take your notes and this article to my room to review. I don't want anything on your person concerning this matter. It is only a precaution for your safety. Obviously, you know you have uncovered something important. I need time to make the connections." He was thankful that Maize was unaware of the true meaning behind the necklace, and its possible implications as it related to this new information, and he was going to keep it that way.

"Thanks Professor Wikki, but I can take care of myself."

Chuckling, Richard stood up to leave, reaching for Maize's folder on the couch. "I'm quite sure you can."

As he walked towards the door, he asked Maize to double lock her hotel door, and not leave the room until it was time to meet him in the morning. "You can always reach me through the hotel phone system if you feel the need. I will meet you downstairs at the front desk in the hotel lobby precisely at 9:30 for breakfast. Don't be late." As he began to open her hotel room door to leave, he added. "And, at that time we will discuss this Lord and Uncle Wikki stuff." He began to take his leave shutting the door behind him when he remembered. "And by the way, what is bees knees gum chew?"

Maize just smiled as she closed the door.

Chapter 16

Richard was looking forward to diving into the information Maize uncovered. Upon entering his hotel suite, he turned the lamp light on nearest to him as he took off his sports jacket and laid it neatly over the arm of the couch.

Something wasn't right.

Richard observed the large window in the parlor area was open and the ceiling fans were moving; both he left intentionally closed and turned off. Realizing his room was on the top floor of the hotel, he thought it was unlikely anyone came through the windows. As he cautiously moved down the short hallway from the parlor, he noticed the lights were on in the bathroom. Richard didn't think he'd left those on either.

Remembering the gun he purposely tucked away in his suitcase, Richard slipped silently to his bedroom to retrieve it before further investigation. He glanced quickly around the bedroom, noticing nothing was out of order. It was obvious his suitcase was untouched. For a moment, he relaxed as it occurred to him all of this could have been the maid bedding down his room for the night.

Suddenly, Richard turned toward the sound of a door slamming shut at the front of his suite. He reached for his gun, and swiftly retraced his steps, looking behind the bathroom door and shower curtain. No sign of anyone. He then checked all the closets and cubby holes as he crept towards the front parlor. Richard intently listened for any sounds which might reveal the intruder. His hotel suite was empty; he was alone. The sound he heard must have been the front door slamming as the intruder left.

Realizing he was alone, Richard set his gun on the dining table and felt his pocket for the amulet. As usual, it was safely nested. As he walked to peer out the opened window, he wondered why someone would break into his hotel room, and not seem to be looking for anything, only leaving a window open, ceiling fans running, and a bathroom light on. Richard shut and locked the parlor window.

He then turned to scan the room once again. He wondered why someone would break into his room for no reason. There was absolutely no evidence that the intruder was looking for something or someone. If it would have been an ordinary burglary or even someone looking for the amulet, there would be a little clutter at least. *Maybe I interrupted a burglary attempt mid-stream and the mission was aborted.* Nothing made sense. He grabbed for his pipe and sat in the nearest chair. *How does one get into a hotel suite on a secured floor for Christ's sake? This was a jail.* Richard's gut told him this was planned. But why? For what purpose? It made no sense.

Since nothing was missing, he decided not to call hotel security. He surmised if security was anything like good ole Rufus, he was better left on his own.

At that moment, it occurred to Richard the intruder might be the same man who was following Jonathan. He questioned. What had he uncovered to attract such interest? And then he thought of Maize. He rose quickly, grabbing for the hotel phone to call the operator to ring Maize's room. He did not like this helpless feeling.

Maize answered as cheerful as ever, with the latest Jazz tunes blasting out of the hotel radio in her room. "Hello??"

"It's Professor Wikki."

"Oh, Professor Wikki, just a sec … I have to turn down the radio … can't hear you … hi, what's up?"

Richard realized the hotel operator was probably listening in on their conversation; they were notorious for eavesdropping. Acting casual as not to alarm Maize and tip off the operator, Richard replied. "Just checking to see if everything is fine before I turn in for the night."

"Yes, everything is fine. Why?"

"Oh, nothing, just thought someone should check in on you."

"Oh, don't worry. I called Mom earlier and let her know I bumped into you. Told her we were going to the Boston Museum tomorrow. She felt better and glad I wasn't alone wandering big bad Boston."

Great, Richard thought to himself. *Now what am I going to do with her? More than likely, Virginia is elated I am around to keep her only daughter safe and out of trouble, with emphasis on the latter.*

Maize noticed the pause on the other end of the phone. Feeling awkward, she tried to explain it wasn't a big deal. "I told Mom I would return in a few days with you. Mom said she will only feel better when I am safely home."

Richard was not at all pleased. He knew he would not be able to do anything about this situation until morning. "Well, make sure you double lock your door. I will meet you tomorrow morning downstairs at the front door at 9:30. Don't be late."

"No problem. See you then." Maize hung up.

Madame Flambeau, a messenger of the Angel of the Night, covered in her black hooded shawl, waited silently, hidden in the dark shadow of a light post outside Richard's hotel window. No one would see her this time of night. The city park closed at 9 p.m., and that was several hours ago. No one was even lingering after hours. The sky was quite dark with no light from the stars or moon; the area seemed to be covered with an eerie dark veil. She was quite alone. While waiting, she lamented. *I hope I haven't sent a fool into a lion's den.* Then suddenly, she noticed someone resembling her young attendant moving slowly and cautiously across the courtyard, hoping not to attract any unwanted attention.

Simon appropriately addressed her as he approached. Bowing, he hesitantly whispered. "Madame … everything has been done according to your instructions. I left nothing out of place, but only evidence that someone was in the room. I had to hide when he entered unexpectedly, and let the door slam when I left as he entered his bedroom. He definitely knew someone had been in his room. No one saw me coming or going."

At that moment, Madame Flambeau noticed Richard looking out his window. She politely moved Simon with her further into the darkness. Only after he had closed the window and walked away did she continue. "Well done. Hopefully now Lord Detective Professor Richard Wikki has no doubt someone is following him … it's just not us. The Angel of the Night will be happy we succeeded in warning him."

When Simon turned to answer her, he found her nowhere in sight. "I hate when she does that."

Chapter 17

Richard rose early the next morning, tired from tossing and turning most of the night. Things were starting to happen and as far as he was concerned, Maize's involvement only muddied the waters. During the early hours of the night, it seemed he awoke every hour on the hour. Richard decided to send Jonathan a wire, updating him concerning the current situation. He wanted Maize's father to hear the latest events cryptically in a Western Union Telegram from him, and not Maize's mother.

Since the events of last night left quite an impression on Richard concerning the now volatile nature of his assignment, he hoped no one was going to intercept his telegram in hopes of extracting his true purpose. Also, following up on a bit of information Jonathan had passed at their recent dinner, Richard had made an early appointment with a member of the local Boston Masonic Lodge historian to fish for any bits of information about the dearly departed Henry Phillips II, via his father's membership. He surmised he should finish both errands in plenty of time to meet Maize at the front door of their hotel.

Richard arrived just minutes before Maize. "You're late," he goaded teasingly.

"I'm not late." She looked at the clock over the front desk to her left. "It's 9:35. I'm fashionably on time," she replied, looking over her outfit.

Rufus was standing in the background, waiting for the correct moment to ask if Lord Wikki needed a car, a cab, or a surrey. "No thanks, we are going to take the trolley," he replied as he swept Maize quickly out the door.

The Boston streets were as busy as the day Richard arrived. People were everywhere. As they entered the trolley looking for a place to sit, Richard mentioned to Maize. "This will take us to a nice place for breakfast, and not too far from the museum where we'll meet Helena at 11:00."

***

"You haven't been listening to a word I've said," Maize admonished, as she took another bite of the eggs on her plate.

Richard, lost in his own thoughts, mechanically ate his breakfast, as he had tuned Maize out a long while before. He was rehashing the latest events, and trying to find the best approach to break the news to Maize that she would not be returning to New Haven tomorrow. Instead, she was going to accompany him on the rest of his vacation. At that revelation, he knew she would be full of questions, and legitimate ones at that.

Until last night, Richard had thought it was more of a lark to investigate Henry II's movements, but now it had become a serious investigation—one that was potentially dangerous—especially for a young, naive, small-town girl.

"Hmm? Oh yeah, I heard you," Richard mumbled coming back to reality.

E.K. Prescott, Ph.D.

"I asked if you came to any great conclusions or revelations about the information I gave you last night."

"Yes, about that. We will get to that … but first, I must talk to you about something … something serious. We need to talk about you."

Leaning back in her chair Maize's eyes grew wide with intrigue. "Me?"

Richard leaned forward, crossing his arms on the table in front of him while looking directly into her eyes. With a hushed voice, he began.

She could tell he was serious, and that worried her.

"Maize, when you first brought me the necklace, everything seemed quite simple. But since that day, things have become quite complicated."

Maize had no idea what he was talking about, but knew from experience not to ask any questions until he was finished.

"Any time someone finds a skeleton buried for quite some time, there are always a lot of questions." He paused, realizing Maize was a smart girl and could put two and two together if he didn't phrase his words carefully. He wasn't sure how much information she should know, mainly to keep her alive. "You did a fantastic job following potential leads."

Maize beamed with satisfaction.

Richard leaned a little closer. "Maize, you must not react to the information I am going to tell you. You must act like we are having a normal discussion over breakfast."

Maize was quite stunned at such definite instructions. The lightness of their conversation seemed to take a serious turn. Trying her best to act normal, she nodded that she understood.

"Events of late, which you are not aware of, have caused a needed change of plans. You are going to accompany me on the rest of my vacation. I cannot explain now, please understand, but tomorrow we are going to visit Danvers, Massachusetts. I have uncovered some information that will now take me … us … to the next leg of my vacation, Salem Town."

Richard could see the questions urging to pop out of Maize's mouth, and diverted his attention to others sitting in the restaurant to avoid eye contact. He was always aware of his surroundings and was not totally sure they had not been followed.

Although he could not identify anyone specifically, his gut told him someone was there in the restaurant watching them.

Richard stood. Laying down the money for the tab on the table, he said, "Maize, I appreciate you understanding how to play the game. We must leave now. I will answer all your questions later. I must ask you to play the part of Lord Wikki's niece as well as you did the other night at the speakeasy."

Smiling and acting on cue, Maize took Richard's arm as they left the restaurant.

Remy rose immediately, abruptly dropped change on the table for his coffee, and followed them out the door.

E.K. Prescott, Ph.D.

Chapter 18

"Mr. Judson, Detective Wilson is here to see you," Lily announced over the phone.

Before Jonathan could acknowledge his secretary's announcement, Detective Wilson burst in his office, assuming red-carpet treatment and looking pompous with a smirk of superiority on his face. He wore a shiny badge precisely placed on his shirt to alert everyone that he was not just any policeman. He was a short man with a big ego, a man who took his relationship with the New Haven chief of police too seriously, as well as his importance to the department.

It was clear that Detective Wilson would rather be anywhere than here delivering a message for the chief, but he knew it would be unwise to go against the chief's wishes. As he entered, Jonathan rose and pointed to the chair in front of his desk. No one spoke as each sat down. Jonathan made an attempt to ease the tension in the air, which permeated each corner of his office, while the detective looked around, staring at the many scattered plants.

"My wife wanted to give my office some life and decided to decorate the whole place with plants. If it wasn't for Lily, they probably would all die of thirst." Jonathan quickly surmised his uninvited guest did not care for small talk or anything else he had to say. "Well then, we'll get to the point. What can I do for you Detective Wilson?" Jonathan knew this type of person, they seemed to crop up everywhere in the newspaper business. He hated titles.

"The chief has asked me to speak privately concerning the skeleton found on the beach a few weeks ago." Detective Wilson sat up in his chair staring straight at Jonathan as if this was an honor to be given special permission to represent the chief in this matter.

Jonathan tried to hide a snicker. He learned a long time ago how to play their game and just nodded in agreement. He felt compelled to remind Detective Wilson that his daughter was one of the girls who discovered the skeleton, and because of that, he too, has a special interest.

"I see," Detective Wilson replied in a manner that suggested he was not aware of this bit of information. "Well, here are the facts. I don't have time to sit here all day discussing unimportant details. The chief wanted me to inform you of …" Pausing, Detective Wilson referred to his notes. "One, the identity of the skeleton is confirmed to be Henry Phillips II. His casket was exhumed and no body was found in it." Checking his notes once again, he continued. "Two, young Henry's father, Phillips I, died in 1889 of tuberculosis—known as consumption—was verified in his medical records as cause of death. And, three, we should be receiving a biological report any day on the fungus found near the body." Putting his small notebook in his pocket, he proclaimed. "That's about it!" He looked very pleased with himself.

"I do have a few questions, Detective Wilson," stated Jonathan.

"The chief thought you would. Shoot, times a wastin."

"First of all, please relay to the chief our original agreement still stands. He will know what I mean." Jonathan paused. "When was the casket exhumed?"

E.K. Prescott, Ph.D

"That's on a need-to-know basis."

"Ok. Well then, tell me, how was a funeral ceremony conducted without a body in a casket? Wouldn't somebody notice no one was inside?" Jonathan was losing patience with this loser.

"Tuberculosis as you know is quite contagious and we surmised they kept the casket closed in order to avoid spreading germs. At the time, tuberculosis was of epidemic proportions."

"I see." Jonathan replied. "Did his father have a closed-casket ceremony as well?"

Avoiding the question, Detective Wilson exclaimed. "I am aware his wife died earlier from the Spanish Influenza epidemic. Apparently it was a tragedy because the epidemic was almost over."

"Did you have approval from his family to exhume Henry Phillips II body?"

"Sorry, that's on a need—"

Quite disgusted, Jonathan cut him off mid-sentence. "I know … on a need-to-know basis. Can you tell me if there was any link between the son's and father's deaths?"

Detective Wilson emphatically replied, "No."

Jonathan sighed to himself. *This is like pulling teeth.* "Are there any suspects?"

"The chief has a few ideas, but they have all been dead ends. He doesn't think there is much use in pursuing such an old case."

A look of utter disbelief passed over Jonathan's face. "Excuse me?"

"Chief said if you want to know anymore you need to talk to him personally."

Jonathan was done with this character and this conversation. He stood up, put his hand out and dismissed Detective Wilson. "Thank you for taking the time to deliver the chief's information. Please tell your chief that I will be in touch." Pointing to the door, he said, "I'm sure you know the way out."

As Detective Wilson left Jonathan's office, you could hear the door slam throughout the building. Noting the meeting was obviously adjourned, Robert entered his father's office to find out what had transpired. Jonathan relayed the short version of the conversation as he stopped periodically stating, "Who do they think they are!"

Jonathan paused at the end of the story, and Robert concluded. "Dad, it's obvious they are covering up something. What do you think it is?"

"I don't know, but I intend to find out. I am waiting to hear from Richard Wikki."

Just then, Lily knocked and announced there was a telegram for Jonathan from Richard Wikki. Jonathan eagerly reached for the telegram and sat back in his chair as he opened it. Lily left the office, politely closing the door behind her. Robert became alarmed as he watched his father's face change from anticipation to shock to worry.

WESTERN UNION TELEGRAM

Boston, Massachusetts

July 10, 1923

Jonathan. Maize is fine. She is with me. Not good for a girl to travel alone these days. She is a great help in teaching me American history. Things are progressing. Maize and I will be moving on to our next historical city, Salem.

More Later.

Lord Wikki

Chapter 19

She was looking forward to meeting Maize and Lord Wikki at the Boston Museum of American History. It was one of many average-sized museums scattered throughout the Boston area; there was also the Museum of Science and Technology, the Museum of the Arts, and the Museum of Automobiles and Trains to name a few. Helena stood in front of the mirror, fussing over her appearance. It wasn't as if she wanted to ignite a relationship; she just wanted his approval. She finally chose a casual, yellow cotton dress that buttoned down the front. The V neck and short sleeves, with the addition of flat tied shoes made her a picture perfect model for the popular American sporty look of the early 1920s. Helena was pleased with her choice of attire; it was not only fashionable, but cooling on a hot summer day. She would not have chosen this outfit back home in Cambridge, England, but it was vogue in Boston. Helena liked the American fashions which seem to give women a sense of freedom, fun and adventure, leaving the restrictive Victorian styles popular at the close of World War I behind.

"So are we going to have a conversation about why you've decided I should now be your niece?" Maize asked as they watched the trolley pull away.

They were standing across the street from the museum. Richard watched as cars and bicycles passed. He especially found the tandem bicycles quite intriguing and wondered how in the world they stayed in sync. He was waiting for the policeman to wave across the street the small group that had gathered.

Ignoring Maize's question, he replied. "I see Helena. She's waiting for us under that little bit of shade to our right." He recalled how easy it was to talk to her last night, and amazed at the fact that he found her quite alluring. He couldn't shake the feeling he had seen her somewhere before, but where?

As they crossed the street, Helena noticed their arrival and waved, smiling from ear to ear; she was glad to see Lord Wikki again. After polite greetings, Helena suggested they quickly step inside out of the heat, only to discover it was still warm, even with the breeze from numerous ceiling fans running at high speed. The large crowd made the inside almost as hot as the outside. Maize couldn't understand why all these people would want to visit the museum on a day like this.

"Well, where would you like to begin, girls?" Richard asked.

Maize loved history and jumped in. "Let's start with the Presidents. See, over there." Maize pointed to the third large display on their right.

"Sounds like as good a place to start as any," replied Helena. "This will be quite educational for me. I know of your first president, George Washington, but not many others." As they walked towards the president's display, Maize couldn't help noticing all the diverse women's fashions. She was amazed to see so many young women wearing a high skirt hem above their knees. She noted that there seemed to be a maze of various skirt lengths among this large group. Maize concluded one wouldn't see this extreme of women's fashions in conservative New

Haven. Interrupting her thoughts, she heard Richard calling her name.

"Maize, come on. We almost left you behind. What are you looking at?"

"Oh nothing." Intentionally changing Richard's focus, Maize exclaimed. "Oh look, they already have a wax figure of President Harding!"

Just then all three turned towards a loud, boisterous voice proclaiming President Harding is a crook and a stooge of a President. "Can you believe his dog has a Cabinet seat, and was thrown a birthday party in a Cabinet meeting?" The small crowd in front of the display laughed. "It's true. It was reported the other day in the *Washington Post*."

"Do you think that is true?" Helena asked, perplexed.

"Well, Helena, earlier reports about our president's behavior suggest that there is truth to what this man is saying."

Helena, trying to find the correct words, added. "I cannot believe the United States would elect such … such … a dysfunctional President."

"Well, we did, for better or for worse," commented Maize.

Richard had enough of the hawkers and suggested that they move on. "Where would you ladies like to go next?" he asked as he led the way out of the president's exhibit hall towards the center of the museum, where all the halls exited.

"Well that was certainly short but sweet," Maize interjected.

"Sorry Helena for your incomplete presidential history lesson, but I could not take that overbearing crowd any longer," explained Richard.

As they re-entered the crowded main lobby, Helena inquired. "Richard you seem somewhat distracted today. Is something wrong?"

Richard had been on edge since discovering someone had broken into his hotel suite. And, he knew that he and Maize were being watched during breakfast and he was confident it didn't end there. He knew they were here too, but where, and who or whom and why? The center lobby was very crowded with men, women and children, and that made Richard very uneasy. Anyone could hide, and unexpected events could easily spin out of his control. That was not a good feeling.

Maize interrupted Richard's train of thought, pointing to a marquee to their left. "Let's look at that sign and see where the Salem Witchcraft exhibit can be found. Since you are taking me sightseeing there tomorrow Unc, let's go get a preview." Richard really didn't care what they saw, as long as they got out of this crowd.

"Sounds like a plan," he retorted as he walked towards the sign, intentionally dismissing Helena's earlier question. Richard could not see anyone out of the ordinary in the large scattered crowd; he began scouting above as he pretended to review the marquee. He wondered where someone would be able to hide yet watch them at the same time.

"There," Maize pointed. "See? It's just across the room."

Great, right out in the open, Richard lamented to himself. Maize and Helena led the way, zigzagging through the crowd while Richard lagged behind, scouting the crowd and the open area above for anything or anyone unusual.

"Children, this exhibit is about what we are studying in history, The Salem Witch Trials. See, there is a portrayal of Abigail and the other girls in court seeing an apparition accusing people of being a witch." The nun lectured in a sing-song voice, escorting a small group of schoolchildren on a field trip.

One of the young students inquired. "She looks young. How old was she?"

"Why she was not much older than you, around thirteen or fourteen," answered the nun.

As Helena and Maize arrived, they heard the children start

E.K. Prescott, Ph.D

talking all at once.

"Is there an exhibit with Tituba?" "Where are the witches?" "I need to go to the bathroom." "This is boring." "I want to go home." The nun was obviously overwhelmed.

Maize talked just loud enough for the children to hear her. "Did you guys know that Tituba was a slave from Barbados in the Caribbean Islands? She brought her Voodoo practices into Abigail's house, sharing them with her and several other young girls. And ... Abigail had been taken in by her uncle after her parents died. Supposedly she saw Indians bash in their heads as they laid in bed on their pillows one night."

Now she had their attention. One young fellow broke the silence. "Nah, you are pulling our legs."

"No, I'm not. Pay attention to your history lessons and you will find out a lot of interesting bits of information." Maize couldn't help but add, "Did you know it is believed Abigail ran away to Boston before she could be charged for her actions and became a prostitute?"

The nun gasped with horror, putting her hands over the little girl's ears nearest her.

Richard politely interrupted. "Okay little Miss Flapper. I don't think you'll make a good teacher of today's young minds." With that, the nun frowned and protectively herded her young charges to the next exhibit.

"Well, I certainly found that interesting," added Helena. "My childhood tutor covered the Salem Witch Trials briefly when reviewing some American historic events. I was schooled at home; Mum thought it better than a private school. I was raised in a small country town outside of Cambridge. I lived with my mum, dad, and nanny in a quaint Château in the hills. My mum and my nanny mainly raised me. My father was gone a lot ... on business." Helena didn't know why she decided to divulge this information at this time, but she did. She hoped she delivered it in a conversational manner not wanting to answer any questions. Helena watched Richard's reactions. She wondered if he connected to anything she had said.

Helena turned her attention to the exhibit in front of them. The schoolchildren had moved on and the three were momentarily standing alone in front of one of the courtroom scenes. "Look, this plaque states that they could tell if someone was a witch if they had a mole, or tit, as they referred to it, and they floated when dunked in a dunking chair in the lake … is that true?"

"Yep, I believe so," replied Maize. "I remember if you confessed you were a witch you wouldn't be hanged or jailed."

"You are kidding," Helena replied.

Maize continued. "I remember my history teacher mentioned that not only Puritans came across from England but many who wanted to flee the country for various reasons, like those that practiced witchcraft. So there were others besides Puritans living in Salem Town."

"What I do know," added Helena "is that there have been reports of witchcraft in Europe since before the 1500s."

"As far as tidbits of history are concerned, I'm in the dark as much as you Helena," added Richard. He continued. "It states here that over one hundred people were hung or burned as witches, and—"

As a loud crack of gunshot echoed through the room, Richard heard people screaming and the thunderous toppling of the exhibit before them. Mannequins were flying every which way, furniture was landing on the museum floor, some splintering into pieces, and others barely missing people who were meandering in the vicinity. And then suddenly a loud crash was heard as someone bolted from behind the scenery landing almost on top of Richard.

"It's an illusion Lord Wikki," the young man yelled as the next bullet lightly grazed Richard's arm. As he grabbed his left forearm and tried to quickly regain his senses, as well as his balance, the intruder ran off, losing himself in the crowd. As Richard began to follow him, he heard another shot fired. The crowd panicked, screaming and running helter-skelter, trying to escape imminent danger.

Moving in between the obstacles of the out of control crowd, Richard soon reached the body, lying alone on the opaque tile floor where once a large crowd mingled. He found a young man no older than sixteen shot dead on the floor.

As he crouched next to the body, he instinctively looked up to see if the shooter could be located. He could see no one. He then dug quickly through the boys pockets looking for identification; Richard only found a piece of paper neatly folded in his front shirt pocket. Upon hearing police car sirens, he immediately shoved the paper into his own pocket. He decided his best bet was to go back and join Maize and Helena; he did not want to get involved. Soon policemen were entering en-mass, guns raised and yelling commands. Richard was positive the shooter left, hidden within the crowd exiting the museum. He knew they would never find the shooter; it was the job of a pro.

In the shadows HE slowly and methodically removed his gloves one finger at a time. Holding his tan calf-skin leather gloves in his right hand, he rhythmically ran them across the palm of his left hand as he patiently waited for the shooter to find his mark. He strategically placed himself across the room and out of the sight of the shooter and any unwanted company, but close enough to be sure his plan was executed properly. Upon hearing the third shot and the roar of the police sirens HE nonchalantly, but with great haste, moved within the shadows to exit the building, unnoticed by all.

"Are you injured?" Richard heard a museum security guard ask Helena and Maize as he reached them. Maize was leaning on what looked like a fallen judge's table, and Helena was standing next to her;

neither one was talking. Richard thought both looked out of sorts, not understanding what just happened. "May I get either one of you a cup of water?"

Both were parched and replied, "Yes." As the security guard left to fetch their water, Maize asked Richard, "Did you catch him?"

"This is not the place to talk. Let me look around the wreckage a minute and then we will leave," Richard answered. "I think you both should relax and find a quiet spot to sit while you wait for me."

While Maize shot Richard a look of womanly disgust, Helena thanked him and motioned for Maize to follow her. "My legs are still a little wobbly."

The large open museum lobby was dotted with security guards, custodians and managers as well as an array of police officers of different ranks. All customers had been escorted out and designated areas were roped off, allowing no entrance. Richard noticed a stocky, middle-aged policeman barking orders, commanding crime scene protocol. Richard thought he looked like trouble and definitely wanted everyone to know he was in charge. He would avoid him.

Richard cautiously weaved his way through the wreckage, not knowing what he was looking for, but hoping to uncover a clue of some kind. Props of all kinds were scattered sporadically over the area. Broken pieces of furniture cluttered his path and parts of mannequins dotted his view. Richard rested upon a chair that was miraculously untouched, sitting as if it was supposed to be there, perfectly set amongst all the debris. It seemed to him this particular scene was demolished for a reason. But what was it? As Richard sat back in the wooden chair, contemplating possible implications to the trial scene, he watched the principal players investigate the crime scene. To him it was like watching a Charlie Chaplin silent picture movie. What a farce!

Believing this was no coincidence, he began to explore

E.K. Prescott, Ph.D.

possibilities. *The trial scene … what about the trial scene,* he said to himself. *What did the young boy say?* Richard remembered he used his name, thus whatever he said was a message for him. But he couldn't hear what the boy said. He only heard the word "illusion." What does illusion have to do with this trial scene? Richard tried to remember what exhibit they last saw, what was it about? It was about the apparition the girls saw during the trial—an illusion. Richard was sorely perplexed. *Okay, I got the illusion part, but what is the illusion, and why did someone risk his life to tell me this piece of information?*

As Richard sat there, staring into space and trying to make sense of the last twenty-four hours, he questioned how this was all linked. It occurred to him all these things didn't start happening until Maize appeared, or was it when Helena entered his life? These events of late were no coincidence, but how were they connected to the skeleton or the amulet? Richard froze. His body tensed as he reached in his breast pocket to see if the amulet was still there. It was. He sighed with relief.

Before he rose from the chair to leave, he remembered the piece of paper he took off the dead body. He stood to retrieve it from his front pants pocket. As he unraveled the crumpled piece of paper, he couldn't imagine what it might contain; maybe a clue of some sort? As Richard read, he became even more perplexed. "WARN LORD WIKKI! –Angel of the Night."

Chapter 20

How in the world did I end up with two women accompanying me to Salem Town? Richard asked himself as he let out a big sigh. The summer air was warm, but the breeze was refreshing and somewhat hypnotic as he drove north to Danvers, Massachusetts; once known as Salem Town. Helena was sitting in the front seat and Maize in the back, squished in between all of Helena's extra baggage. Both were fast asleep, enjoying the smooth quiet drive.

Somehow Helena had wiggled a ride to Danvers, explaining that she was going there anyway and would enjoy the company. Richard didn't realize when he agreed that she would have so many trunks of clothes; there would hardly be enough room for the three of them. He was glad it was a nice day so he could drive the new 1923 Cadillac Model 61 with the top down. As he glanced over at Helena, soundly sleeping and basking in the warm sun, he was beside himself trying to figure out where he had seen her before. He couldn't shake the feeling she had ulterior motives, and was not quite what she seemed to portray. But he was attracted to her anyway, and that really bothered him.

Next he glanced in the rearview mirror to check on Maize. A

smile came across his face as he remembered her playing "little miss flapper." She was a young woman of the twenties: smart, full of energy, and talented. Her personality was full of life—illuminating everything around her. Her curiosity seemed to drive her actions, laying out her feelings whether good, bad or indifferent for everyone to see. He liked those qualities about her. She reminded him of his daughter.

Richard was glad to have some time to himself with no questions or chattering. Out in the country between Boston and Danvers, there seemed to be very few cars this time of day, an early afternoon on a weekday. Once in a while, he ran across a tractor moving from one part of a farm to the next, slowing down his pace. At thirty miles an hour and halfway to Danvers, it would only take less than an hour to arrive at their destination. They would arrive at the Danvers Congressional Hotel, special courtesy of Rufus and friends, so he explained when Richard asked for a car upon checking-out of the Boston Congressional Hotel.

Weird things kept happening and that made Richard extremely uneasy. How did Rufus know he was going to Danvers and would need a car? It must have been Jonathan, he surmised. Funny, he didn't mention the car last night when he talked to him on the phone. Richard grabbed for his pipe he had laid on the dashboard earlier in the trip and began to gnaw on the end as usual.

Jonathan knew the answer to an important clue, and one extremely timely after the earlier incident at the museum that day. Richard concluded Jonathan didn't care if he was overheard by a nosey telephone operator as he proceeded to tell him the fungus had been identified. It was mainly hemlock. He said they identified the ingredients; poison hemlock and poison parsley as well as traces of beaver poison and something called Musquash Root, with traces of henbane, which causes immediate death. Jonathan explained that he had asked Sam to research hemlock and its use. Outside of the intent to kill someone, Sam discovered it was also used in ritual ceremonies related to witchcraft and other spiritual medium cults. It also supposedly helped induce insight to the astral plane, and rubbed on magical knives to empower the beholder. Jonathan and Richard agreed that someone killed poor young Henry II by the ingestion of a hemlock concoction laced with arsenic, but how, and by whom, and why?

As Richard rehashed the phone conversation in his mind, he recalled Maize's newspaper article stating that during that time, many young men were dabbling in the dark arts. Could there be a link? Young Henry did not seem to be a saint, and would probably gravitate to such mischief. Add the museum catastrophe at the Salem Witchcraft Trials exhibit to the mix; Richard believed the clues were starting to pile up. He remembered the note from the dead body. Someone named Angel of the Night wanted this young man to warn him. Who is this person? How did this person know he needed to be warned? Warned of what? An illusion? Why was this person involved? Why would someone feel he needed to be warned? Why did someone kill the person who was sent to warn him? All these questions had no answers, just more ambiguous clues. Richard realized there were several people involved in this puzzle. He could put them in two very general categories: ones that wanted to help him and ones that wanted to stop him. Both of which had no faces and no names.

So what was the illusion surrounding Henry? He laid the pipe on his lap and instinctively felt for the amulet in his left pocket. Patting it, Richard thought to himself, *No one knows I have it, or do they?*

As he went to reach for his pipe on his lap, he noticed a car in the rearview mirror. Even though it seemed a ways back, he thought it resembled the car that first drove behind them as they left Boston. Richard already knew he was being followed but not why or by whom, so it was not anything new. But he did hope no one would approach him while the ladies were in close range of potential danger—lethal danger—as it suddenly occurred to him. Richard shook his head back and forth, symbolically erasing his thoughts. He told himself it was just another lazy day traveler and quickly dismissed any alternative conclusion.

Richard's mind soon wandered to his visit to the Boston Masonic Lodge yesterday morning. *Was that yesterday?* So much had happened in a short period of time, Richard wondered if he had been followed and if anyone questioned the staff as to why he was there. The historian had been helpful to a point. He had verified the Phillips lineage membership which included young Henry's father, but not Henry. And, that many ancestors before and including Henry I held very prestigious positions in the higher workings of the Masonic Lodges here in the United States and internationally. Richard wasn't sure where this piece of information fit, but he was sure it would be important in the future.

Considering the Phillips' past, Richard felt he needed to create a profile of young Henry to aid in his investigation in Salem Town. It was obvious he was a troubled child, having been asked to leave one school after another. It appeared his parents didn't know what to do with him, so they sent him to work at Boston Congressional Hotel; not too far away from home but far enough to avoid unwanted attention in the elite social circles of New Haven. Then, apparently, during Jonathan's investigation, he discovered Henry didn't last long there and was sent to Danvers Congressional Hotel—owned by the same person—and seemingly a friend of the Phillips family.

He believed young Henry more than likely did not have a good relationship with his father. Richard tried to think of possibilities such as if young Henry was one of the radical bad boys of New Haven's youth dabbling in the dark arts, maybe he continued his interests while in Salem? The embarrassment to an elitist family alone would be cause to

E.K. Prescott, Ph.D

send him away. *But,* he questioned, *if all of this is an illusion, why does it all seem to fit?* What he did know was this good-looking bad boy was bound to leave his mark in Salem like he did everywhere else. He just needed to find it. As Richard once again thought of the amulet and what it represented, he couldn't for the life of him figure out how Chaos Magick and the amulet itself fit in the picture.

The honk of a car horn jolted Richard out of his thoughts. He hadn't realized they had reached the outskirts of town and traffic had picked up.

"What … uh … what?" Both women awoke, trying to decipher the noise which disturbed their tranquil slumber.

"Well that didn't take long," Helena commented as she read the "Welcome to Danvers" sign.

"Of course not," Richard replied. "You slept like a log the whole way."

"Better sleeping than having a backseat driver," Maize chuckled.

Richard pulled up to the curb in front of the hotel where a bellhop had obviously been waiting for their arrival. Nodding to acknowledge the ladies, the bellhop greeted his new guests. "Hello Lord Wikki. Welcome to the Danvers Congressional Hotel, formerly the remodeled historical Salem Town Inn. My name is William. May I take your bags?" The bellhop began to walk around the car to open Richard's door.

"Thanks William, I can open the car door myself, but you can fetch our bags." For that, Richard was thankful; Helena's trunks were very heavy, having been packed for a long vacation in America. He motioned for Maize and Helena to stay with the car until he verified their reservations. With that he walked into the hotel alone.

"EXTRA! EXTRA! Man shot in Boston Museum identified as John Doe! EXTRA! EXTRA," yelled the young paper boy as he walked past

Maize and Helena standing beside their car in front of the hotel.

"Whoa," gasped Maize as she and Helena stared at each other, fixated in thought.

Helena reached for her purse and pulled out a fifty cent piece; money wasn't a problem. "See here, young man," Helena called out, dangling the coin to entice the newspaper boy to double back pronto. This would provide him with a hefty tip since the paper only cost a nickel.

"Wow, thanks ma'am," the young lad said as he bit the fifty cent piece, checking for its authenticity. Deciding it was, he tipped his cap. "Have a nice day."

Helena read the front page. Yesterday's incident had made the headlines.

Maize leaned over, trying to read silently as Helena began to read aloud. "Yesterday at the Boston Museum of History, there was a shooting among a record-breaking crowd. One was shot dead as others incurred minor injuries while escaping certain danger." Helena silently read through the rest of the article until she came near the end. "The young man was around sixteen years of age. There was no identification found on his body. There were no results in attempts by the Boston Police Department to identify the body. They named him John Doe."

"That's odd," Maize proclaimed. "Look at that picture." She pointed at the picture at the bottom left of the front page. Maize was dumbstruck. "I recognize him. Why, he's … he's…." Maize quickly realized it was probably best not to inform Helena that she and Professor Wikki were being followed. Trying to cover up her outburst, she continued. "Oh, I guess I'm mistaken."

As Helena continued reading the paper, Maize decided to inform the professor about the picture, mumbling an excuse to enter the hotel. To Maize's relief Helena politely suggested she would stay to guard the open car.

E.K. Prescott, Ph.D

Chapter 21

The morning showed promise as a slight breeze flowed through Danvers, formerly known as Salem Town. Richard could feel it in his bones that answers were here, hiding and waiting to be uncovered. It was a familiar and welcome feeling when his gut signaled an investigation was about to turn in his favor. Normally a hint of danger wouldn't cross his mind, but now Maize was accompanying him and he felt responsible for her safety. He had to admit, Maize could prove useful as the investigation progressed. He chuckled as he realized that she kinda grew on him; of course he would never fess up to that fact. Richard had observed for some time that she possessed a natural instinct for investigating. He concluded she could be helpful, acting as his eyes and ears when he couldn't be in two places at once. Richard had less than two days in Salem to uncover any clues; every moment was precious. *This might work*, he thought to himself.

And then there was Helena. She was a puzzle to Richard. He couldn't pinpoint it, but he was sure he had met her before. After they had arrived at the hotel, Helena expressed her desire to meet him and Maize for an early dinner then go her own way. That seemed a little weird to Richard, but he had no reason to be offended. She was just an acquaintance, having met her just two days earlier. Was it an accidental meeting? He couldn't help thinking that all of the events the past two days seemed to coincide with her arrival into his life: that seemed too coincidental for Richard. Unfortunately, at this point the only thing Richard was sure of was Maize, and that in itself was an unusual placement of his trust, especially when he liked to work alone. Too many of his comrades at Scotland Yard were out to make a name for themselves and he was afraid he would get killed in the crossfire. New Haven was not Scotland Yard, but there seemed to be an element of danger and he knew from past experience working alone kept him alive.

"Good morning, Uncle." Maize greeted Richard, who was deep in thought while enjoying the cool morning breeze, bringing wanted relief from the heat of the past few days.

Maize was full of anticipation and ready to be a part of Lord Wikki's holiday. She knew it didn't take a rocket scientist to figure out this was more than a vacation, especially since she saw a picture of the man who was following them in yesterday's Danvers Times. Professor Wikki didn't seem impressed when she told him about the picture, but she knew better. In addition, it was totally unbelievable that her overprotective father gave his blessing for her to stay and travel with Professor Wikki. In Maize's mind, things could not have worked out better. On a lark, she had come to Boston purposely to deliver important information she had uncovered, and since then, her life had become a roller coaster. Maize was determined to prove herself a competent partner, posing as Lord Wikki's niece.

Since it was such a beautiful morning, Richard had chosen a table outside of the restaurant. He looked up as Maize continued. "I see you are looking for places to visit today." Maize pointed to the Salem Village brochure lying on the table next to his finished breakfast plate.

Richard had made arrangements before retiring last evening to meet Maize around nine o'clock at the quaint mom and pop restaurant around the corner from their hotel. As she pulled out a chair next to him, she noticed he had intentionally selected the same type of spot as usual, a table next to a back wall, or window in this case, offering him a panoramic view. *How odd*, she thought to herself. She made a mental note to ask him why at another time.

Maize leaned over whispering to Richard that they never really discussed the man in the newspaper. "You know the man that followed us to the museum … what is going on? Does this have anything to do with the information I brought about young Henry? This all seems to be too weird if you ask me!"

Richard knew this time would come sooner or later and had rehearsed what he wanted to say. But everything flew out the window as she pinpointed certain events. He could not ignore her any longer. Richard looked straight at Maize, keeping his voice low while intentionally relaxing his body. Body language was extremely important for anyone possibly watching them which at this point, was more likely than not. "Maize I'm going to trust you just as I did when you first visited my office. You must discuss this with no one except me."

Maize was not about to lose Professor Wikki's trust. She felt privileged to be involved with his work at her young age. To her, this was not only a chance of a lifetime, but exciting as well. Thus Maize decided her best action was to just nod her head in compliance and not say a word.

"I don't want to insult your intelligence and tell you that there is not a connection between the man you saw at breakfast and the young man killed at the museum. Obviously we were being followed for some reason, and someone wanted that young man killed. I'm not going to sit here and try to convince you not to worry. We are being followed. I believe it has to do with the skeleton."

Maize started to interject but Richard raised his hand to silence her. "Please let me finish. I think you were followed from New Haven to Boston. That is why your father and I thought it wasn't safe for you to travel home alone. Continuing with me on my holiday seemed the safest decision." Richard was walking a fine line, the less she knew, the better, for her own good. He didn't think it was prudent for her to know about her father's involvement, so he decided to keep the story focused on him. "This is a business trip for me, not just a vacation. I was interested in learning more about the skeleton … ya' know, getting back in the saddle so to speak."

Again Maize decided to just nod, knowing he wasn't finished.

"I had a few leads and thought it would be fun to resurrect some of my old investigative skills. It is obvious to some people you have uncovered something very important. But the problem is, we don't know what that is. And I'm not sure if these people are trying to keep us from discovering this information or trying to kill us before we do."

Maize sat uncharacteristically speechless. Richard had taken a gamble to include her in his journey. He sat waiting for her reaction. As he watched her internalize all this information with her blue eyes wide open and mouth closed tightly, he gave her time to digest what he had just said.

While sitting in silence, Maize's mind raced. Rationally she knew this all seemed to be true, but emotionally it never seemed real … just a dramatic game like she and Leslie used to play. As she watched Professor Wikki's face, she realized he was serious; this was real. Maize had a million questions, but she knew answers would not be forthcoming. She also knew he was waiting for a response. It was obvious to her how she reacted would determine how Richard included her from here on out.

E.K. Prescott, Ph.D

"Sounds like you are the big cheese who will keep me from getting zotzed," she replied with a mischievous smile across her face. "So when do we start Unc?"

Richard, not really sure how she would react, let out a sigh of relief. She was smarter than he gave her credit. She obviously knew when to hold 'em and when to fold 'em. "Follow me."

Richard left money on the table and motioned to Maize for her to follow him as he started walking north towards downtown Salem. They did not speak until they were within shouting distance of the restaurant. Richard broke the silence. "We are going to walk a few blocks until we reach 310 ½ Essex St. It's Judge Jonathan Corwin's original home; it's now a museum. He was one of the influential judges during the witch trials. It said in the brochure that he purchased it when he was twenty-four, and that he is buried in Broad Street Cemetery located somewhere around here. I recall from your little outburst with those middle school students, you know quite a bit about Salem's history."

As they continued to walk towards their destination, Richard reviewed the story of witchcraft and Salem Town. "I think it's good to keep this part of history fresh in our minds. The information may prove handy … you never know. I didn't realize until Helena mentioned it that there has been witchcraft since before the 1500s in Europe."

Maize didn't want to seem condescending, but believed she knew a lot more than Professor Wikki about the history of Salem. "That was new to me as well. Did you know witches organize themselves in covens? Covens usually consist of twelve individuals and when more members are added, they create a new coven. Several covens make up a district ruled by a Grand Master. The chief work of the covens was the performance of magical rites, either public or at a witch's house."

"You do seem to know a lot of background. Good. It may come in handy." The walk seemed to be a little longer than Richard originally thought, but it was a beautiful day and both seemed consumed with their investigation.

Maize thought he appreciated the information and wouldn't take offense to her adding more. "Did you know the Devil was the instructor of the witches?"

Richard's eyebrows rose.

"The witches wrote their rituals and meeting notes in a journal called the Devil's Book."

As they walked, discussing the history of witchcraft and Salem Town, Richard kept an eye on every passerby and then some. Everyone they passed seemed to be happily enjoying the break in the hot weather. He also noticed Maize seemed quite engaged in their adventure, especially being able to add to their conversation. She was becoming invested, and to him, that was a good thing for a partner. Well at least a potential partner which was a temporary situation … a necessity of the moment, he thought to himself. But his main concern was their safety as he kept an eye out for anyone following them.

Maize continued. "Did you know the word coven comes from the word convene? Witches had to convene at Esbats and Sabbaths. The Devils, the head of the covens, were the officials, and witches kept the reports of every meeting in the Devil's Book."

Richard slowed down his pace and stared at Maize. He realized there's more to this girl than meets the eye. He was intrigued.

"What?" Maize questioned his gaze. "Scouring stacks of potential information as a reporter leads one to a lot of information. Information you don't think you will ever use … but see here." Maize seized the moment, adding as Richard picked up his pace, eyeing the museum just ahead. "Witches were also required to conduct several rituals a year as well as attend district and yearly rituals."

"Here we are!"

E.K. Prescott, Ph.D.

Maize stopped and looked up. "How interesting, the Judge's home is now a museum named The Witch House."

The main room by current standards was quite small, with the original fireplace as the main focal point of the room as in the past. Simplistically designed furniture sparsely filled each room with very few decorations. Puritans kept possessions at a minimum as well as their dress, usually plain gray or black with no additions of any kind. Nothing in their lives was to bring attention to oneself, otherwise it would be the work of the Devil.

Judge Corwin was quite wealthy and although he kept simple accommodations not to draw too much attention to himself, he owned the largest home in Salem Town. Other rooms were basically adorned the same, but with added sale items, such as sight-seeing pamphlets, books, original artifacts, trinkets, and costumes, almost any souvenir a tourist could possibly desire. Clerks of all ages were dressed in Puritan clothes of the time period, prepared to welcome and help any customer.

Recognizing her friendly welcome, Richard nodded at the stout gray-haired elderly woman dressed in a long black full dress with a high collar, long sleeves, and a white apron. He noticed her friendly smile and brilliant blue eyes; she gave the house a sense of authenticity.

Maize signaled that she wanted to look at the book presentation across the room. A large sign advertising a new book about witchcraft in Europe caught her eye. Richard nodded and decided to go into the next room to wade through souvenirs and artifacts. As he entered the small room, he noticed a display of authentic witchcraft artifacts from 1836, among which was a variety of amulets of all sizes and shapes. The descriptions tied to many of the amulets suggested their use and meaning. Most denoted a certain belief or status. He searched for one that resembled the Chaos Magick amulet he had in his pocket. The only ones that were similar were ones etched with east-west-north-south designs. He did not think it prudent to take the amulet out of his pocket, but he recalled there were four distinct elongated arrows at the east-west-north-south sides of the circle. Richard had no idea what this similarity might mean, but he would store this information for future use.

As Richard walked into the main room, he saw Maize ecstatically waving at him to join her. The book she was holding contained a clue; well at least she thought it did. When he reached her, Maize showed him the cover of the book. "Look!" She pointed to the cover. Maize tried to contain her excitement in order to circumvent unwanted attention from the customers now filling the tiny museum. She whispered. "*The Witch Cult in Western Europe: A Study of Anthropology,* published in 1921."

Richard gave her a puzzled look, not knowing what she was trying to tell him.

Maize turned to the table of contents pointing to the Appendix 111 A: Covens, and Names of Members. Richard still did not see the connection.

Maize turned to the back of the book to page 253. She pointed to the third section. "Look! All the covens mentioned here are in Europe except this one … look!"

Richard read silently.

Hartford, Conn.
(Though the published records are incomplete, the number of names surviving suggests that a Coven existed here.)

1. Andrew Sanford	5. Mary Sanford	9. Goodwife Ayers
2. Elizabeth Seager	6. Nathaniel Greensmith	10. Goodwife Grant
3. James Walkley	7. Rebecca Greensmith	11. Goodwife Palmer
4. Judith Varlet	8. William Ayers	12. Goodwife Sanford

Richard could not believe what he was reading. He gently took the book into his own hands to review it further. There, in the middle of naming numerous covens in Europe, lay the only one in the United States, and it happened to be only a hundred miles to their west, just north of New Haven. Richard quickly concluded that witchcraft or some form of it was evident in other areas of the eastern United States besides Salem. If witchcraft was, and probably still is, in Hartford, it would seem logical it would be in New Haven as well. Thus the newspaper story Maize showed him had more to say than was reported.

"I'm going to purchase this book," exclaimed Richard. "I need to review more of its contents." He moved to the back of the room to the only register he could see in use. Many tourists had filled the museum while he and Maize had been there, and now all seemed to be standing in line to purchase something. He decided to just step back to the far wall, pretending to browse around. Out of curiosity, he opened the door on the back wall. The opening to wherever it led was bricked over. As he ran his hands over the bricks, he noticed how aged and gritty they were. As he viewed the entire brick wall, he noticed a hole near the bottom left where several bricks were missing; it seemed like they had been kicked in. *If only I could get through to see what was behind those bricks.*

"Can I help you?" asked the clerk as she peered over the checkout counter.

Startled, Richard closed the door to the basement and answered the clerk as he walked toward the counter. "Why yes, I would like to buy this book."

Maize wondered what Professor Wikki was up to. He gave her a puzzled look. She knew that look. The look that said "don't ask, but I'm onto something." Maize joined him as Richard checked out.

"Miss, do you know why the door is bricked over?" Richard asked matter-of-factly.

In a nonchalant manner, the clerk stated. "Ya' know, I really have no idea. I've been told it's been that way since before the owners bought the house many years ago." She leaned closer to Richard across the counter and whispered. "To tell you the truth—" She paused to check if anyone was listening or watching. "Sometimes late at night when I clean the house … I do that for extra money … I hear strange noises coming from down there." She pointed to the door.

Richard tried to act like a curious tourist instead of an intent investigator. "Really! What kind?"

"Well ya' know the house has a history and that history is … shall we say … shady, to say the least. And let me tell you, those noises are eerie. I hear voices from a whisper to a chant."

"What kind of chanting?" Maize asked.

Richard noticed the clerk draw back. "It's ok. She's with me."

"I couldn't hear the words but it had a slow eerie rhythm to it … almost seductive like."

A customer shouted across the room for the clerk's attention, breaking her concentration. "Yes ma'am, I'll be right with you."

As she finished the transaction, Richard nodded to Maize, noting it was time to leave. Their work was finished and yet, just beginning.

As they walked towards the entrance, the same pleasant woman greeted Richard again. "Thank you for coming."

As Richard turned to look at her, their eyes locked.

A strained, concerned look came over her face an in a hushed voice, she continued. "You are swimming in a sea of illusions. Be careful … you are getting caught in the undertow."

To Richard, it seemed to be an eternity before their eyes broke contact. But in fact, it all happened in a blink of an eye. He paused on the sidewalk as he and Maize exited The Witch House. Wanting affirmation of what he just saw and heard, Richard immediately stepped back through the entrance, but no one was there. He looked in each room, but she was not there. He inquired about her and no one knew of an employee who greeted customers. No one saw or heard her but Richard.

Maize was patiently waiting outside on the sidewalk when Richard returned, looking perplexed. He made an immediate left and briskly walked silently back to their hotel. Maize found herself trying to constantly stay in step as she tried to accompany him. It bothered her that he did not want to talk, but she just remained silent. Richard did not acknowledge the hotel staff as they greeted Lord Wikki upon his return. Maize found herself following him to the elevator and to her room. As she unlocked her door Richard warned with a tone of worry.

"Maize, be sure to securely lock all your doors, and do not open your door for anyone except me. We are going to get an early start in the morning. I'll ring you about 7 a.m."

As Richard turned to leave he explained. "We are going to Hartford … without Helena." He then said good night and returned to his room to think. As Richard entered the elevator, Maize, quite bewildered, closed her door and locked every lock possible.

Chapter 22

"Maize, are you awake? It's Professor Wikki." Richard whispered as loud as he could without being heard as he tapped lightly on Maize's hotel door. He looked around to see if he had disturbed anyone as he continued to tap on Maize's door, calling her name.

Maize had fallen asleep on the couch earlier that evening reading a book which was now lying open across her stomach. She awoke slowly upon hearing her name. As her mind cleared, she recognized the professor's voice. She rose slowly trying to shake the sleep from her eyes. *What time is it*, she wondered. Maize looked at the clock on the fireplace mantel; it was midnight. As she unlocked every lock she had locked several hours earlier, Maize wondered what in the world the professor wanted at this time of night. Upon opening the door, Richard put his fingers to his mouth signaling to be quiet. He cautiously entered her room, shutting the door quietly behind him. Maize stood silent, wondering what was so urgent.

Richard realized he probably looked a little strange dressed all in black this time of night as he explained. "We are going back to The Witch House." As Richard put down the satchel he had been carrying, he continued. "I will answer your questions later. I need you to change into something all black as quickly as possible. We need to leave now."

Everything was moving so fast; Maize didn't have time to think. In retrospect, she knew she would have panicked if given the time to realize what was about to happen.

She dressed in silence.

***

Detective Wikki moved in, out, and around with expert precision. *Old dogs never lose their tricks*, he thought. He could feel the familiar rush that always overtook him when he was about to jump into action. Locating a jarred window behind The Witch House was almost too easy. If he didn't realize the house most certainly had settled during the years, leaving windows unbalanced for easy entry, he would have thought due to recent events, someone was aiding his investigation.

The elongated window was not far from the ground, which made entering simple. Richard threw his satchel in first and then worked his way through the window. Retrieving his flashlight from his stash, he immediately began to search the inside, lighting areas throughout the room. Once he knew it was safe, Richard opened the door to the backyard and motioned for Maize to enter. Richard checked her hands, making sure Maize had put on the extra pair of cotton gloves he gave her before he climbed through the window moments earlier. He made sure both he and Maize were wearing gloves so no fingerprints could be detected. Although fingerprinting was a new technology with lots of flaws, it still was a popular technique to identify criminals.

It was pitch dark, but there was a full moon shining high above, which lit their way from the hotel to the museum, but once inside, they would need flashlights. As Maize entered, Richard pulled from his satchel another flashlight for her use.

Reaching for it, Maize began to babble. "Geez, I can't believe I'm doing this. This is unbelievably spooky. You told me you would answer my questions later; what's going on? I know you can tell me something. I'm not going any further until you talk to me." Maize couldn't quit chattering, her nervousness showing. As she stopped to take a deep breath, Richard interrupted her soliloquy. But before he could begin, a thunderous noise jolted them both. It seemed to come from downstairs as both turned quickly towards the sound. Professor Wikki was the first to speak as he shone his light through the open crack at the bottom of the brick wall that had been erected to close off the basement.

Carefully and quietly, he began to unravel the brick wall. Whispering to Maize while working, Richard explained. "That was a very solid slam like maybe something closing hard." He could see the question on Maize's face. "I wouldn't be dismantling this wall if I thought someone was down there." The loud noise had moved their attention to the basement, thus Maize never heard the answers to her questions. Soon there was a large hole, big enough for Richard and Maize to safely step through. Richard rose and motioned for Maize to join him, whispering for her to stay close behind him. They were going down to the basement. Maize quickly surmised she was in a no-win situation, as she didn't want to be left up there alone and she didn't want to go down there. But down there was where Professor Wikki was going, and where he was, she knew would be the safest choice; he would protect her … she hoped.

Richard held his flashlight so it shone into the dark abyss. He could see only as far as a few rotten and splintered wooden steps, which seemed to continue descending into nothingness. Common sense told him this was a normal full set of stairs descending into a basement, but what was waiting for them at the bottom was obscured by the dense darkness of the cellar. He then turned his attention back to viewing one step at a time. As he began to take his first step, Richard noticed there were gaps in each step, making descending safely a little tricky. It was no big deal to him, but Maize was another story. He turned once more signaling her not to speak. Whispering, Richard cautioned her to stay directly behind him, step only where he stepped, and to hold on to the rail to their left. At a snail's pace he led the way, cautiously testing each step before he put his full weight upon it. Maize did the same. The first step was safe. She grabbed the rail to her left as Professor Wikki had instructed. The weathered, rickety, wood railing shook in her hand, causing Maize to struggle with her balance. She gave out a squeal. It was obvious if she added any more pressure she and the railing would tumble to the basement floor. Richard paused to check if her squeal was serious or just her; a little of both he thought, and then continued. They walked in tandem, slowly testing each step. Richard paused what seemed to be halfway down the staircase, annoyed that Maize was following him so closely. He could feel her fast paced nervous breathing on the back of his neck. He turned slightly, giving her a reassuring look to ease up. Richard couldn't tell if she was scared to death or utterly enthralled. As he turned around to take the next step his right foot rolled over an out of place rock, causing him to tumble down the rest of the staircase. Maize froze. She was in complete darkness except for the beams of light shooting helter skelter all over the room. All she could hear was Richard cursing, then a thud, and then complete silence. Maize fumbled with her flashlight trying to feel how to switch it on.

"Ok, you can turn yours on any time now," Richard yelled as he sat upright banging his flashlight to resume its illumination.

"Well you certainly are fine," Maize replied blinding Richard as she shined her light in his eyes. Richard had fallen the last four steps to the basement floor.

"You really didn't have far to fall for all the commotion you made." As Maize cautiously descended the few remaining stairs Richard stood as he regained light.

Maize was surprised at the huge sigh of relief she felt when first stepping on solid ground. As she used her light to look deep into the cellar, she began to feel the cold and dampness of the basement. "Anyone throughout the whole house could have heard you. If we don't get killed by someone, we will by the stench of the mildew down here." She moved her light across the top of the cement shelf that separated the basement from the wood floor upstairs. As Maize followed its outline which seemed in sync with the path of the floor immediately above them, she noticed the beady eyes of numerous whining scattering mice. She shivered. Nothing about this idea appealed to her.

As Richard's and Maize's eyes were adjusting to the dim light of their collective flashlights, Richard took the lead, moving further into the room. "If someone was here, they certainly would have made their presence known by now," Richard remarked.

They found themselves alone in the middle of a cold, dark, damp cellar, slowly illuminating all parts of the room. Corroded candelabras of all sizes and shapes filled the room. Some, still standing, held their original burned candles, while others were collapsed and sprawled about. There were a few old wooden chairs towards the right corner providing a home to the largest cobwebs Maize had ever seen. Just ahead of them stood a long wooden table with at least an inch thick layer of dust concealing what seemed like old books, papers, and other junk. To their left were remnants of what seemed to be a circle of chairs at one time. Underneath their feet was a tattered, mildewed, oval rug with several rat bitten holes obstructing the view of a faded ornate design of some kind. As they continued to their left, lighting the cement wall which led to behind the staircase, they discovered a huge solid wooden door. It was rounded at the top with its right side connected to the cement by oversized black metal plates and screws.

"I bet that door closed, causing the loud noise we heard earlier."

"Why would it close? Nothing is down here!" retorted Maize.

"I guess we'll find out when we open it."

Maize gave him a look. "You mean when YOU open it!"

Richard decided to discover what was behind the door after they had a look around. Seeming not to be in any immediate danger, Richard was curious as to what was on the table. "Well since no one is here, let's look around first."

Relieved, Maize eagerly agreed. "I will look over here. There's a small table toppled near the door."

Richard fumbled through the few sheets of fragile papers; he had no clue as to what he was reading. To him it was full of unending lists, some kind of recipes, and numerous odd illustrations. His eye, not catching anything of importance, moved on to some of the artifacts sitting nearby on the table. They were grimy and full of dust and critters. He picked up a tarnished pewter cup of some kind with etched insignias on all sides. Not impressed, he moved on and noticed other items resembling rusted cooking utensils; some were engraved with similar etchings. The oversized ledger opened in front of him was full of the same grimy dust. As he brushed the dust and grime off the opened pages, he noticed its contents seemed to be handwritten notes describing meetings.

"Maize, I think I've found something." She quickly joined him.

"This seems like some kind of ledger. Look at the handwritten notes." Maize reached to turn the book over.

"Careful, it's fragile," Richard cautioned.

As Maize rubbed the dirt from the cover, both stared at the title of the book: The Devil's Book.

Richard spoke first. "Well, that explains why all this junk is lying around. It's what you were talking about earlier today—witch notes and stuff."

"It's more than that. It's an accounting of the witch covens, members, ceremonies, spells, and meeting notes." Maize was excited; to her, this was a goldmine taking her back to Salem's diabolical past. She quickly turned back to where the book was originally opened. Turning the pages with much care, she began to read. "Look! Here are the member's names of one of the witch covens with the date of their meetings and special ceremonies."

Richard did not understand why his gut told him he would find clues down here. This didn't make sense. He continued to investigate the artifacts and papers before him, looking for clues of any kind to move the investigation forward.

As Maize continued turning pages, she noticed a familiar name. She froze. "What is it?" Richard asked. He drew his flashlight closer.

Maize didn't speak. She just ran her finger under the handwritten notes …

Our youngest and newest member, Henry Phillips, will be leaving us tomorrow to join our sister coven in Hartford. We will celebrate his journey with the sacred service of.…

In their silence, Maize jumped, startled. "Shhh … did you hear that?"

"No," Richard commented as he continued reading. He could not believe what he was reading; this seemed too easy.

"Shhh … there it is again! It sounds eerie, like that chant stuff the clerk talked about earlier today."

Richard stood very still trying to locate the sound. "I think it is coming from behind that door."

He shined his light at the door, lighting his path as he walked towards it. He listened. "Yep, it's coming from behind this door."

"You are not seriously going to open that door?" Maize exclaimed as she followed him.

"Of course I am." And with that Richard gave the door handle a big tug.

Both Richard and Maize struggled to keep their balance as a fierce wind blew in like a monsoon. Upon regaining their composure after the wind died down, Maize and Richard stood in awe of what they saw in front of them. There were three large well-lit tunnels. One went straight ahead, one went to their right, and the other to the left, all intersecting in front of them. The passages all ran beneath the street just above. All seemed well-maintained with brick floors and smooth interiors, illuminated with large sconces holding lit flambeaus. Richard and Maize turned off their flashlights, but kept them just in case.

"This is an underground passageway. It would be my guess with its superb condition that it is an important crossroads," Richard surmised.

"Wow, an underground city."

"I wouldn't go that far."

"I wonder where they lead."

"We'll follow the music which is coming from that direction." Richard pointed straight in front of them.

Maize choked. "What do you mean WE?"

Richard ignored her and took her by the arm as he started walking towards the chanting. "I am not leaving you here alone."

Resigned to her fate, Maize walked along cautiously, noting all the etchings along the way. Both sides displayed life-sized images of mythic gods and goddesses. She recognized Isis, Thoth, Aphrodite, and Hercules. As they neared the large wooden door similar to the one in the basement, Richard slowed his pace. He noticed the door was ajar;

someone had not closed it properly when they entered or exited. Maize and Richard could hear the hypnotic rhythm of the chanting quite clearly now.

As Richard peeked into the room through the slight opening, it seemed to him to be a cloak room of some kind with capes and clothing hanging on large hooks. He whispered to Maize. "It's an empty dressing room."

"You're sure it's empty?" she whispered in return.

Richard opened the door cautiously as he checked for any unwanted persons. He waved for Maize to follow him. "I think this is the basement of the house across the street from the museum," surmised Richard.

Looking around the room, Maize remarked. "Well the interior of this basement is certainly the polar opposite of its neighbor's." It was well lit with electric lamps, and sufficiently filled with tables of all sizes, cushioned couches and lounging chairs. "Seems like someone spared no expense."

Richard moved quietly, continuing to walk toward the music. It was coming from the next room, behind another door, which was made of the same materials of the exterior door, but of lighter weight. The interior door was covered with unusual ancient carvings and hosted a small squared window near the top.

Richard and Maize couldn't decipher what the carvings signified, but they were positive these carvings held a special meaning, a clue to who these people were. Richard ever so slowly turned the door handle to get a view of the events. Maize slightly nudged him in his back, giving Richard an uneasy look alerting to the possibility they might be discovered. As Richard squatted low to the ground, Maize raised herself a little above him so she could observe as well.

There, in front of them were twelve witches—both men and

The Ivy League Chronicles: 9 Squares

women—sitting in a circle in the center of the room. All dressed in long black gowns tied at the waist with gold ropes adorned with large tassels hanging from both ends. The dim mystic hue that permeated the room was attributed to a myriad of shiny, golden-lit candelabras of all sizes and shapes. An oversized mahogany table standing to the left of the room was filled with ritual artifacts with a large ledger lying directly in the middle. It all seemed to be a replica of the grungy artifacts just across the street behind them; a mirror image. To the left of the room were floor to ceiling gold, black, and red velvet curtains. Large scarves hung from the dark iron curtain rods, draped decoratively over the velvet curtains; designs within the texture of the scarves were the same as the etchings on the door Maize and Richard were hiding behind.

All of a sudden, the witches stopped singing and bowed their heads. After a noticeable pause, someone appeared from behind one of the drapes dressed in a red, velvet, floor-length cape and hood accessorized with a black and gold oversized sash. He too, had his head bowed and hands clasped directly in front of him as he walked towards the circle. As the guest moved closer to the circle, a member of the group stood on cue and left his chair as the guest moved to stand in front of it. If Richard hadn't known better, he would have thought this special person resembled a Catholic Cardinal.

Maize whispered. "That is the Devil. This must be a special meeting of some kind." As the Devil mumbled, the others raised their heads answering in unison.

It was time to leave. Richard had seen enough. After quietly closing the door, walking cautiously across the dressing room and then through the back door to the underground street, he commented. "Well it looks like witchcraft is alive and well in Salem Town."

Maize, uncharacteristically silenced by what she had witnessed, just nodded in agreement. As they entered the basement of the museum, Richard approached the table to his left before ascending the basement stairs.

"What are you doing?" Maize asked.

Without answering, Richard quickly ripped several pages where the ledger was opened and ascended the stairs with Maize directly behind him.

As Richard shut the door to the basement of the museum and locked it so no one would notice the dismantled bricks, he alerted Maize.

"We need to get some sleep. We have only a couple of hours until sunrise, and we need to leave for Hartford immediately. With that, both left through the back door. Richard checked to see if the back door was locked and the window in which he entered was closed before they both walked silently back to their hotel.

Chapter 23

Upon their arrival at the Hartford Congressional Hotel, Maize demanded time to sleep, complaining she hardly slept the precious few hours before the ungodly time that Richard wanted to depart from Danvers. She said she needed rest and not to be alarmed if she slept most of the day. She told Richard she would be in touch and asked that she not be disturbed.

Richard jokingly agreed, "Aye, Aye, Captain," and safely tucked Maize into her room. He would check on her later in the day. He found himself alone in yet another sterile hotel room, just a different city, pacing absentmindedly like a Cheshire cat waiting to pounce. But pounce on what? Since he had ripped out the few yellowed pages from The Devil's Book, he hadn't time to totally review their contents.

Even though Maize apologized profusely for needing rest, Richard was relieved to have some time alone to relax and think. He wanted to unravel what they had seen the night before. He took a few minutes to set up the suite's sitting area in order to easily access the massive investigative information he had acquired. He moved a couple tables and chairs here and there near the couch, establishing a work area. Richard then pulled out the information Maize had brought from home, his many papers of notes, the book he purchased from The Witch Museum, and the delicate papers he had torn from the BOOK, spreading them over his makeshift working area for easy access. He then reached for his signature pipe he had left in the bottom pocket of his jacket lying over the chair next to the couch. He was ready to start his review. As he gazed quickly over all the investigative materials while gnawing on the tip of his pipe, he pondered where to begin.

As he made a third pass over his layout, something caught his eye; a drawing. A drawing that resembled the diagram he saw etched on the rug in the basement across the street from The Witch House during what Maize seemed to think was a special witch meeting. It was a circle with north-south-east-west markings.

Instinctively, he reached for the amulet tucked in his left pants pocket. He gently placed it on top of the larger drawing from the papers he had taken from The Devil's Book. It seemed like almost an identical miniature. *Think, think*, he told himself. He began pacing around the furniture, not taking his eyes off the amulet. *If the amulet is a key, a key for what had not been established, and it is connected to a witch ceremonial ritual, it must relate to some organization that uses the same circle configuration for a ritual of some kind.* With that being quite plausible, now there were a lot more questions than answers. He sat in the empty chair near the couch where his jacket laid, stretching out his legs in front of him. *Relax*, he told himself.

Richard reached for the amulet, absolutely sure this was the key to unlocking the truth. But what truth, and how was it connected to Henry II? Or did its importance have nothing to do with young Henry? He couldn't understand why people were following him and willing to kill for what he knew? What was ironic to Richard at this point, was that he wasn't sure of what he supposedly knew. One thing he was sure of was that no one knew he had the amulet … well … he was almost sure of that. He couldn't see how anyone would know. He continued to sift out key points. *If this was pulled off of someone and the skeleton … Sarah! That's it*, he thought. In the notes from his meeting with Sarah in the library, she talked about that east west stuff. He gathered his personal notes and began to rifle through them until he came to their meeting. So much had happened since their meeting he had almost forgotten. He skimmed his notes until he saw…

Chaos Magic with a "k" … a movement that believes anyone can move energy to change both your subjective and objective reality.

As he continued to read, it all came back. Richard concluded, *This amulet is used somehow as a key to manipulate energy to attain an objective.* He recalled Sarah talked about Quantum Theory and The Second Theory of Thermodynamics and how they fit with Chaos Magick and something being studied called the Butterfly Effect, but that was all out of his league.

What he did understand, whether he believed it or not, was that this use of energy kept the true goal from being seen by the masses because everything was in a chaotic state, and that the main goal was obtained under the disguise of chaos. He sat back, mouthing his pipe with his notes lying on his lap. Now how does witchcraft fit into this? Why is he following Henry's path, which identifies him as a witch and part of a coven; moving from one coven to another. And, most likely since he died in New Haven, he was a member of a coven there. Then there is the fungus that was diagnosed as hemlock laced with arsenic, which was associated with witchcraft … so he was poisoned on the beach, maybe by another witch … and Henry pulled off this amulet from his killer's neck … and it had a special purpose. So this killer knew about witch's brews and was connected with an organization that uses energy mixed with chaos for its own purposes.

All these facts muddled Richard's brain. The probability of all of this seemed quite bizarre, yet outside of the heebie jeebie stuff of witches, Sarah's information confirmed what was iffy to be a scientific fact. Somewhere in between all of this information, he was sure he'd find the truth. And the truth was what he wanted to uncover.

Richard decided he needed some fresh air. After scooping up all his investigative information, he phoned the concierge to bring the car around. It was still a little early to disturb Maize, and a nice drive in the country would help clear his head. He double-checked to make sure the amulet was safely tucked in his right coat pocket, his pipe in his left coat pocket, his pistol stuffed behind his back under his belt, concealed by his jacket, and all his investigative information filed in a briefcase. All would accompany him on his outing.

Richard really didn't care in which direction he drove; he just wanted out of the hubbub of the state's capital city, Hartford. Whimsically, he decided to drive west to take in the quiet countryside. The further he drove, the less traffic and buildings dotted the landscape, and more green, vacant fields, and blue skies. Once in a while, he passed an antiquated farm or small home dotting the middle of a pasture. He was in no hurry to go anywhere, and with very little traffic, he slowed down to about fifteen miles per hour.

As he leisurely drove, enjoying the scenery, Richard noticed a large odd looking building several acres from the road to his left. Since time was not a factor he decided to drive down the dirt road and investigate; always the investigator. As he crept closer to the building it looked more like a resort. The pristine Victorian architecture was enhanced with large southern white pillars and a very large veranda that seemed to wrap around the whole building. It looked about five stories high, and as if it was a hotel of some kind, Richard was sure it held at least 500 rooms. What seemed out of place was the roof; it was topped with Moorish chrome looking domes. The immediate grounds looked like an agricultural paradise with eons of fruit trees, rose bushes of every color, hanging green plants, and all types of greenery filling in between.

Upon reaching the structure, Richard noticed no signs of life outside besides the abundant foliage. No animals and no humans. It seemed empty but full of life at the same time. *How odd,* he thought to himself, *to find a place like this out in the middle of nowhere.*

As he sat looking at this beautiful building, Richard realized there were no other automobiles and no place designated to park. So he decided to park on the front lawn several yards from the porch. He left his car there and moseyed around the front yard. The wide front steps with the oversized veranda and white pillars gave it a look right out of the old south. The house had such a tranquil, alluring appeal that Richard felt no harm would be done to walk up the stairs and knock on the door.

The Victorian Manor covered six acres of land and was a quarter-mile long. The roof housed numerous Moorish turrets, domes, and minarets towering heavenward and shining in the early afternoon sun. The gingerbread-colored architecture was a fireproof structure with poured concrete and reinforced steel rails and cables between floors. Most of the sleeping rooms had their own bathroom, electricity, and telephone. The inside was as opulent as the outside with exotic furnishings, porcelains, Venetian-style mirrors of all sizes and shapes, and European sculptures and paintings. The white iron lattice pillars along with the wrap-around veranda added to this sense of luxury. The grounds were as awe-inspiring as the hotel itself—covering over 150 acres. In the back of the house were over twenty-one buildings used for necessities and pleasure: maintenance, automotive garages, green houses, a barn yard with chickens, goats, and horses, stables, kennels, an athletic house, and much more. In contrast to the solitude in the front of the Virctorian House, the back was full of life.

"We've been expecting you, Lord Wikki," echoed two young girls dressed in full-length navy skirts and white laced Victorian blouses as they pushed open the oversized front doors to The Victorian Manor. "Won't you come in?"

Richard nodded in compliance as he stepped into a large, domed room. He felt the soft cross breeze from the opened large matching doors on the opposite side illuminating the lively backyard. He stood in awe of the many people obviously not in a hurry; they were meandering, talking, and reading inside and out. All seemed busy doing something or going somewhere.

"Come this way, please. She has been waiting for you." Still taking in his surroundings, he sluggishly followed the girls. He noticed the domed ceiling seemed etched, resembling something Michelangelo would paint; the large rotund room was filled with paintings, sculptures, greenery, and an array of seating. This room seemed to be the focal point of the whole building, situated in the center of two long wings; one to the north and the other to the south.

"Ah, excuse me." The girls paused and turned back to Richard. "What is this place?"

"It is called The Victorian Manor. I'm sure you will have all your questions answered in good time. Please follow us."

"Wait a minute … who's been waiting for me?" No one answered.

When they arrived at the oversized room near the end of the north wing, one of the girls paused and asked Lord Wikki to wait until she announced his arrival. The other stayed with Richard. Richard peered down the long wing they had just walked. "Nice carpet … looks like a

Persian design."

Politely, she answered. "Yes, most of the furnishings here at The Victorian Manor are from Madame's travels to Europe, the Middle East, Africa, West Indies, and South America. We kid that she needs to quit traveling or we are not going to have room to move about."

Richard thought to himself, *That's the name of the someone who is expecting him, Madame?* "What do you do here?" he asked.

"We all have jobs. Mine and Suzanne's is one of hostess, which mainly oversees everything is working smoothly."

"What happens if something isn't working smoothly?"

"We notify the person in charge of that particular area."

"What is the purpose of The Victorian Manor? It looks like a hotel."

"I'm sure all—"

Interrupting their conversation, Suzanne opened the door and politely asked Lord Wikki to enter. "Madame is ready to greet you."

As Richard entered the room, Suzanne closed the door behind him. It was quite dim, as most of the light came from myriads of candles of all sizes and shapes spread around the room, as well as sconces hanging from the walls. As his eyes began to focus, he noticed a woman on the other side of the room sitting at a large rectangular walnut table with a small electric desk lamp, providing just enough light to complete her paperwork. Her head, draped with a sheer white scarf, was down, reviewing the stack of papers lying in front of her.

Richard stood, believing it was prudent to be silent until she acknowledged his presence. Richard noticed the room seemed very comfortable with Victorian couches and chairs set about. Heavy walnut book shelves filled the walls from corner to corner with all sizes of books, and numerous artifacts lay amongst all the furnishings. He missed the hint of vanilla perfuming the air.

Within a few minutes Richard noticed her stir. As she rose,

removing the scarf from her head and resting it around her neck on her shoulders, she began to walk towards Richard. She was in her mid-fifties with salt and pepper hair loosely pulled back away from her face in a high loose bun adorned with a large gold comb resembling a Spanish ornament. She was dressed in a loose-fitting turquoise georgette dress adorned with two long stands of pearls. She had an average matronly frame and stood about his height. As she walked around the table towards Richard, he noticed she moved with courtly grace. Her eyes were as blue as the sky and her porcelain complexion in the hue of the candles captured her angelic appearance. Her voice was friendly, calm, and warm.

"My dear Lord Wikki, how nice it is to finally meet you face to face," she said greeting him, holding out her hands to clasp his in hers.

Richard, who was usually not stirred by much, was speechless. He thought the best approach was no approach. He had no idea what he had walked into.

"Please, won't you sit down?" Madame motioned toward the two chairs sitting on the right side of the room near one set of many bookshelves. As they both sat, Suzanne entered and asked if Madame needed anything. "Yes, please bring us some tea." She looked at Richard for a response, and he nodded affirmative. He thought to himself, *When in Rome, do as Romans do.*

"Richard, I'm sure you have a lot of questions. I will be happy to answer them in time."

"Madame, I would really like to know the purpose of this place. One of your hostesses mentioned that it is called The Victorian Manor. And, how do you know my name?"

"Those are two fair questions. First, we have work to do here, and when our work is done we will move on. Next, I've been watching you for some time. You are an important person in clearing the web you have stumbled upon."

Richard had a hard time connecting the ambiguous explanation with the obvious sincerity of the speaker. She was serious and he could tell this was no game, but nothing made any sense. Suzanne entered with the cart of tea. She rolled it over to Madame and Richard and politely poured for both. "Thank you, Suzanne."

Suzanne nodded her head and left, closing the door behind her. Tea was not exactly what Richard had in mind, but he was thirsty. Politely, he took a sip as she continued "It's not by accident that you arrived at The Victorian Manor on your journey to investigate the untimely death of Henry Phillips II."

Richard couldn't believe what he was hearing. *How in the world did she … out in the middle of nowhere in another city … know what I am investigating?* He tried not to look astonished. As a detective, he had been in a number of unexplainable situations, but nothing like this.

"I can see that you are surprised that I know your name and what you are doing in Hartford."

"You could say that." Richard said, trying not to sound annoyed at this unwarranted intrusion into his life.

Madame sat her tea cup down on the cart and rose. "Come, please walk with me and I will try to explain."

Leaving her door open, Madame led the way back to the center dome.

Not wanting to wait for more double-talk, Richard decided to ask more questions. "Madame, you certainly possess the presence of a well-versed woman and one quite capable of overseeing … whatever this place is … but … who are you?"

"That question is not as easy to answer as you might think. Our ancestors go way back; back to a time when greed and overambitious desires of power caused a whole continent to blow up and sink.

Several survived, fleeing to nearby countries such as Egypt, South America, and India. Our ancestors—some referred to them as the Kaloo and others as Atlanteans—helped their new friends tap into individual personal inner skills that lay dormant until the appointed time. Thus, the Ancient Mystery Schools began; helping each to achieve their potential, working for the greater good of mankind. As decades passed, the Essences were given special gifts to protect a sacred journey; a journey which embodied pure perfection and love. Others have been known as The Way and some the Druids and Magdalenes; all given special talents. Down through the ages, all had a similar purpose; to help establish the balance of the world. One of our missions is to protect the Great Mysteries and search for new information until time for their unveiling. And that my dear Richard, will depend on millions of people such as yourself."

Madame stopped at the north side of the center domed room in front of a wide ascending staircase with a caged enclosed elevator off to its left. "Here we are. Just to the right behind the staircase you will find a most magnificent ballroom." Madame continued to walk toward the outer door to the ballroom slightly behind and left of the staircase. As she walked, many greeted her either by nodding or whispering a simple hello. As she opened the ballroom door, they stepped inside. It was as unique and decorated as the rest of the Manor. "This is where we hold our worship and meetings."

As Richard looked around the ballroom, he felt the presence of something special, he could not describe it but he knew it was there, and he knew it was kind. *How odd,* he thought, *to feel something you cannot see or hear.* He frowned.

"Richard, I'd like to show you a special room," replied Madame. "It is across the dome in the south wing." With that, they both left the ballroom and crossed the center room. As they strolled down the southern wing, Richard asked. "What are you talking about … ancient mysteries?"

Madame did not answer until she came to the third room on their right. "I think this will help answer a few questions," she commented as she waved her hand unlocking the door to an oversized room. "This is a very special room—it's our library. You can see by its condition that we are running out of space." Madame motioned for Richard to follow her. "Here we have saved coveted information down through the ages. As you can see, our information takes many forms." Richard walked around the room. He stopped at the shelves filled with antique scrolls of old.

"What are these?"

"This room is a library of knowledge which represents secrets of the past, present, and future: ancient mysteries. These scrolls in front of you have been passed down through the ages. The Vatican is not the only place that owns a library of secrets. They are mostly papyrus and written by hand." Madame walked across the room where oversized volumes of books were shelved. "These are from a time where if a book was to be duplicated, it was recopied by hand. We progress to the time of the printing press over here. And over here, you see large crystals of all sizes and shapes. They hold much knowledge. Our ancestors preserved special information in what you might call a time capsule. Here you see many crystals providing light for this section of the library."

Richard had never seen anything like this; he wondered if the Vatican library looked anything like it.

"A large part of our work, as I referred to earlier, has to do with traveling the world, collecting knowledge. Much has been buried, and is waiting to be unearthed. Many here find it of great interest to travel and bring home important teachings from the past which help us understand the present and the future."

The Ivy League Chronicles: 9 Squares

"What does all this have to do with me?"

"In good time my, dear Richard. I'd like to show you something." Madame walked to the bookshelf which housed smaller books of print. "Here it is. This is Nostradamus's book of predictions which so many believe is a big riddle or fake." She handed it to Richard to peruse.

To be polite, because he really didn't care, Richard opened it to the publishing page. There, he read "Published in 1752." Carefully closing and handing it back, Richard asked. "So what else do you do around here?" It was obvious to him by now that Madame was only going to divulge what she wanted him to know.

"Let me take you further down the hall where one of our most learned teachers and researchers is instructing two promising young men who want to become researchers much like their teacher."

As they left the library and continued walking to their right down the south wing Richard asked, "What do researchers do?"

"When those who travel bring home new information, the researchers study and prepare it for the library. Many times a researcher asks an elder to review the materials in order to shed further light on what has been found."

"Who and what are the elders?"

"I am one. We have great insights and gifts which are held in high esteem by all here at The Victorian Manor. We see what others cannot see."

"What do you mean by that?"

Madame stopped. "We are here."

"Forgive us, Timothy, for interrupting your studies with these fine young men. We have a visitor who now is part of our journey. I am giving him what you could say is a bird's eye tour."

Timothy nodded. "Welcome."

"What are you studying?" Richard asked, trying to act like he was interested.

"We have just received some scrolls found in Alexandria, Egypt. I am demonstrating how to examine such an artifact and how to log specific information."

Richard uncharacteristically didn't know what to say, so he just nodded his head.

As Madame and Richard exited the classroom and walked back to the center dome, Richard asked, "What did you mean back there … my being part of your journey?"

"Each of us is put on this earth with the ability to create our own path from life to death; it's called free will. Albeit that our environment and genetics does help form who we are, we all have choices as to how we build and live that journey. At this point in time, our paths have crossed and now we are a part of each other's journey. One may say this was destiny or because of decisions you made from this point back in your life. For example, when you decided to take the visiting professorship, or when you accepted the dinner invitation at the Judson's, or when you wanted to see the necklace or when you had lunch with Jonathan Judson and accepted his offer to investigate young Henry, each choice you made took you to the next choice. And you made the choice to stop here and see what this house was all about. So here we are … our paths have crossed."

As they walked towards the back doors in the center room, Madame continued. "Here, please let us sit outside and enjoy some lemonade in the shade and I will explain."

The afternoon sun was beginning to go down, but Richard hadn't noticed. His mind was captivated but skeptical about what he was seeing and hearing. No alarms were signaling anything devious or hurtful was occurring, in fact it all seemed quite normal. That fact alone made him uneasy. He did not know what he was going to believe about this whole adventure, but he planned to let it play out; even though it unnerved him how Madame knew those little details … choices … of his recent past. He would finish this conversation and never return. He did not like the feeling of not being in control.

They crossed the large veranda and walked down the steps to a beautiful manicured park area to their immediate right. As he sat himself in one of the large high-back cane chairs next to Madame, a group of children playing caught his eye. Upon noticing Richard watching the children, Madame wondered if he had seen Madame Flambeaux outside his window in the Boston Congressional Hotel.

"They are learning about … you might say science. See the teacher, Madame Flambeaux? She is showing them how all things are made of energy, geometry, and harmonics; that is a fundamental genesis of everything in the universe. You and I are also made of the same materials. She is teaching them that grass, flowers, and rocks are created using these three forces."

At the point of being rude, Richard felt it was best not to state his opinion. Instead he asked, "So what do you feel is my part of this combined journey?"

"I know this all seems quite, shall I say, bizarre, to you. But I assure you all is very real. More real than the movie you have created of your life. I need you to understand as you continue your life's journey that there is a very delicate balance on this earth of positive and negative energy. To skip to what you call 'the chase,' the ancient mysteries have been given for preservation until it is time for them to be revealed, not to be exploited. But there is an energy misusing them for personal gain, which is causing an imbalance on the earth. Many of us are concerned. We work very hard to maintain positive loving energy so Mother Earth does not destroy us or we her. There will be a time, if we are ready, that all will be healed."

Madame could see Richard did not understand, or more importantly, believe, anything she was telling him. "As you continue your journey home you will understand. You will remember what I have told you. What is most important is that you realize there are negative and positive forces protecting these mysteries. And, as you are confronted with these energies, you have choices to take you to the next choice. Be sure you make the right choice to create the most loving path. The universe will respond to the loving path ... I promise."

Out of the corner of his eye Richard noticed someone running towards them, and then urgently whispered in Madame's ear. Madame's face looked very concerned at what she was hearing. Calmly, Madame informed Richard, "I have just been told that the hotel in which you are staying is aflame."

Whatever she said from there after was a blur to Richard. He stood frozen in fear for a moment. "MAIZE!"

Chapter 24

Shades of yellow, blue, and red consumed the dense, starless night. Radiant flames shooting high in the sky were slowly tamed by gallons of water erupting from the firefighters' hoses. It was a five-alarm blaze and they had arrived too late; it was out of control, burning to the ground. All that could be accomplished was the dampening of the inferno so the nearby forest would be preserved.

Firefighters' voices could be heard yelling orders to move here and there; small groups of inspectors from Scotland Yard were grouped sporadically across the countryside, collaborating on how to solve the dilemma and asking who would do such a thing … who were Richard's enemies? Amidst all of the chaos, one broken man sat devastated, on a nearby hill, overlooking the inferno.

Richard stumbled, leaning on a nearby lamp post, as he watched the Hartford Congressional Hotel engulf in flames. Trembling and frozen by fear, he entered another time and place …

Why did she want to move to the country? Why did he agree? He had found a clear patch on a hill, sitting alone, watching the events unfold in front of him like a silent movie. His head was buried in his hands, unable to face the reality stabbing his heart and mind. It had only been a few hours since he kissed his wife Veronica, his five-year-old daughter Julianna, and patted his faithful Irish Setter Yaxley goodbye. He was working on a case which required him to work late into the night. He would be home by daybreak.

"Detective Wikki … Lord Wikki … RICHARD!" yelled Richard's one time professor, mentor, and friend Dr. Dunby. "It's me, Professor Dunby. Richard!" Richard, hearing a familiar voice, slowly emerged from his hidden place; a place of deep and desperate sorrow—a place where only he could go—a place no human would want to be. He looked up at his dear friend, not fully comprehending his surroundings and wondering why his mentor would be calling his name. Dr. Dunby joined his protégé, sitting next to him on the grassy hill away from all the commotion happening below.

"Richard, your comrades called me. They thought I might be of some help. You had not responded to their voices—they were obviously concerned about your well-being." Trying to keep his dear friend in reality, Dr. Dunby tried to engage Richard in some kind of conversation, even if it was in monosyllables.

"Richard, tell me what happened." Numb both mentally, emotionally, and physically, Richard rehashed the events of his day, stopping periodically to regroup his focus; the grief was so devastating tears could not come to his eyes.

Someone grabbed his arm, bringing him back to the present. "Sir, are you ok?" asked Deputy Frank, who had been perusing the area for anyone in need of help.

"I … why yes, I just needed some rest," replied Richard.

"Are you staying at the hotel, sir?"

"Yes. I am looking for someone."

Richard didn't know if Maize was safe; he couldn't handle the idea of losing another female friend or family member; this was not an option. Many areas around the hotel were closed off by work horses and tape holding at bay a growing group of concerned citizens. Six fire trucks and numerous police cars surrounded the hotel with their lights glaring. Hotel guests and staff were mingling around the area— some were yelling, some were crying, some just were. The intense, uncontrolled noise made it difficult for the deputy and Richard to hold a conversation.

"Her name is Maize. She's about eighteen … so high … short brown hair … she is my niece."

"That description could fit a number of young ladies. Why don't I help you work your way through the crowd to locate your niece. I'm sure she is fine."

HE watched Richard and the deputy make their way through the crowd while he meticulously removed his white cotton gloves, one finger at a time. He stood hidden away from the crowd under a large tree, surveying the perfect execution of the final phase of his plan. HE was pleased, and so would be Davenport.

Deputy Frank barely managed to maneuver through the crowd. "Sir, please stay with me. I promise we will find—" His words fell on deaf ears as Richard spotted Maize. He peered over heads, bumping into almost everyone as he tried to reach her, excusing himself as he pushed his way through the overanxious crowd. He saw Maize standing near a fire truck to his left. He wondered who could be conversing with her. As he moved closer he couldn't believe his eyes. There stood Maize, wrapped in a blanket and chatting with Helena.

Upon noticing Richard walk towards her, Maize dropped the blanket and ran to him. Hugging him tightly Maize exclaimed with tears in her eyes. "Profess … oh, I mean Uncle, where have you been? I've been so worried. I couldn't find you."

"Let me look at you Maize. You're not hurt?" Richard's single most concern was that Maize was alive and well. His inner relief was disguised by a frown as he noticed from the corner of his eye that Helena was watching them. "What a surprise to see you Helena? Where did you appear from?"

Unlike Richard, Helena was glad to see him again.

Maize piped in first. "Uncle, when I came down to the lobby to get something to eat … I didn't want that new thing called room service … there was Helena, waiting to check in. And then all hell broke loose."

Instinctively, Richard's hand nonchalantly moved to check if the amulet was still in his inner breast pocket as Helena started to explain her arrival at the Hartford Congressional Hotel. The amulet, whatever it was, had become an extension of his body. He tried not to show his relief when he realized it was still there; he had not been mindful of it since he left Madame's.

"I had decided to continue my journey to Hartford to tour the state capital and then finish my trip in New Haven to visit Yale University. I was sad I did not get to say goodbye to you and Maize before you left Danvers. So, you can imagine my surprise and joy when I saw Maize in the hotel lobby."

I'll bet, thought Richard. This was all too coincidental.

"We chatted a little and then everyone started screaming as the firemen came running into the hotel. Maize and I stayed outside together, protected by the firemen. And that's about it."

"I'd like to take a look around," mentioned Richard. The two women followed him as he took in the damage. The top floors seemed to be the ones most affected by the fire. They just happened to include the floors he and Maize occupied. That alone did not sit easy with Richard. He wondered if he was being paranoid, or had they once again,

E.K. Prescott, Ph.D.

been targeted.

As he looked up to the top of the hotel, Richard surmised. "Maize, it looks like we have lost everything … it all looks pretty scorched to me. The important thing is you are alive and unhurt." He was secretly very pleased he had taken everything of importance with him on his joy ride; everything else could be replaced.

"What are we going to do Uncle Richard?"

"My car is over there still packed with suitcases. Since this trip has been cut short I think I will be on my way to New Haven. I would love to repay the drive and take you home to New Haven," offered Helena.

Richard thought this all was a little too convenient, but now was not the time to think. "Just a minute," Richard stated as he quickly ran to where he had left the borrowed hotel car and retrieved his briefcase. Returning, he informed Helena they would take her up on her offer.

"Maize, let's go home!"

Chapter 25

It had been several weeks since they returned to New Haven from Hartford. As Richard sat overlooking The Green through his office window, as he had done numerous times before, he could not stop revisiting the fire. The fire that changed his whole life; the fire that was the sole reason he was here living and working in New Haven instead of London.

Before the fire, he was Detective Wikki of Scotland Yard. Now he was Professor Richard Wikki, Chair of the criminology arm of Yale's Law School. He was numb to the point of believing this must have happened to someone else as if an out of body experience. Richard knew that remembering would unleash a series of events he did not want to deal with any time soon. He had managed to keep this disaster at bay, creeping up only once in a while, luckily to be quickly buried to avert total memory; hoping the pain would not set in his heart like a boulder—a pain no one could escape.

And now it was Maize who—because of his need to protect her—opened the flood of agony he now could not put aside any longer. Richard understood he had to deal with this tragedy or it would consume him, but not now!

The Green was void of students, being that the summer session was now over and the dog days of summer had everyone fleeing for shade of some kind. Several ceiling and floor fans were moving full force in his office, but Richard still sweltered in the stifling heat and humidity. The open windows did not support the usual welcoming breeze from the harbor across town. He thought most of the boats would probably not be at bay, but out in the Atlantic Ocean, searching for respite from this heat. He made a mental note to purchase a sailboat one day; he loved sailing with his father as a child. It was one of the few pleasant memories he had of his childhood.

Richard intentionally diverted his thoughts, leaving the past behind him, to the amulet he held in his hand. As he rubbed his fingers over the amulet, he realized his vacation trip to Boston, Salem, and Hartford had triggered something within him. He now knew he missed being a detective for a number of reasons, but most of all it was the ability to use his mind to connect seemingly unrelated clues. And that's what he knew he now had accomplished.

Richard had not seen Maize since their return. It was a gigantic relief to hand her safely over to her father. However, he felt it was not the time to discuss what he learned on his vacation; there were still a few loose ends. He looked at his watch, checking how much time he had before his appointment with Dr. Diane Granite, the Director of Archival Research at the newly constructed Sterling Memorial Library.

The library was built with funds from the bequest of John W. Sterling, a New York attorney who graduated from Yale in 1864. Designed by James Gamble Rogers, the library was built to house 3.5 million volumes in a book stack tower intended to be a dominating feature. The interior of the tower was a self-supporting, unified structure of steel which was the largest welding project ever undertaken at the

E.K. Prescott, Ph.D.

time. Although technically seven stories high, the book tower actually contained sixteen levels of stacks. The library was largely surrounded by small buildings; the sheer size of the tower stunned its viewers. The impression of the size was heightened by the semi-Gothic style tower, its rather plain façade and elaborately crenellated battlements. The ornamentation of Sterling Memorial Library was beautiful, detailed, all pervading, and symbolic of the history of the university and libraries of the world. The artwork contributed much to the unification of form and function in the building that affirmed the value of knowledge and scholarship at Yale.

Attention to artistic detail pervades all of Sterling Memorial Library. As a general rule, the ornamentations of each library area were designed to be in harmony with the intended purpose of the room being decorated. A second floor room originally designated as the English Study has window decorations portraying King Lear, Hamlet, and Lady Macbeth; the offices of the Babylonian Collection were given windows bearing the human-headed winged bulls of Nineveh and the Babylonian lion. In larger areas, design schemes were even more elaborate. The entrance hall related, in stone and stained glass, the history of the Yale Library. Carved stone panels below the windows represented such events as the meeting of the Branford ministers in 1701 to form a "college of the colonies," the Saybrook pleas for retention of the library, and the British invasion of New Haven in 1779. The windows above the panels had decorated panes that interweaved the story of Yale and New Haven; the windows showed everything from the portrait of Elihu Yale to ox carts that brought the books from Saybrook.

Richard turned his chair around and laid the amulet in the only clear patch on his desk which was right in front of him. As he leaned back in his chair, staring at the amulet, he retraced his path as he followed young Henry from New Haven to Boston to Salem Town to

Hartford and back to New Haven. This wayward youth had found some kind of self-satisfaction in the world of witchcraft.

Although Richard had not uncovered direct evidence, Henry did return to New Haven to become an important member of a witch coven; all pieces led to that conclusion. From the piece of paper Richard had ripped from The Book of Shadows in the basement of The Witch Museum, he knew Henry had earned a promotion so to speak and was moving to fulfill that position in a coven in Hartford. And now Henry's skeleton was identified as the one found on the same beach where Richard now resided, Long Island Sound Beach in East Haven. Thus, it was logical to assume Henry returned to New Haven. In addition to this piece of evidence, the authorities disclosed the greenish-brown algae, which was found near his body, was comprised of hemlock and other poisonous herbs used by witches, plus arsenic.

Now feeling this part of the puzzle was solved, Richard could not understand how the amulet representing chaos with the Sherman Coat of Arms etched in the middle had anything to do with what he had uncovered about young Henry. Richard recalled the position of the amulet when removed by Maize from Henry's hand and outstretched arm indicating he had pulled this off of someone. But who, and when, and why? Was this person his killer? Did he know this person? Was the killer part of a coven in which he was a member?

Richard believed the images portrayed by the shape and indentions of the amulet told a story of someone who was part of an organization who used energy to ignite chaos in order for his or her workings to be undetected by the masses. Richard was excited in that he knew he was close to the truth, but he didn't know what truth—the truth about Henry and witchcraft or the truth about the meaning behind the amulet. He was beginning to think they were two separate truths but interconnected in some way. With that, he glanced at his watch and decided he would leave a little early for his appointment. He was hoping Dr. Granite might have some information which could help him tie the clues together. Richard grabbed for his pipe on top of the highest stack of ungraded papers on his desk and then for the amulet, carefully securing their safety by hiding both on his person as usual; it was routine.

Richard was in his own investigative world as he nonchalantly walked across campus to the new library. Uncharacteristically, he did not notice George Seymour crossing the University using the intersecting sidewalk Richard was now approaching.

"Well hello, Dr. Wikki."

Regaining clarity, Richard replied. "Well, hello Dr. Seymour. Surprised to see you here."

"Just on my way to a meeting and running late as usual. Looking forward to seeing you at the Elihu Society celebration honoring our new members tomorrow, and don't forget there is a reception afterward at the Taft … as in Hotel."

"You mean I am not exclusive? Darn!"

"No such luck Wikki," George chided as he continued to cross the campus. "See ya' tomorrow."

Richard continued towards the library, quite aware George did not have a meeting to attend and obviously seized the moment only to remind him to show up and on time.

Dr. Diane Granite, the Chair of Archives Research for the new Sterling Library at Yale University, was born and raised in New Haven and earned several degrees at Yale, including her doctorate. She possessed a rich, personal understanding of New Haven's history as well as a hefty researched historical prospective.

Diane immediately befriended Richard upon his arrival at Yale in 1921. Loving inquiries of any kind, she was naturally interested in his history, especially his life at Yale's sister school Cambridge as well as his work as a Scotland Yard detective. Dr. Granite, much to Richard's dismay, was also one of the few people who had discovered he held the title of Lord of Foxworthy; she had a special way of prying information. Believing most professors possessed an overinflated opinion of themselves, Diane was surprised how much she respected Professor Wikki—from her point of view he was a cut above most of the celebrated faculty. Richard was looking forward to seeing her as she was him. He knew she would be the perfect person to fill in some of the few holes remaining in his investigation. Richard decided he would start with something easy like the history of The Green, leading up to who really is Mr. Davenport? He knew there was more to this man than owning a lot of hotels and being a member of almost every committee and club in New Haven.

As Richard entered Sterling Library and walked towards Dr. Granite's office, he felt the regal ambiance that he believed demanded reverence and respect from all who visited. The presence of history filled every corner—a special unique history which embodied the essence of New Haven and Yale's American/European roots.

"Good day, Dr. Granite. I thought I might find you here, hiding in the Rare Books section." Professor Wikki commented, introducing his presence. Dr. Granite was taking a well-deserved break from the continuous grind of writing detailed research reports.

Not surprised to hear his voice, Diane replied. "It's time to take a break when the lines start waving and everything is a blur." Raising her book, she continued. "It's time for something frivolous and less taxing on the mind … *This Side of Paradise!*"

"Mum's the word, Dr. Granite," smiled Richard. "We wouldn't want anyone to find out your secret."

Diane had taken a liking to Richard immediately. If truth be known, she searched him out, wanting to see the new man on campus. His background alone as a detective from Scotland Yard, plus his connection with Cambridge, gave rise to a lot of interesting research questions worth inquiry. She found his conversations informative and always uplifting. To her, Professor Wikki seemed to be a series of contradictions: self-assured but at times looked out of place, a loner but lonely, aloof but friendly and he definitely masked a great sadness. He apparently had no family here or abroad. He was obviously astute and quick-minded; she loved picking his brain.

To Dr. Granite, Richard was a research project worth uncovering and analyzing every bit and piece of information. She never wasted her time on too many faculty members at Yale; most of them were "climbers" in her eyes and she hated politics. Politics was not her idea of a good time; she had that in common with Professor Detective Wikki. Granted, as head of the Archival Research Department, there was some song and dance work, as she called it, but she could excuse it as a necessary evil to survive. But Diane never let it impede her boundaries, which waffled from time to time, if truth be told.

"Dr. Granite, now is it? It's Diane to you, young man." She grinned as she patted the seat next to her, signaling for him to come and sit. "You have found my hiding spot." Closing her book and laying it on the side table next to her, Diane continued. "I know it's very unlike me to read something so frivolous. Now, my dear boy, what are you up to?" She loved mothering him, and Richard really didn't mind.

"I thought I'd take a break and visit my favorite person," smiled Richard.

"You mean from all that detective investigation work," Diane replied with a mischievous grin. "You know how I love your stories."

Richard knew he would have to appease her unsustainable appetite for mystery and think of something quick and short, so he began. "The Domestic Strangler was on the loose one fine night ... it was a full moon."

"Oh you mean like the one we are having now."

Richard hadn't remembered it was a full moon, but nodded his head in agreement. "We knew very little about him ... oh we were sure it was a he. We had uncovered from credible sources that he wore a butler-like costume, thus the Domestic name, and he loved to strangle his victims leaving his deathly trade mark—a black bowtie."

"How bizarre. What happened?"

"To make a long story short, he actually caught himself."

Diane's eyebrows rose questioningly.

"He apparently met his match because the chosen victim became the killer." Richard knew Diane wanted the details but he hurriedly changed the subject. He turned, looking at her fondly. "I need your help with something."

"Sure," she replied, disappointed that it was obvious Richard wasn't going to provide the details.

"In my temporary office on the fourth floor of Phelps Hall, I have a large window overlooking The Green. Throughout the last year or so I have heard bits about its origin and such ... like it was part of the first planned Puritan colony which came to America from England in 1638. Since it has been in existence up until now, I figure it must be a very important piece of land."

"Yes it is. There are whole books written about the history of The Green. From its beginning, it was meant to be the center of the town. It was first called The Market. It was used for cattle grazing, the town hall and police buildings, schools, and even had stocks for punitive judgments. Originally, there were seven people who collectively held the land title for The Market. These people became the overseers of the property. It is a coveted position—the Proprietors are appointed until death. Usually the position is passed down generation after generation and only to the elitists of New Haven. Through the years, The Green became more park-like as New Haven grew. One point I always found quite fascinating was that in the late 1800s, the Proprietors, among others, were able to convince the federal government they were entitled to sole responsibility of the land. I do believe the agreement still stands today. No federal, state or local government has any jurisdiction. The Proprietors run the whole shebang. Even Indian land is governed by Tribal Councils overseen by the Federal Bureau of Indian Affairs."

Richard tried not to reveal his surprise.

"I do believe it is the only land in the United States—outside of Indian land—that is not ruled by any form of government."

"So you are telling me that there is no accountability to anyone concerning The Green?"

"Only amongst themselves … and since there is no accountability, they do not have to submit notes of their meetings for public record. Come to think of it, I don't think I've ever seen one."

"Who are the Proprietors of The Green?"

"Well that piece of information is of public record. Since I have a great interest in its history, I have discovered there is no one document listing all the members since its beginning, but I do know for a fact Roger Sherman's descendants have always held the position of a Proprietor."

"Were most of the Proprietors Yale graduates?"

Diane nodded. "Mostly."

"Were they members of Skull and Bones?"

"Matter of fact, many of them were."

Richard started to think out loud. "So you are saying many of these Proprietors were wealthy, politically connected, graduates of Yale, held long political genealogies from conception, and were members of

Skull and Bones—"

Interrupting his train of thought, Diane answered. "Quite of few of them, yes."

Richard was now sure there was more to this small group. He knew they were connected to an underground political current of some kind. It only made sense. "Is Mr. Davenport one of them? I guess it's easy enough to check the public record."

"Why yes. He is very influential in this town. No one seems to question anything he says or does. He is a hometown boy with ALL the right credentials. If you know what I mean."

"Mr. Davenport, through the help of Dr. Seymour, submitted my name to become a member of the Elihu Secret Society. He said I was the perfect example of an Elihu man. I will be jumping through the hoops tomorrow afternoon."

Diane leaned forward, lowering her voice. "You know Richard, we have a lot of secret societies around here. But actually, there are more underground than above."

There was a long pause. To Richard, the word "secret" seemed to be used a lot lately.

He thought he should change the subject before Diane's research antenna started asking too many questions. "Have you been keeping up with our newest murder investigation these days?"

"You mean the horrible skeleton that was found on Long Island Sound Beach a few months back? Of course. I love intrigue."

Diane looked around for any unwanted ears. She wanted to show off her investigative skills to Richard. "The word is he is the son of a past Prior who also died under mysterious conditions."

This wasn't news to Wikki, but he did not want to let Dr. Granite know. He whispered. "Diane, this is something we are keeping hush hush."

Her eyes widened. Putting two fingers to her lips, she whispered in return. "I understand."

Diane was feeling very special like Richard had hoped. He didn't want to go any further with this discussion, thus it was time to make a polite departure. He would be in touch soon.

Before he returned to his cottage, Richard thought he would take a walk on the beach near the lighthouse. Barefoot, with pipe in hand and the amulet in his pants pocket, he was ready to be swept away by the sounds of the ocean.

As he walked slowly, feeling the heated sand from the days in the sun on his bare feet, he felt a warm summer breeze slowly nudge him forward. The beach was usually deserted this time of day during late July; it was just how Richard liked it. Outside of a few birds moving with the wind, he could only hear the tide flow in and out.

As he approached the lighthouse he stood, still trying to capture a moment—a moment in time when Henry was enjoying the sounds of the beach, just as he was presently, and then abruptly snuffed to nothingness. Richard decided to pause and sit in the sand. He stretched out his arms moving his hands over the sand, releasing the granules gradually through his fingers. As Richard sat in limbo mesmerized by the sparkling water mirroring the sunset he could not help but wonder. *What brought Henry to this spot that fateful night? Was he alone and surprised by the killer or was the killer with him?* What could the sand tell him?

At that moment, Richard noticed a small anomaly. The sand particles next to him had begun to spin into a small funnel-like shape, somewhat like a water spout, he thought as he watched the funnel take shape within just a few minutes. And then as fast as it formed, it fell back to individual sand particles. "Interesting," he said aloud. Richard had never noticed a small breeze do that before on the beach. *Maybe I was never close enough to watch this strange occurrence.*

He started thinking of related words. It was a game he often played to find focus with seemingly random items. Wind … movement … energy … energy of the wind caused the sand particles to take a form and the molecular structure changed into a swirling cone. *Yes, yes keep going,* he told himself. He was on to something. Energy … transformed something into fact … it had been chaotic … and energy made a specific intention out of it … a sand funnel. Richard was on a roll. The energy moved the dispersed chaotic particles into an object. He chuckled at himself. How simple yet so intricate! Now he understood what Sarah was trying to tell him. Could this be related to thermodynamics or something called quantum theory? Could this be a simple demonstration of how energy can be used to form new thoughts and movement?

Richard jumped to his feet. He began puffing on his unlit pipe and walking faster towards his cottage. The faster he walked the more he puffed on his pipe. It was beginning to get dark, but the full moon was illuminating the beach as far as the eye could see. All of a sudden, he stopped dead in his tracks and looked out at the moonlit ocean. *Boy, you are good,* he thought to himself. He held the amulet in his hand, truly beginning to understand for the first time the potential power behind this once mistaken necklace. As Richard turned and walked across the grassy knoll and across the dirt road towards his cottage, he heard his phone ringing. It echoed in the silence of the night.

Grasping at the pile of mail in the doorway which had been shoved through the mail opening earlier that day by the postman, Richard rushed to answer the phone.

"Professor Wikki, am I catching you at a bad time? You sound out of breath?"

"Hello, Maize."

E.K. Prescott, Ph.D.

"How did you know it was me?"

"I think you are the only one I know who lets the phone ring this long."

"Oh, I'm sorry am I disturbing you?"

"No, of course not." In fact, Richard was glad to hear her voice. He had wondered how she was doing since their return. "What's up?"

"I want to invite you this weekend to hear Edgar Casey speak at the Shubert Theater. I thought you might find him interesting after all the unusual events we encountered while on … vacation." Maize knew she had to be careful, one never knew who was listening. "His topic is going to be about…."

As Maize rattled on about Casey's interpretation of scientific fact as it related to metaphysics, Richard began unconsciously filing through the mail he had laid on the table while half-heartedly listening to her soliloquy; he knew she would get to the point sooner or later—she always did. Suddenly, Richard stopped abruptly. He stared at a letter addressed to him using pasted cut out letters from a newspaper or magazine. *How strange*, he thought.

Resting the receiver on the table, he opened the envelope; Richard pulled out a plain white sheet of typing paper with more pasted letters. He grabbed the phone receiver. "Maize sorry to interrupt, but I need to go. I will be glad to accompany you. I'll be in touch." And without waiting for a reply he hung up the phone and read the letter.

YOU WALKED IN A SEA OF ILLUSIONS

AND NOW THE

ILLUSIONS ARE ILLUMINATING…

Who sent this?

Chapter 26

"Well, there you are! We were beginning to think our favorite new member would not attend his own celebration party." Richard hated the ceremony and knew he would hate the reception. But, he had made the decision to play along, and play along is what he would do. Dr. Winehart, a well-known New Haven surgeon and Elihu's membership director, approached Richard upon his late arrival, extending his hand for a predetermined and staged ravenous hand shake. Richard's relaxed demeanor hid his total lack of interest and disgust for all this pomp and circumstance. As all eyes were watching his every move, Richard smiled graciously, trying to pry his hand quickly from the clutches of Dr. Winehart's.

Built in 1911, the Taft Hotel on College Street opened its doors to the public on New Year's Day, 1912. The elegant hotel is near the Shubert Theater. Former President William Taft, for whom the hotel is named, lived there for eight years while he was teaching at Yale Law School. Before the Taft Hotel was built, other hotels and taverns stood on the site, including one in which George Washington stayed in 1775. The Taft's immediate predecessor was the New Haven House, designed by Henry Austin, which was built in 1858 and was razed in 1910.

The Taft, as it is known, is the host of many Broadway actors, politicians, and dignitaries. Since the Shubert Theater is right next door, Taft Hotel draws people from all over the world, becoming a popular hot spot for both locals and out-of-towners. During the early years of prohibition, the Taft Bar and paneling were dismantled and resurrected on the second sub-basement, creating a speakeasy. It is quite notorious, providing entertainment that rivals the famous Cotton Club in New York City's Harlem District.

The welcoming party organized itself near the far right of the Taft Hotel lobby. It was a diplomatic meet and greet until the real celebration started in a private room downstairs in the speakeasy. The grand hotel lobby gave the rotunda area of the United States Capital Building a run for its money—large, tall, white pillars stood grandiosely from floor to ceiling, framing the stark, white, rotund sculptured ceiling with a stained glass and wood intricate design in its center. It took one's breath away.

Richard needed fresh air; he was tired of mingling. It was becoming quite stuffy. He wasn't sure if it was the hot air from his pompous company or the hot air of August. He politely excused himself from the mindless chatter and left the celebration to wander the halls of the Taft Hotel.

The confusion in the hotel lobby had died down as most had left for the speakeasy. There were only a few meandering hotel guests delaying their return to the hot sun, and one young couple with a "Just Married" sign on their luggage stacked next to them while waiting at the counter for a hotel clerk.

As Richard approached the right side of the main lobby, he noticed a secluded hallway to his immediate right. Richard hoped he would find a men's room somewhere down the hall. Soon he realized no

E.K. Prescott, Ph.D

men's room was to be found on either side as he reached the end of the hallway. He paused, leaning against the wood-paneled wall, enjoying the solitude.

As he peered down the deserted corridor in which he just came, he thought it quite unusual that there was not one entrance to anything, just a hallway to a dead end. He noticed the lighting was diminished considerably as one came closer to the end. *How odd*, he thought.

Leaning his head against the wall to relax, his eyes fixated on something etched at eye level on the wall across from him. Not thinking much about it, he stepped across to investigate this oddly placed indention. He took a minute to examine the etching, running his fingers across its awkward shape. Suddenly it struck him that this apparent etching was the exact size and shape of the amulet tucked safely in his upper inside coat pocket.

Richard nonchalantly took a look down the hall for any unwanted set of eyes. *Good*, he thought to himself, *all clear*. Feeling more at ease, he took a closer glance, methodically tracing the outline of what seemed to be an exact replica of a Chaos Sphere. It was too risky to take out the amulet in his pocket to check his hypotheses, but he was 100 percent sure it would fit exactly into the indention etched in the wall. How strange. In the middle of nowhere, at the end of a hallway to nowhere, he discovers an engraved replica of the amulet in his pocket. It has to be a key of some sort, Richard surmised.

As he stood contemplating what was in front of him, he heard a voice call his name from down the corridor.

"There you are," George shouted as he walked towards Richard. Not wanting any undue attention, Richard walked towards George, meeting him half way. "We wondered where you had run off—"

Interrupting, Richard stated matter-of-factly, "Nowhere special.

I was looking for a breath of fresh air in hopes of finding a men's room. But alas, to no avail." Richard maneuvered his position so both men were heading back towards the celebration.

"Tell me about it. This whole ordeal can become quite tedious. But sometimes it is a necessary evil to become part of the brotherhood," George cajoled as he put his hand on Richard's shoulder.

Richard cringed. Not that word again, and what's with the good ole boy pat on the shoulder. He did not like the sound of this. Richard would never be beholden to anyone, and certainly not to them! They have the wrong man.

As Richard walked with George down the hall and across the lobby to where a few Elihu men still lingered, he knew he would return later tonight to see where his newest clue would lead. As he excused himself and crossed the lobby to find the men's room, he realized this was going to be a long night.

***

It was about twenty minutes before midnight when Richard scanned the outside of the hotel for any unwanted do-gooders. The lobby was empty and no one was at the registration desk. He walked towards the designated hallway which was near the hotel's infamous ballroom. His only thoughts were to enter and leave the Taft Hotel unnoticed; as if never there. The light at this time of night in that part of the hotel was illuminated from the bright full moon shining through the large elongated windows facing College Street. There was sufficient light to guide Richard's walk, even though it dimmed considerably as he neared the end of the hallway. No one would have cause to notice this area of the hotel, much less this hallway which was extremely dark and went nowhere.

Upon finding the engraving, Richard pulled out the amulet.

He hesitated for a moment, eying the amulet and the engraving. It would be a perfect fit. He slowly placed the amulet into the wall. It fit. He waited, but nothing happened. He decided to refit it and try a little twist. Suddenly, the panel now housing the amulet, opened slowly inward. Immediately upon entering, before the panel closed behind him, Richard grabbed for his amulet and rested it safely back into his upper inside jacket pocket. There, in front of him was a long staircase to what seemed to be some type of basement. Slowly and methodically, Richard reached for his .38 caliber Webley Mark VI revolver, which was the standard arm of the British Navy, and proceeded down the steps.

As he descended the stairs to what initially appeared to be just another basement, Richard realized as the light grew brighter, that there was a shiny paved corridor at the end. Upon entering, he stood, dumbfounded. There before him was a well-lit boardwalk with no apparent light source. The corridor was immaculate with a cobblestone narrow walkway as far as the eye could see. A little ways to his left was a street light fixture—with no light—standing next to a park bench surrounded by various sizes of green potted plants. This ensemble decorated the hallway about every twenty feet, rotating from side to side of the corridor. On both sides of the corridor, the walls were painted like a continuous mural depicting a blue sky; some areas with clouds, some areas more sunny, some with birds. As he walked cautiously, alert for anything, Richard noticed a street sign post to his right. It read "Welcome to Elihu Village." The other post with an arrow pointing to his left read "General Information."

He had discovered an underground city of some kind; a totally bizarre concept to Richard. Excited about his discovery, Richard decided to start with General Information. He opened the large, wooden double doors into what looked like an empty upscale lawyer's office.

He assumed everything was deserted this time of night, just like the corridor, but still proceeded with caution. To him, it seemed like an average-sized receiving room with top of the line interior decorations. The furniture included a sofa, side and coffee tables, large chairs and a large redwood receptionist desk. *Someone spared no expense*, he thought. All accessories such as lamps, figurines, decorative bowls and urns, and artwork tastefully filled the room.

As Richard passed the sofa table, he noticed today's *New Haven Gazette* newspaper headline featured another great feat by the infamous baseball player Babe Ruth. There were also several magazines scattered on the table such as the first issue of *Time* magazine, dated March 3, 1923; *Screenland* magazine featuring child actor Jackie Coogan; and the latest sports magazine featuring the New York Yankees and New York's new baseball stadium, The House That Ruth Built.

Richard walked around the room looking for anything unusual; something that would give him more information. Unfortunately, since he knew absolutely nothing about art, Richard did not enjoy the originals before him as he moved from wall to wall. He only studied them for clues.

Finding nothing, he decided to tackle the receptionist desk. The desk top was neat and clean with only normal secretarial artifacts and paraphernalia. He also found nothing unusual in the desk drawers which he found to be unlocked. Behind the desk stood a large redwood matching book case. It was filled with the normal stuff: books, pictures (of whom he had no clue), more figurines, and vases.

One particular antique gold figurine in the upper left of the book case caught his eye; it looked unusual. It was a hooded monk-like figure with a necklace pendant resembling his amulet. In disbelief, he tried to lift the figure for a closer look. It wouldn't budge. As he tugged harder it leaned towards him. The base was bolted to the shelf, but the figure moved towards him as he pulled. While thinking how strange it was, a panel to the left of the bookcase opened. Richard's jaw dropped. *Cool ... just like in the movies!* As he cleared the entrance yet another panel closed behind him.

As Richard looked around the twelve-by-twelve sterile metal room lit by an unknown source, he realized he was in some kind of holding room. He did not move as a direct beam of light from above moved from one end of the room to the next inspecting everything in its path: Richard was not sure what the beam was searching for. As soon as the beam finished its cycle the opposite door opened as if this holding area acted as an elevator.

Although he did not feel the room had moved, he could sense a calm but eerie noiseless movement; he was positive he had landed deeper into the earth. He paused for a moment to get his bearings and adjust his vision; it was extremely bright in the elevator room and quite dim in his new surroundings. The marble domed-shaped room before him was a small entrance of some kind to yet another room. As he paused, Richard heard people talking in the room ahead. Once again, he pulled out his Mark VI which he had pocketed earlier in the receptionist area.

As he crept silently through the entrance, it occurred to him the direction in which he had taken should have led him directly underneath The Green.

Before him was a sight to behold. There were eight square pillars forming a perfect circle almost as high as the ceiling. He worked his way slowly to the closest pillar to hide his presence. As he touched the pillar to steady himself, Richard noticed the pillar was comprised of a soft smooth metal; its consistency was nothing he could name. It seemed to be a solid four-by-four block stretching from the floor to about five inches from the ceiling. The pillars formed a circle around an inner circle etched on the floor in the middle of the room. The large circular room was bare except for the pillars, the ceremonial circle, and the hooded figures within it.

The circle was colorfully divided into fours with each axis labeled North, South, East and West, and at each marker stood a hooded person chanting in a low soft tone. Another hooded person stood directly in the center of the circle where all interconnected. All were humming in unison with their heads hooded and bowed with hands folded just below their waists as if in prayer.

Richard decided he could not go any further without disclosing his position. He had stumbled into some kind of ceremony but what and by whom? All of a sudden, the tones changed to a five-part harmony and as if on cue, all five heads raised towards the ceiling in unison. Their chanting became increasingly louder and somewhat piercing to Richard's ears. As their voices rose higher, the chanting became louder. Suddenly, something resembling lightening bolts ascended from the bottom of each pillar, illuminating their entire interior.

The only sound was the harmonized chanting as the light source rose higher and higher within the pillars. As this light, resembling some kind of energy source, reached the top of the pillars, the ceiling began to open, exposing a large triangle positioned just below the decorative water fountain placed in the middle of The Green directly above. Again as if on cue, there was a large crack sounding like thunder as each top of the pillars sizzled, connecting their inner energy with outside energy sources moving upwards towards the circling triangle. At that point, in silence, all five men removed their hoods and dropped their ornate ceremonial robes to the ground. The man in the middle raised his head towards the triangle circling high above uttering something that sounded like Latin to Richard, and then raised the hanging item around his neck above his head towards the large triangle slowly spinning in mid-air attached to nothing.

As his chant became more intense, a streak of light from each pillar connected with the small object the man was holding. Within seconds another white bolt of light connected all four necklace pendants with the one in the center; all becoming one. From the amulet held by the center figure, a colorful illumination extended, attaching itself to the triangle above. The revolving triangle acted as a conduit, filtering the energy of the full moon and the earth's electromagnetic field connecting with the amulets' energies just below the center of the nine squares.

It was quite a silent light show.

Richard was startled when the amulet in his pocket started vibrating. Realizing this amulet was somehow connected to the ones used in the ceremony; he quickly removed the amulet and repositioned it in his front right lower jacket pocket. He hoped since that side of his body was entirely hid by the pillar it would shield any connection with the light source. He was right, although still glowing within his pocket, it stopped vibrating entirely. Richard thought he must be in possession of an exact replica of the amulets held by these men before him. He wondered how the one in his pocket was connected.

As he stood behind the pillar watching the light show before him, he observed wind forming a swirl within the confines of the pillars. Soon it became a large cone-shaped funnel moving upwards and through the ceiling towards the sky. Even though the clothes and hair of the men flapped with the intense wind, everyone stood still as if bolted to the floor like the figurine Richard had seen earlier in the receiving room. The hurricane-force wind did not spread outside of the pillars; Richard was not affected. As he watched this spectacle, the continual swirl of the wind-shaped funnel reminded him of the tiny sand swirl he had watched evolve from nothing on the beach the night before.

The four men at the north-south-east-west axis kept a low hum as the man in the middle, who Richard thought he recognized, stared upward towards the sky and spoke quite loudly.

Richard could only make out a few words, "*universe … movement … intentions.*" The voice of the man in the middle began to rise, "*collective … mind … change … rulership … America.*"

Ending his request, the man in the center lowered the pendant and the other four followed. Then, just like rewinding the image before him, the wind died down, the energy left the amulets and the light in the pillars began to descend. Richard knew it was time to leave if he wanted to come out of this alive.

As he turned to leave, the amulet's chain, loosely hanging outside of his lower jacket pocket where he had hastily placed it earlier, caught on his hand and fell, making a clanging noise when hitting the floor. Damn! He cursed under his breath while he bent to retrieve the amulet, nuzzling it safely in his inner left breast pocket.

One of the hooded men closest to Richard turned at hearing the muffled sound. The others were alerted to this unusual change in movement by their comrade. Richard froze, hoping no further noises would alert them. Instinct took over as he decided not to wait for his unknown guests and returned quietly to the elevator in which he entered. He could hear their hushed voices inquiring what had happened as he tried desperately to find the elevator lever. He could hear them questioning if they had been seen.

As the men began to make their leave, Richard, having no immediate plan, decided if he did not find the opener soon, he would think of something; he always did. Just as the men entered the corridor which eventually led to the elevator, it miraculously opened; he'd found the lever. Richard wasted no time in entering and closing the door, leaving the collective five behind in the Grand Ceremonial Chamber

E.K. Prescott, Ph.D

underneath the nine squares to regain their faculties and execute their individual prearranged alibis.

Chapter 27

The next morning, as he did most mornings, Richard watched the sun rise while drinking coffee on his front porch, enjoying the sounds of the Atlantic Ocean. He had been reviewing over and over in his mind the events of the night before. What seemed incredible, he now believed could be explained by combining Professor Gibbs's thoughts about the Second Theory of Thermodynamics and Quantum Theory with Madame's teachings concerning the Ancient Mysteries— abilities secretly passed down through the ages from Egypt— rationally connecting the truths of science with metaphysical nuances. Sarah was correct with her Chaos Theory discussion as well. There was an underground force manipulating world events while chaos ran rampant just above the surface, disguising their real purpose—world power. *Who were these people?*

Richard recalled when he met with Jonathan a few days earlier and reported his findings. He agreed—even though he was successful following the clues surrounding the mysterious Henry Phillips II—that his death was still a mystery. A mystery which was obviously a secret someone was trying to bury in the past.

As they discussed the unanswered clues of the case, Richard could not bring himself to disclose the amulet. The events from the night before made it quite clear this amulet had powers not known to the average person. Richard recreated in his mind the image of the energy moving up the columns and connecting eventually with all five amulets. This was some kind of strong power; power that could move things. It was obvious this amulet that young Henry held in his hand belonged to one of these men of that time, but who? And who are they? Richard was positive these people were a powerful underground force with a common mission; of what he did not know. It occurred to him when meeting with Dr. Granite in the Sterling Library that she made an off-hand comment about more secret societies underground than above ground. Is she privy to what he saw?

Richard realized he could tell no one. The only person whom he thought might even believe what he had seen was Sarah; but knowing this information could be fatal. He did not want that on his conscience; he must now act on his own. It was crystal clear to Richard that his investigation was just beginning.

His mind jumped from one thought to the next as he watched the waves crash upon the shoreline. He thought to himself, *There must be a storm out at sea to cause such intense waves.* He couldn't help become aware of the visual manifestation of energy … all is energy. Richard was beginning to believe.

With that, he thought of his trip and the new women in his life. What had ever happened to Helena? She was such an enigma to him. He seemed attracted to her, but he wasn't sure who or what she was. He had seen her across the nine squares a few days ago, but decided not to communicate. He knew not why. Apparently, she had not decided to return to England as of yet. Interesting.

And what about Maize? Richard had grown fond of her. She

did add a spark to his life, even though at times she reminded him of his young daughter, a painful memory. He liked her willfulness. If he wanted to continue investigating crimes on the side, he would need an assistant. Hmmm. Surely the Dean would allow him a research assistant upon request. Putting down his empty coffee cup on the side table he made a mental note—ask the Dean.

Now finally awake, Richard reached for the *New Haven Gazette* thrown on his porch earlier that morning. The headline read:

August 2, 1923
PRESIDENT HARDING DIES OF HEART ATTACK
SUSPICIOUS!

Richard sat riveted, staring at the headline. Sadly, he now realized with utmost certainty, he may never know who exactly killed young Henry Phillips II or why, but what he did know was that the murder was committed by one of the past Proprietors. *That was the connection!* And much to his chagrin, it was apparent there were powerful forces at work—so powerful, he now feared for the future of the United States of America.

EPILOGUE

"Have you acquired enough cedar, sandalwood and juniper to keep the Fire of Azrael burning until the tide waters completely smother the embers?" The Consoler was a stickler for details and did not tolerate any problems. Everyone knew you would pay if things were not followed and carried out to the letter. The severity of the penalty depended upon his mood, which was highly unpredictable to say the least.

Henry, though outwardly displaying a cool façade, was glad his long robes masked his nervous, shivering body. Organizing, implementing, and participating, as well as the co-conductor of the Seaside Ritual, was his right of passage as the newly appointed High Priest to the governing High Priestess. He was not going to screw it up. This was the first thing he ever took seriously in his life. He wanted to show everyone—including his father—that he was not a total loss to society and an embarrassment to his family, as his father reminded him of this fact time and time again.

"Yes, Consoler," Henry answered with conviction as he looked up into the Consoler's expressionless eyes. "I have everything set. All white foods are on the menu, from sea scallops in white shells to little crescent honey cakes for dessert. It will be a feast appropriate for the high standards and expectations of the Moon Goddess. In addition, since dogs are sacred to the Moon Goddess, we have asked our members to bring their dogs if they can be relied upon to stay close at hand."

Although the Consoler was pleased with what he heard, he knew that the implementation of these plans was as crucial as the planning, and until the Seashore Ritual was over and the last ember extinguished, he would not be able to relax. As the oldest and wisest member of this

Order, the Consoler could not afford for anything to go wrong. He had a sterling reputation and was going to keep it that way until he left this place called Earth. His stature alone, a large, sculptured, towering body with a masculine chiseled face that seemed to lord over everyone he met, demanded the utmost respect and obedience from everyone he encountered.

"Well, Henry," hating to admit it, "you seem to have everything in hand. Just remember the implementation of your plans is crucial, and the High Priestess does not want to be embarrassed appointing a bumbling idiot as High Priest. She has put a lot of faith in you … more than I would have … but what is … is what is."

With that, the Consoler turned abruptly to continue what he was working on, dismissing Henry without a word.

Where is he? He knows how important this is to me. My one chance to show him I've made something of myself and he's going to miss it, he thought to himself. Henry paced back and forth on the grassy mound just above the sand bank. They had agreed to meet near the historic Southwest Ledge Lighthouse (later to be renamed the Five Points Lighthouse).

Henry had chosen a part of the beach that was a respectable distance from the gathering, but close enough to keep a hawkish eye on all pre-ritual proceedings. Everything had to come off perfectly. Too much was at stake, and his pride was the least of importance. It paled in the magnitude of the approval of the High Priestess, and the approval of his father. His father was a self-made man, a well-respected, aristocratic lawyer, and a prominent member of the Proprietors of Common and Undivided Grounds. Young Henry could never figure out why the latter appointment was so damn important. These men only watch over a little piece of land in the middle of New Haven. People treated his father, Henry Phillips I, as if he was something special; someone to placate because you yearn for his approval and not his wrath.

Young Henry was not sure if it was a curse or blessing he resembled his father. Henry Phillips I was only his father; a father of a prominent, high society, a dysfunctional family, and a self-proclaimed sir; no big deal. Henry had decided at a young age he would never measure up to his father's expectations and found it easier to be a problem rather than a protégé. That was the major reason he intentionally decided to flunk out of school at age fifteen. He left home to move northeast and make his own way in life. To Henry, it didn't matter what the way was, as long as it was away from the overbearing umbrella of his father's influence.

The night was brightly lit with the full moon shining almost at the peak of its height in the dark sky. The shadows it cast were ominous, creating a mystic illusion that left one feeling uneasy. It made one feel unsure, wondering if what was being seen was real or part of an unveiling of a dark truth—a truth that held many secrets.

As he saw his father finally arrive on his favorite black stallion. He tried to literally shake this dark, nagging feeling. *Everything is going to play out perfectly*, he told himself. *It has to!* He screamed inside his head as his dad slowly slithered down the hill to greet his son, a son he did not know or understand. Cordial niceties were passed between them as Henry kept glimpsing to his right at the crowd preparing to take their places for the Seaside Ritual.

As usual, his father arrived just before an event, making a dramatic entrance as if everyone was waiting just for him before the proceedings could finally begin.

As they walked side by side down the beach to the site prepared for the ritual, looking like clones only distinguishable by age, Henry whispered, pointing to their left.

"Dad, you need to stand over there next to those other guests.

Please do not move from that position."

His father jerked, not used to being told what to do or where to stand. Before he could spit out a rebuttal, Henry continued.

"The ritual is a very sacred event and must not be interrupted at all costs."

Henry paused as they both reached the small gathering. He faced his dad, not sure what to say. All he could think of was, "Thanks for coming."

His father, expressionless, nodded and walked slowly to the spot Henry had suggested. Everyone was now in their proper place, even the High Priestess had withdrawn behind a rampart in order not to be seen until the appointed time.

At Henry's signal as High Priest, he would meet the Maiden face to face across the unlit fire, parallel to the edge of the sea. The rest of the Order arranged themselves in a semicircle between them, facing the fire and the sea.

Sir Henry Phillips I could hear the Maiden's words clearly from where he stood. "Be ye far from us, O ye profane, for we are about to invoke the descent of the power of Isis. Enter her temple with clean hands and pure heart, lest we defile the source of life."

Henry's father's thoughts gladly muffled the pathetic, unimportant speeches. His son had always been an embarrassment to him and this would end tonight. He was not here for Henry, but for the preservation of what was most important. The security of the secret was not negotiable and must be protected at all costs.

Interrupting his thoughts, young Henry loudly spoke his part. "Let us show forth in a rite the dynamic nature of the Goddess, that the minds of men may be as fertile as their fields."

The Maiden replied. "Be ye far from us, O ye profane, for the unveiling of the Goddess is at hand."

Sir Phillips I watched with disguised disgust as he smiled and nodded compliantly to the people standing next to him. His eyes followed the Maiden as she walked slowly around the fire, joining his son. He wondered how her white, soft, youthful skin would feel hovering over his toned, aging body. Then his son and the Maiden lit the fire together. When it was lit and burning satisfactorily, the Order and the Maiden sat down in the semicircle.

The High Priest remained standing. "O though that was before the earth was formed …"

Shutting out young Henry's voice, his father tried to look nonchalantly at his watch. He recalled Henry had told him this … whatever it is … would only last an hour. It had only been ten minutes. *Damn!*

No one must know what he was about to do. It was enough to know he was preserving his destiny and the secret, as he fingered the medallion around his neck. He had every detail planned, it was foolproof. As he lingered in the complexities of what must be done, he saw his son raise his arms high and wide. *What was he doing*, he thought, thoroughly disgusted. Then, the High Priestess emerged from around the mound of earth to the left of the fire, walking to where the water covered her feet and paused. She raised her arms high and wide for a moment as she faced the sea, then she lowered them and walked in a stately manner towards the fire. When she reached it, she stood facing the High Priest, Henry.

The High Priest lowered his arms and bowed to her. The High Priestess then raised her arms with her palms up and started to sing. "I am she who ere the earth was formed …"

Where did they get this woman? Henry's father's thoughts were random now, trying to keep his sanity while endeavoring to keep his wits about him. He must control the rage that was burning inside, the rage that only his son could ignite. He was a self-made man, powerful, loved and loathed. He didn't arrive at this place in time by always playing by the rules. His son had become a stumbling block, an embarrassment, and a threat. *Oh thank God, she finally finished screeching*, Henry Phillips I thought to himself.

The song over, the High Priest kneeled and the High Priestess lowered her arms. The seated Order changed to a kneeling position, and the High Priestess walked around and laid her two hands on each head, starting with the High Priest. As she left each person, he or she took a sitting position. Finally she sat down and faced the High Priest.

Henry spoke. "Let us now commune with the fire."

The whole Order, including the High Priestess, gazed into the fire and spoke of what they saw. The High Priestess guided this part of the ritual, encouraging and calming members as necessary. *These people are nuts*, Sir Henry exclaimed to himself. *They actually believe they can see something in the flames of the fire? They are a menace to society.* He would have to do something about them. But, he would deal with them another day, first things first.

Young Henry jolted back to the proceedings when the High Priestess called for the moon-food, which was brought forward and shared, as was the wine. The Order stayed with the fire until the incoming tide quenched all the embers. When the quenching of the fire was complete, the High Priestess spoke. "Those who have received the Touch of Isis have received the opening of the gates of the inner life. For them the tides of the moon shall flow and ebb and flow and never cease in their cosmic rhythm."

The High Priest then brought her the food which had been kept aside; she then threw the food onto the water as an offering to the sea. Finally, she stretched her arms out over the sea. After a moment she lowered them again and turned, and then she and the High Priest led

E.K. Prescott, Ph.D

the Order away.

Young Henry let out a huge sigh of relief. He had done it … *it was perfect*, he thought to himself as he walked side by side with the High Priestess. He had made it a point not to look in the direction of his father during the whole ceremony, and he wasn't about to now. He was afraid of what he would see. He must take solace in the fact that his father attended the ritual at his request. That would have to be enough. He knew his father would not understand anything that took place. That fact alone would make him agitated.

As people started to mingle, Henry tried to locate his father. He noticed him at the far northeast corner of the ritual area where the sand ended and grassy knoll began, talking to the small group of honored guests. Fortunately, his father's back was turned towards him. *How typical*, Henry thought. As usual he was the only one talking and everyone else was acting like they were listening.

All of a sudden, Henry's attention was diverted to someone standing further up the grassy knoll. As he focused his view, he realized it was the Consoler. His face was expressionless as usual but was not tense with disgust. It was obvious he was overseeing the proceedings from afar. Close, but not too close. Close enough to step in if needed, far enough to not be detected. In the blink of an eye, the Consoler seemed to disappear from sight. *What a strange man*, young Henry thought to himself. He was not alarmed because he knew he did well, more than well, he was *perfect*.

Suddenly, his attention was diverted again by the quick disbursement of the crowd as rain drizzled from the illuminated sky. Everyone soon left Long Island Sound Beach looking for drier conditions. The rain was not going to dampen the euphoric feeling exploding within him. Soon Henry found himself standing next to his father, walking towards the lighthouse.

"Son, I have to say I did not understand a word, but it was obvious you played a major role during the ceremony."

Young Henry did not know how to react. This was such an unexpected response.

He continued. "I thought of what I could give you and felt a little father-son ceremony of our own would be appropriate."

Stunned, Henry decided silence was the best reaction at this point. What did his father have up his sleeve? When they approached the lighthouse, Sir Henry stopped and faced his son, pulling out two tiny vessels from behind his back. He had collected these earlier from his saddle bags, and had prepared them before his son joined him. They contained a special liquid for a special toast. He removed the seals and handed Henry his vessel. "To my son, may this symbolize a change in direction for us both!"

As Sir Henry sipped his vessel, young Henry followed … without question.

HISTORICAL BACKGROUND

THE GREEN

All information surrounding The Green, affectionately known as the "9 Squares" is true, with exception of the underground city. In 1638, a group of Puritans from London, England landed on Long Island Sound. They viewed the barrier island as protection and the harbor and surrounding waters deemed lucrative for trade. The new settlers immediately established a protected area of land in the middle of New Haven Colony called The Market, which is now referred to as The Green.

The original purpose of The Market was to provide an open area of land for 100,000 people to gather in order to be lifted up into Heaven for the Second Coming of Christ. In the meantime, it housed other things including a prison, a cemetery, a school, and an open market. It was mainly used as a general meeting place for political and religious purposes.

The Center Church at that time was known as the Congregational Church, and it was also used for religious and secular meetings. It was of Puritan denomination. Seven men—prominent landowners and governing officials—were chosen to oversee The Market. This oversight continues today, but with five Proprietors of The Green instead of seven. The appointment is held until death. When a member dies, the other four go into seclusion until they have chosen the new member.

THE SPOT

Frank Pepe's Pizzeria Napoletana, known locally in the twenties as "The Spot" and today as Pepe's, is a popular pizza restaurant in the Wooster Square neighborhood of New Haven, Connecticut, at

163 Wooster Street. It opened in 1925, and is one of the oldest and best known pizzerias in the United States. Frank Pepe was allergic to tomatoes and cheese, so he created the white pizza, topped with freshly shucked littleneck clams. This became one of the restaurant's famous specialties.

THE PROPRIETORS OF THE GREEN

The information of their history and role is true, as mentioned above, but all names are fictitious, as well as the implication that they are members of a shadow government. Their position in the story is fictitious, but represents a great truth.

COUNCIL OF FOREIGN RELATIONS

The earliest origin of the Council stemmed from a working fellowship of about 150 scholars, who were given the task of briefing President Woodrow Wilson on options for the postwar world when Germany was defeated. The scholars were referred to as "The Inquiry."

Throughout a year beginning in 1917, this academic team, which included Wilson's closest advisor and long-time friend, "Colonel" Edward M. House, and Walter Lippmann, gathered at 155th Street and Broadway at the Harold Pratt House in New York City to assemble the strategy for the postwar world. The team produced more than 2,000 documents that contained detailed and analyzed political, economic, and social facts that would help Wilson in the peace talks.

Their reports formed the basis for the Fourteen Points, which outlined Wilson's strategy for peace after war's end. The scholars traveled to the Paris Peace Conference in 1919 that would end the war. The Council and its British counterpart, the Royal Institute of International Affairs in London (now known as Chatham House), was created at one of the meetings where a small group of British and American diplomats and scholars gathered on May 30, 1919.

Among the meeting's participants were Herbert Hoover, Edward House, Paul Warburg, Harold Temperley, Lionel Curtis, Lord Eustace Percy, Christian Herter, and American academic historians James Thomson Shotwell of Columbia University, Archibald Cary Coolidge of Harvard, and Charles Seymour of Yale.

The Council on Foreign Relations, a sister organization to The Chatham House, was formed in 1922 as a noncommercial and nonpolitical organization whose goal was to support American foreign relations. The Council was bipartisan from its inception, and welcomed members of both Democratic and Republican parties. It also welcomed Jews and African Americans. Women were initially barred from membership.

Its proceedings were completely private and confidential. Of the 502 government officials surveyed from 1945 to 1972, a critical study found that more than half of them were Council members.

Today, the Council has about 5,000 members which have included senior politicians, former national security officers, bankers, lawyers, professors, former CIA members, senior media figures, and more than a dozen Secretaries of State.

THE TEAPOT DOME SCANDAL

In April of 1922, Albert Bacon Fall, President Harding's Secretary of the Interior, secretly leased the rich Teapot Oil field north of Casper to a newly formed company, Mammoth Oil. In exchange, the grateful head of Mammoth, Harry F. Sinclair, had rewarded Fall, who owned a large ranch in Three Rivers, New Mexico, with prized livestock and close to $300,000 in so-called Liberty Bonds, (government-issued bonds that yielded at least 3 ½ percent tax free).

However, Colonel James G. Darden claimed that he owned some

of the Teapot field, and by mid-summer, he had already begun drilling operations.

When Fall learned what the colonel was up to, he demanded that Harding send in the U.S. Marines to put a stop to it, by force if necessary. Harding reluctantly granted his request. As a result, Wyoming is the only state in the U.S. ever to be invaded by the U.S. Marines.

CHAOS THEORY

Chaos theory describes systems that are apparently disordered, but chaos theory is more about finding the underlying order in the disorder.

In 1960, Edward Lorenz was the first to experiment in chaos. A meteorologist, he was working on the problem of weather prediction. Using a computer, he created a set of twelve equations to model the weather. It didn't predict the weather itself, but it did theoretically predict what the weather might be. This effect came to be known as the butterfly effect. The amount of difference in the starting points of the two curves is so small that it is comparable to a butterfly flapping its wings.

The flapping of a single butterfly's wing produces a tiny change in the state of the atmosphere. Over a period of time, what the atmosphere actually does diverges from what it would have done. So, over a period of time, a tornado that would have devastated an area may not necessarily happen. Or maybe one that wasn't going to happen does.

THE BOSTON CONGRESSIONAL HOTEL (THE LIBERTY HOTEL)

The Liberty Hotel held some of Boston's most notorious criminals for 120 years. In 1973, the jail was declared unfit and in violation of the inmates' constitutional rights after prisoners revolted because of the

E.K. Prescott, Ph.D.

poor living conditions. The remaining prisoners were moved to the new Suffolk County Jail in 1990.

Massachusetts General Hospital acquired the property in 1991 and sought out proposals for its use, requiring that significant elements of the building be preserved. In 2001, Carpenter & Company entered into a lease agreement with MGH for the land and the jail to develop the project.

The jail was constructed between 1848 and 1851 according to plans designed by architect Gridley James Fox Bryant and prison reformer, Rev. Louis Dwight. It was designed according to the 1790s humanitarian scheme known as the Auburn Plan. The original jail was built in the shape of a cross with four wings of Quincy granite extending from a central, octagonal rotunda with a ninety-foot-tall atrium. The wings allowed segregation of prisoners by gender and category of offense, and thirty arched windows, each thirty-three feet high, provided ventilation and natural light.

The jail contained 220 granite cells, which were eight feet by ten feet in size.

The jail housed a number of famous inmates including James Michael Curley, Malcolm X, Sacco and Vanzetti, World War II prisoners from the German submarine Unterseeboot 234, and suffragists who were imprisoned for protests when President Woodrow Wilson visited Boston in 1919.

THE TAFT HOTEL

The Taft Hotel opened its doors in 1912 on New Year's Day. Notables in theatre, society, art, and politics called the Taft Hotel home.

William Howard Taft lived in the hotel that bears his family name for eight years after his presidency, while he taught law at Yale University.

With the Shubert Theater located next door, many celebrities visited the hotel before or after Broadway shows, including Gloria Swanson, Mary Martin, Al Jolson, Eddie Cantor, Katharine Hepburn, and Alec Guinness.

Rodgers and Hammerstein created the Broadway tune "Oklahoma" In their rooms at the hotel, and several famous movies scenes were filmed at or near the hotel, such as *Splendor in the Grass*, *Death of a Scoundrel* and *All About Eve*.

Before the Taft Hotel was built, other hotels and taverns had stood on the site, including one in which George Washington stayed in 1775. The hotel is now known as the Taft Apartments, but the building still has its historic tap room on the ground floor, which was restored and reopened as Richter's Cafe in 1983. What was once the hotel's grand ballroom is now a restaurant called Downtown at the Taft.

SPEAKEASY AT THE TAFT HOTEL

Richter's Tap Room dates back to 1858, when the New Haven House Hotel, designed by Henry Austin, was built at the corner of College and Chapel Streets.

After Prohibition was repealed, the pub was a hot spot from the 1930s to the 1950s, until the building was sold and sat empty for ten years while the hotel was renovated.

In the fall of 1981, Richter Elser, a recent Yale grad, accidentally discovered the boarded up Tap Room, restored it, and re-opened the historic bar in 1983.

HARDING'S PRESIDENCY AND MYSTERIOUS DEATH

Rumors began to circulate within minutes of Warren G. Harding's death on August 2, 1923. No one is able to give a correct time of death, not even the physicians who cared for Harding during the week leading up to his death, and no one is sure as to who was with the president when he died in the San Francisco hotel room. Some say he suffered a heart attack, or was it a stroke?

It could have been both, exacerbated by the ptomaine poisoning that he may or may not have experienced a few days earlier in Vancouver. An autopsy could have confirmed the cause, but Mrs. Harding would not permit it. Within an hour of his death, he was embalmed, rouged, powdered, dressed, and in his casket. Within twenty-four hours, he was on a train to Washington, D.C.

Many people questioned the circumstances of the death of the twenty-ninth President of the United States. Many asked how an event so important to the nation be handled so badly. Conspiracy theories arose. Was it suicide? Was it murder? We may never know.

THE VICTORIAN MANOR

The Tampa Bay Hotel was built by railroad magnate Henry B. Plant—to anchor his rail line—at a cost of over $2.5 million.

The hotel covers six acres and is a quarter-mile long. It holds the first elevator ever installed in Florida, which is still in use today.

On the 150-acre grounds of the hotel sit 21 buildings, a golf course, bowling alley, racetrack, casino, and an indoor heated swimming pool. The hotel has six minarets, four cupolas, and three domes, which were all restored to their original stainless steel state in the 1990's.

The 511 rooms were the first in Florida to have electric lights and telephones. Most rooms also included private bathrooms. The price for a room ranged from $5.00 to $15.00 a night at a time when the average hotel in Tampa charged $1.25 to $2.00.

During its operating period from 1891 to 1930, the hotel catered to many celebrities. When the Spanish-American War broke out, the United States military used the hotel as a base of operations.

Generals and high ranking officers stayed in its rooms to plan invasion strategies, while enlisted men encamped on the hotel's acreage. Colonel Teddy Roosevelt and his Rough Riders also were at the hotel during this time. Roosevelt retained a suite, and during the day led his men in battle exercises on the property.

Sarah Bernhardt, Clara Barton, Stephen Crane, the Prince of Wales, and the Queen of the United Kingdom also stayed at the hotel, as well as Babe Ruth, who signed his first baseball contract in the Grand Dining Room.

REFERENCES

BOOKS:
Boutell, Lewis Henry. (1896). *The Life of Roger Sherman*. A.C. McClurg & Co. Il: Chicago. NY: Mineola.

Cirker, Blanche: Edited by. *Victorian House Designs in Authentic Full Color*. Dover Publications. Inc. NY: Mineola.

Cirlot, J.C. (2002). *A Dictionary of Symbols*. Dover Publications. NY: Mineola.

Cunningham, Scott. (2nd Ed. 2006). *Cunningham's Encyclopedia of Magical Herbs*. Llewellyn Publications. MN: St. Paul.

Cunningham, Scott. (1999). *Earth, Air, Fire & Water: More Techniques of Natural Magic*. Llewellyn Publications. MN: St. Paul

Doyle, Arthur Conan. (1975). *The Complete Adventures and Memoirs of Sherlock Holmes*. Gramercy. NY: New York.

Druesedow, Jean, L (1990). Selected and Introduction. *Men's Fashions Illustrations from the Turn of the Century*. Dover Publications, Inc. NY: Mineola.

Farrar, Janet and Stewart. (1984). *The Witches' Way*. Phoenix Publishing. WA: Custer.

House, Edward Mandell. (1920). *Philip Dru: Administrator, A Story of Tomorrow*, 1920-1935. B.W. Huebsch. NY: NY.

Laubner, Ellie. (1996). *Fashions of the Roaring '20s*. Schiffer Publishing, Ltd. PA: Atglen.

McCartney, Laton. (2008). *The Teapot Dome Scandal*. Random House. NY: New York.

Morrison, Dorothy. (2003). *The Craft: A Witch's Book of Shadow*. Llewellyn Publications. MN: St. Paul.

Murray, Margaret Alice. (1921). *The Witch-Cult in the Western Europe: A Study in Anthropology*. Clarendon Press. England: Oxford.

Osterweis, G. Rollin. (1976). *The New Haven Green and the American Bicentennial*. Archon Books. Connecticut: Hamden.

Zeitz, Joshua. (2006). *FLAPPER*. The Rivers Press. NY: New York.

PAPERS:
Samuelson, Eric, J.D. An Introduction to the "Little Sister" of The Royal Institute of International Affairs: The U.S. Council on Foreign Relations
http://www.sweetliberty.org/issues/shadow/cfrintro.htm.

The Rockefeller Bloodline
http://www.theforbiddenknowledge.com/hardtruth/the_rockefeller_bloodline.htm.

OTHER SOURCES:
Archives and Manuscripts. The Sterling Library: Yale University. New Haven, Connecticut.

New Haven Museum and Historical Society. New Haven, Connecticut.

New Haven Branch of Allen County Public Library. Reference and Archives.

WEB SEARCH:
Blavatsky Net – Theosophy
http://www.blavatsky.net/theosophy/theosophy-checklist.htm.

Biography of Roger Sherman
http://colonialhall.com/sherman/sherman.php.

Illuminati News
http://www.illuminati-news.com/2007/0313a.htm.

Newspaper Archives
http://newspaperarchive.com/.

Sherman's of Yaxley
http://www.soysite.com/researchbooks.html#FamiliesEssex.

Winchester House
http://www.prairieghosts.com/winchester.html.

E.K. Prescott, Ph.D.

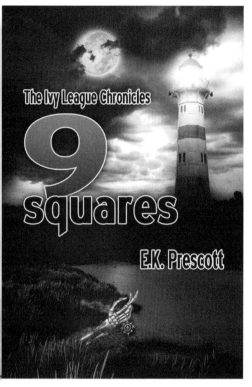